SMALL VICES

Books by Robert B. Parker

CHANCE

THIN AIR

WALKING SHADOW

PAPER DOLL

DOUBLE DEUCE

PASTIME

PERCHANCE TO DREAM (*a Philip Marlowe novel*)

STARDUST

POODLE SPRINGS (with Raymond Chandler)

PLAYMATES

CRIMSON JOY

PALE KINGS AND PRINCES

TAMING A SEA-HORSE

A CATSKILL EAGLE

VALEDICTION

LOVE AND GLORY

THE WIDENING GYRE

CEREMONY

A SAVAGE PLACE

EARLY AUTUMN

LOOKING FOR RACHEL WALLACE

WILDERNESS

THE JUDAS GOAT

THREE WEEKS IN SPRING (*with Joan Parker*)

PROMISED LAND

MORTAL STAKES

GOD SAVE THE CHILD

THE GODWULF MANUSCRIPT

SMALL VICES

Robert B Parker

SMALL VICES

NO EXIT PRESS

This edition published in 1999 by No Exit Press
18 Coleswood Road, Harpenden, Herts, AL5 1EQ

http://www.noexit.co.uk

A CIP catalogue record for this book is available from the British Library.

ISBN 1-901982-58-0 Small Vices

2 4 6 8 10 9 7 5 3 1

Printed by Caledonian International Book Manafacturing, Glasgow.

For Joan: You may have been a headache,
but you've never been a bore.

Through tattered clothes small vices do appear;
Robes and furred gowns hide all. Plate sin with gold,
And the strong lance of justice hurtless breaks;
Arm it in rags, a pygmy's straw does pierce it.

—KING LEAR

chapter 1

THE LAST TIME I saw Rita Fiore she'd been an assistant DA with red hair, first-rate hips, and more attitude than an armadillo. She'd had a drink with me in the downstairs bar at the Parker House, complained about men, and introduced me to a blowhard from the DEA named Fallon, who answered more questions about the cocaine trade than I'd asked. This time we were alone, in a conference room on the thirty-ninth floor of the former Mercantile Building, with a view of the coastline that extended north to Greenland and south to Tierra del Fuego. She still had red hair. She still had the hips. And she was still tougher than Pat Buchanan. But she wasn't a prosecutor anymore. She was the senior litigator for Cone, Oakes and Baldwin, and a member of the firm.

"Coffee?" she said.

"Sure."

I had decided that I was more alert with coffee than without it. So I decided to have a couple of cups each day, to keep my heart rate up. This one would be my third, but my heart was still a little sluggish. Rita sent a female underling for the coffee, and leaned a little back in her chair and crossed her legs. Her skirt was a little short for business, just as her hair was a little long. I knew Rita knew that, and I knew she didn't care.

"Still got the wheels," I said.

"Yeah, and I'm still spinning them."

"Beats the view out of Dedham District Court," I said.

"Oh, yeah. Professionally I'm a big goddamned success. But am I married?"

"Gee," I said. "I wish I could help."

"You had your chance."

I grinned.

"Reminds me of an old joke," I said.

"I know the joke," Rita said. "And never mind."

The female underling came back with two coffees in real cups, with a cream pitcher and sugar bowl on a silver tray. Everything bore the firm's initials.

"Discourages the clients from stealing stuff," Rita said.

I put some sugar in, and some cream, and had a sip. It was lukewarm.

"I thought you got married," I said.

"I did. Twice. Both jerks."

"Probably ought to stop doing that," I said.

"Marrying jerks? Yeah, I should. But you eliminate the jerks, and who you going to marry?"

"A woman needs a man like a fish needs a bicycle," I said.

"How come that's the only feminist remark guys can quote?"

"There's another one," I said, "something about whore to her husband, slave to her children? Have I got it right?"

Rita grinned at me.

"Could you maybe just shut the fuck up?" she said.

"Sure."

Rita drank some of her coffee and made a face.

"Limoges china on a silver tray and they can't get the coffee hot," she said.

I looked out the window. The ocean was gray today, and the far sky was the same color, so that the horizon was hard to distinguish and the distance just seemed to fade away. I could see the wake of a nearly indistinguishable power boat as it pushed past one of the channel markers in the outer harbor.

"About a year and a half ago, when I was still prosecuting, we had a guy named Ellis Alves. Charged with the murder of a Pemberton College student named Melissa Henderson."

"I remember," I said. "You got a conviction."

"Yeah, what a challenge. He's black, had two priors for sexual assault. She's white, honor student at Pemberton. Father owns eight banks. Her grandfather was once Secretary of Commerce."

"And?"

"And I did what I was employed to do. I prosecuted. I won. Ellis is now at Cedar Junction. Forever."

"Way to go, Rita."

"Yeah. It was easy. He had a public defender one year out of law school, Yale, I think. Kid named Marcy Vance. Serious. Talbots suits. Just a little lipstick. Knew more law probably than I'll ever know. Knew nothing at all about criminal defense. I could convict Santa Claus if she was defending."

She finished her coffee and put the cup aside.

"You're not smoking anymore," I said.

"The patch worked for me. I been off three and a half years."

"Good," I said.

"What do you care," Rita said. "You're in love with Susan."

"This is true," I said. "But it's not monomania."

"Nice to know," Rita said. "Anyway. I didn't like the case, but it was there to be cleared and I cleared it. While I was clearing it, I was interviewing here, and a couple weeks after I cleared Ellis right over to Cedar Junction, I came to work here and started drinking coffee out of china cups."

"So?"

"So last spring who shows up here, wearing more makeup, but still dressing Talbots? My old adversary, Marcy Vance. And as soon as we get reintroduced she starts in on me about Ellis Alves. He was framed. She was too green to conduct a proper defense. He was the victim of racial discrimination."

"You believe her?"

"I believe Alves had a lousy defense. I believe it is easy to get a conviction on a black man whose victim is a rich white woman."

"You believe he was innocent?"

"Most of the people I've convicted aren't."

"True," I said.

"But Marcy says he didn't do it. She admits freely that he's a bad man and probably a career criminal and probably guilty of a lot of other things. But she says he did not have anything to do with the Henderson kid."

"If she's right it means somebody else did. And got away with it."

"Yeah."

We were quiet for a moment. The power boat was out of sight now, out in the bay somewhere. The gray sky seemed to have lowered, and the panorama had closed in considerably as we talked.

"You think she's right?" I said finally.

"I'm not sure she's wrong."

"Ah ha," I said. "So there's more to this than just the chance to flash your legs at me and remind me of what I missed."

"Well, that's the primary purpose, but the firm is also prepared to employ you to look into the matter of Ellis Alves at our expense."

"And if I find out he didn't do it?"

"Then we would be very happy to have you ascertain who did."

"Probably would have to anyway," I said. "It's a sure way to prove he didn't do it."

"Let's be clear on this," Rita said. "The firm's not hiring you to clear this guy. The firm's hiring you to establish the truth."

"And you a lawyer," I said.

Rita smiled.

"I know, I'm not comfortable with the idea either," she said. "But there it is."

"Well, okay, if that's the way you feel," I said.

Rita took a thick cardboard envelope off her desk and handed it to me.

"Trial transcript," she said.

"I'll read it," I said. "Though not happily. And I probably ought to talk with Marcy, and then I ought to talk with Ellis. How's Ellis feel about white people?"

"He feels that some of them put him away for life."

I nodded.

"Be better if I can talk with him here," I said.

"Why?"

"Bring him in, sit in a conference room, give him a decent lunch, have Hawk join us. Anybody in Corrections owe you a favor?"

"Hawk?"

"Might ease the black-white thing a little."

"Yeah, I can pull that off. He'll probably have to be shackled."

"Leg irons only," I said. "And no guards in the room."

"Ellis is kind of a dangerous guy," Rita said.

"You can be right outside," I said.

"Yeah . . . Hawk with anybody?"

"Always, and not for long," I said. "I don't think he's husband material."

"No," Rita said, "he's not. Be a hell of a weekend, though."

"I've heard that about you," I said.

"Really? Where?"

"I think it was written in pencil on the wall of a holding cell in the Dedham jail," I said.

Rita grinned.

"And the sad thing is, I wrote it."

chapter 2

"AND I HAVE to face it," Marcy Vance told me, "a lot of this is my fault."

We were sitting on stools at a high table for two in a sandwich shop on State Street, looking at the lunch menu.

"How so," I said.

"Have you read the transcript?" she said.

I nodded.

"He wanted to plea-bargain," Marcy said. "I told him no. If he were innocent, we should fight. He said they were going to convict him anyway. I wanted to prove him wrong, prove to him that the system would work. I even put him on the stand. He's not an articulate man, but I believed in his innocence and I felt that, you know, truth will out."

"Everybody starts out young," I said.

I was considering the club sandwich.

"I started out younger than most," she said.

She was a lanky woman, still younger than most. Not thirty yet, with pale skin and green eyes, and straight brown hair efficiently cut. There was a hint of freckles that no suntan had ever intensified. Her hands were big, with long fingers. She wore no jewelry, and her only makeup was a pale lip gloss.

"And I asked one of the detectives in cross-examination a question that permitted him to mention Ellis's record. The judge allowed it. Said if I were going to ask questions to which I didn't know the answer, I was going to have to live with the consequences."

"But it's Ellis that's living with them."

"Yes."

It was a given that if I had a club sandwich, I would get some of it on my shirt. What was under consideration was whether I cared or not, which was related to how I felt about Marcy. Which I hadn't decided.

"Why do you think he's innocent?"

"He said so. I believed him."

"That's it?"

"And it doesn't fit. His previous assaults were on black women in his neighborhood. The rest of his record is all of a piece. Petty street crime, extortion, possession with intent, that sort of thing, all within a mile of Ruggles Station."

The waitress was rushed. She didn't want to wait for me to evaluate my feelings about Marcy before I ordered. Marcy ordered carrot soup. I played it safe.

"Ham on light rye, mustard," I said. "Side of coleslaw. Decaf coffee."

The waitress flat-heeled away at high speed and

slapped our order on the service counter. There were maybe ten other order slips already there.

"Ellis own a car?" I said.

"No."

"He got a credit card?"

"I don't know. Why?"

"Could rent a car if he had a credit card. Hard to do without one."

"I never thought . . ." she said.

The waitress hurried back. Put a white mug of decaf in front of me, and a Diet Coke in front of Marcy.

"Be good to know how he got out to Pemberton," I said.

"He says he wasn't there."

"Be good to know where he was."

"He says he was with a woman, doesn't know her name. Her place. Can't remember where it was. They were drinking."

"Hell of an alibi," I said.

"Don't you think if he'd done it, he would have had a better one?"

"Not necessarily. Not everybody in jail is a thinker."

I drank a little coffee. It was just as good as if it were caffeinated. Or almost just as good. At least it was hot.

"What was the case against Ellis?" I said.

"Two eyewitnesses picked him out of a lineup."

"Two?"

"Yes, a Pemberton undergraduate and her boyfriend. They said they saw him drag Melissa Henderson into a car near the campus."

"They call the cops?"

"No, not then," Marcy said. "They thought it was just some kind of lover's quarrel, and they didn't want to seem racists, you know, a black man and a white woman?"

"Which was a racist thing to worry about," I said.

Marcy frowned, and looked puzzled, and looked as if she wanted to argue. She settled for a shrug.

"But they appeared after Melissa turned up murdered," I said.

"Yes. They went to the Pemberton Police and reported what they'd seen."

"How'd they connect to Ellis?"

"Pemberton Police got an anonymous tip."

"And they grabbed Ellis and put him in a lineup and the two witnesses pick him out."

"Yes."

"And the arresting officers find the victim's underwear in Alves's room."

"Yes. The DNA tests proved they were hers."

"What's Ellis say about that," I said.

"Says the police planted them."

"They ever find the rest of the clothes?"

"No."

The waitress rushed by again and dropped off some carrot soup for Marcy and a ham sandwich for me. There was a small paper cup of coleslaw on the platter beside it. Marcy got a dinner roll with her soup.

"There's something else," Marcy said. "It sort of got me what you said about the eyewitnesses not calling the cops—that it was a racist assumption anyway."

"You sort of thought deep in your heart that Ellis was guilty," I said. "So you overcompensated because you know that it was an impure racist thought that you were harboring."

"How did you know?"

"I'm a trained sleuth," I said.

"I was terrified of him, too."

"Probably with good reason," I said.

"Maybe, but I was, no, I *am*, ashamed of it."

"Well, you've confessed it to me," I said. "Maybe that'll help. You got a home phone in case I need to reach you after hours?"

"Yes. I've written it out for you. And I wish you wouldn't laugh at me."

"Sorry," I said. "It's a character flaw. I laugh at nearly everything."

She handed me a piece of lined yellow paper with her name and address and phone number handwritten on it with a felt-tipped pen in lavender ink. Maybe Marcy was more exotic than she looked.

chapter 3

I WAS THE only white guy in sight, sitting in an Area B cruiser on Seaver Street, near the zoo, with a cop named Jackson, who was the Community Service officer for District 2. He was a slow, calm, burly guy with gray hair. He had one of those profound bass voices which adds portent to everything said, though he didn't talk as if he knew that.

"Ellis got the same story most of the kids you can see got," Jackson said. He made a graceful inclusive gesture with his right hand.

"His mother's about fifteen years older than he is. She and him live with her mother, his grandmother. Nobody's working. Don't know who the father is. Mother does some dope 'cause she got nothing else that she knows how to do. Grandmother does what she can. Which ain't

much. She's got no education. She's got no money. She
don't know who fathered her daughter. When Ellis was
born, his grandmother was about thirty-two. Ellis don't
go to school much. Nobody at his house seems able to get
up early enough in the morning to get him there. He's a
gang banger soon as they'll have him. Ran for a while
with The Hobarts. By the time he's a grown-up he got his
career mapped out. He does strong arm, dope dealing,
small-time theft. For recreation he molests women.
Anybody he seen in his whole life, that he actually
knows, who's a success, that's what they do. Michael
Jordan may as well be from Mars."

"You think he did the woman in Pemberton?"

"Could have. Don't much matter to me. He's where he
should be. I don't never want to see him get out."

"His lawyer thinks he was railroaded because he was
black."

Jackson shrugged.

"Probably was. Happens a lot. Because he's black.
Because he's poor. Either one is bad, the combination is
very bad."

I watched the kids walking past us on the sidewalk.
They looked pretty much like any other kids. They were
dressed for each other. Oversized clothes, sneakers, hats
on backwards, or sideways. Most of them tried to look
confident. Most of them were full of pretense. All of them
were a little overmatched by the speed at which the world
came at them. But these kids weren't like other kids, and
I knew it. These kids were doomed. And they knew it.

Jackson watched me as I looked at the kids.

"Shame, ain't it?" he said.

"Been a shame for a long time," I said.

"Went to a meeting, couple weeks ago," Jackson said.
"Some politician thought it'd be a good idea to get some

influential folks together, talk about how to save the children. Asked me to stop by, maybe answer some questions."

"And let me guess," I said. "How many of them had grown up in a project."

"Just me," Jackson said. "They're all white. They all feel that the parents needed to be more involved. They say that they all have faced problems in their schools. Students been defacing desk tops in Marblehead, and they been writing dirty words on the lavatory walls in Newton."

"Better get a police presence in there quick," I said.

"And the whole evening nobody uses the word 'black' or the word 'Hispanic.' Like there ain't a racial thing going on. Like there's a bunch of white Anglo kids in the inner city, walking around looking for the fucking malt shop. So I say, you people have simply got to stop talking 'bout fucking *inner city* when you mean black. And you really got to stop talking about fucking *parents*. Kids in the *inner city* got the usual biological folks. But mostly they ain't got no fucking *parents*. Mostly the only family they got is the gang, and the only thing that they can insist on is respect. And the only things they got to insist on it with is balls and a gun."

"Makes you tired, doesn't it?"

"I'm used to it."

"Well, at least they're asking the right questions," I said.

"They ain't asking the right people," Jackson said.

"Hell," I said, "even if they were."

Jackson nodded.

"Yeah. Only thing will help is if people change."

"You think they're going to?"

"Been a cop thirty-four years," Jackson said.

"Yeah."

We were quiet. It was the second Monday after Labor Day, and the kids who went were back in school. It had been a dry summer, but it was promising to be a rainy fall. It had been ominous for five straight days and each day seemed heavier with rain than the last one. The TV meteorologists were almost climactic.

"Just don't get romantic on this one," Jackson said. "Ellis is a bad guy. Maybe he didn't have much choice about that, but it don't mean he ain't bad. You get him loose, you may be doing him a favor. You ain't helping anyone else. And you probably ain't helping him. You get him out, he gonna go back."

I nodded, looking at the still-green leaves stirring apprehensively in the overcast.

"You think you can eliminate crime?" I said.

Jackson snorted.

"So what do you do?" I said.

"Do what I can," Jackson said in his deep slow voice. "There's nobody perpetrating a crime on this corner, right now. That's 'cause I'm here. Somebody's perpetrating something someplace else, maybe, but right now this corner is okay . . . It's not much. But it's all there is."

"Yeah."

Jackson looked at me for a while. Then he nodded slowly.

"Okay," he said. "You too. Okay."

We were quiet again. The street was almost empty now as if everybody were inside somewhere, waiting for the storm.

"Just don't expect too much from Ellis Alves," Jackson said.

"I expect nothing," I said.

"Be about what you'll get," Jackson said.

chapter 4

SUSAN AND I were sitting together on the couch in my place in front of an applewood fire. She had come straight from work without changing, so she was in a dress and heels. The dress was black and simple and set off with some pearls. Her black hair was shiny and smelled like rain. I had my arm around her, which I was able to get away with, because Pearl the Wonder Dog was asleep on her back, in the armchair next to the fireplace, with her feet sticking up in the air.

"I always felt that Rita Fiore had designs on you," Susan said.

"Me too," I said. "I've always liked that about her."

"I suspect, however, that you are not the only one."

"Boy," I said. "You spoil everything."

"You think I'm wrong? Me, a shrink? And a female shrink at that?"

"No," I said, "I think you're right. That's what spoils it."

"How many times she been married?"

"Twice, she told me."

"Any kids?"

"Not that I know of."

The fire, being expertly built, settled in on itself as the logs burned. Pearl twitched a little in her sleep and made a snuffing sound.

"What do you suppose she's dreaming about?" Susan said.

"Everybody always says chasing rabbits," I said. "But how do they know. She might be dreaming about sex."

"The baby?"

"Maybe," I said.

"I hope not," Susan said. "Are you going to try and get this Ellis person out of jail?"

"I'm going to try and find out the truth," I said.

Susan bumped her head on my chest a couple of times, which seemed to mean approval.

"That's almost always the best thing to know," she said.

"We both have to believe that," I said. "Don't we."

"It's more than wishful thinking," Susan said. "There's a lot of ostensive evidence to support the opinion. Happiness is not the art of being well deceived."

"So much for Alexander Pope," I said.

"So much," Susan said. "You have any champagne?"

"Sure," I said.

"Well, let's drink some."

I got up quietly so Pearl wouldn't wake up and went and got a bottle of Krug and an ice bucket and two glasses. But to get the champagne and the ice for the bucket I had to open the refrigerator door. And Pearl can hear a refrigerator door open anywhere in the northern hemisphere. By the time I got the ice in the bucket, she was beside me, looking in at the open door. I gave her a small piece of the roast chicken we hadn't finished and closed the door and went back to the couch. Susan had her feet stretched out on the coffee table, and when I put the ice bucket down, Pearl jumped up beside her where I had been and went into an unyielding snuggle. I poured us two glasses, put the champagne in the bucket to chill, gave one glass to Susan, and sat down beside Pearl, who was now where she wanted to be, between me and Susan. But she wasn't big enough. I could still reach past her and put my arm around Susan. Which I did. Pearl looked at me. I did not stick my tongue out at her. It is important to win gracefully.

"Have you ever thought of having a child?" Susan said.

"Excuse me?"

"A child. Haven't you ever wanted one?"

"Well, Paul's sort of like my kid," I said. "Not to mention the princess dog."

"I'd like to adopt a baby," Susan said.

I drank my champagne and reached over and got the bottle and poured some more. I drank a little of that.

"You and me?"

"Yes. How long have we been together?"

"We met just after school had opened, about this time of year as a matter of fact, in 1974," I said. "Of course there was a gap back there in 1984/85. . . ."

"And there won't be another one," Susan said. "But I would like a baby."

"A baby," I said.

"Yes."

"And would we move in together and take turns looking after it?"

"No. We could live as we do. I think we need to. The baby would live with me. You would be its father."

"What kind of baby would we get?" I said.

"I don't know. I thought we could talk about it."

"Oh."

"It's not that hard," Susan said. "There are only two choices."

"Yeah."

I finished my champagne and poured some more. Susan's glass was empty so I poured her some as well, which emptied the bottle. I got up and got another bottle and jammed it into the ice bucket to chill.

"So what do you think?" Susan said.

"I don't know. It's a little sudden," I said.

"Yes, I know. I didn't want to broach the subject until I was sure myself."

"A little one," I said, "like a month old?"

"Yes, as young as possible. I'd like as much of the full experience as I can have."

"How much do they weigh when they're that age?" I said.

"Oh, twelve, fifteen pounds perhaps."

"About the size of a small turkey," I said.

"About," Susan said.

I nodded. We were quiet. Susan sipped her champagne, staring into the fire. Pearl's head was in her lap. I patted Susan's shoulder a little.

"I can't make this decision for you," she said finally. "But I don't want to do this alone."

"Be difficult alone," I said.

"More than that, it isn't fair to the child. A child benefits from having a father."

"If he or she can," I said. "Probably better having one good parent than none."

"I don't think I'll want to do this without you," she said.

"You'll never have to do anything without me," I said.

"I know," she said.

And she leaned her head back against my arm and the three of us sat there and looked at the fire.

chapter 5

A STATE COP from the Norfolk DA's office patted Hawk
and me down and ushered us into the conference room on
the thirty-ninth floor at Cone, Oakes and Baldwin. A
couple of guys from the Bureau of Corrections brought
Ellis Alves wearing leg irons and handcuffs into the room
and sat him in a chair with a great view out the picture
window of places he might never visit. They took off the
handcuffs and left and it was just Hawk and me and Ellis.

Ellis was tall and bony with high cheekbones and his
hair cut short. There were prison gang tattoos on his
forearms. He sat straight up in the chair and stared
straight at me.

"My name's Spenser," I said.

"So what you gonna do?" he said to me.

"Find out if you did what you're in jail for."

"Sure," Ellis said. He looked at Hawk. "Who this? Your butler?"

"I don't know," I said. "He followed me in."

Hawk looked thoughtfully at Ellis.

"We know you bad, Ellis," Hawk said. "Don't have to keep showing us."

"You ever been inside, bro?"

"Been almost everywhere, Ellis."

"You be inside, bro, you know there's black and there's white and you got to choose."

"Damn," Hawk said. "I been trying to pass."

"What's your name, bro? Your name Tom, maybe?"

"My name's Hawk."

Ellis was too full of jailhouse self-control to look startled. But he was silent for a moment staring at Hawk. Then he nodded slightly and looked back at me.

"So what you want from me, Spenser?"

"Tell me your story," I said.

"I got no story, I'm just another nigger framed by the man."

"Sure," I said. "How'd it happen?"

"How you think?"

"I figure they kidnapped you from church," I said.

"Naw. They come busting in, about eight of them, while I was still in bed. Ten o'clock in the morning. I had a bad hangover. State cops, I think. I never did know for sure. And they haul my ass out to Pemberton. And stick me in a cell in the back by myself. You know, man, my whole life I never been in Pemberton? 'Cept for doing time, I ain't been five miles from Seaver Street."

"You didn't kill this girl."

"No. I tole them that and every time I tole them that the one cop doing all the investigating, State cop, I think, big tall guy, blond hair, real pink cheeks, he talk a lot of trash, 'bout how they know how to handle a buck nigger goes around raping their girls."

Ellis paused a moment thinking about it and shrugged.

"After a while couple of people I never heard of pick me out of a lineup," he said. "And then they gimme some preppy bitch probably never been laid, to be my lawyer, and you know she walks me right into the joint."

"You got a theory?" I said.

"Sure, same old honky shit. Something goes down, find a nigger and clear the case."

"How'd they pick you?"

"They want to get me off the street anyway."

"Who they?" Hawk said.

"You ought to know that, bro."

"Yeah, but they a lot of white folks, Ellis. Which one want to get you off the streets?"

"What's the difference?" Ellis said. "They ain't going to help you get me out."

"We're not looking for help," I said. "We're looking for information."

"Well, I already give you all I got," Ellis said.

I looked at Hawk. Hawk shrugged.

"He got no reason to hold back," Hawk said.

I nodded, and looked at Alves.

"You got anything else to say?"

"The cop doing all the talking, out in Pemberton, cop name of Olson? Maybe he know something."

"We'll talk with him," I said.

Ellis looked at Hawk again.

"I heard about you," Ellis said.

"Un huh."

"You willing to work with him?" Ellis nodded toward me.

"Un huh."

"You trust him?"

"Un huh."

Ellis, still sitting rigidly erect in the chair, looked at me like I was a specimen. He shook his head.

"You ain't got no prayer. They gonna land on you like a truck-load of sludge. You gonna get buried. Like me."

"Probably not," I said.

"They want it buried—they gonna bury it. Even if you white, you helping a nigger, you ain't white no more."

I didn't see anywhere to go with that so I let it pass.

"You got no idea how they happened to pick you to take the fall?" I said.

"None."

"Okay," I said.

I got up and went to the door. I opened it and nodded at one of the guards. They came in, put the cuffs back on Alves, patted him down, and led him out. He stood absolutely straight as they did this, and when they took him out he didn't look back.

"You in for life," Hawk said after Alves was gone, "hope will kill you. You going to survive, you got to keep your mind steady."

"I know."

"Ain't much else in there but hate and power."

"Better than nothing," I said.

chapter 6

THE CAMPUS OF Pemberton College was like Collegeland at a theme park: stone buildings on hills, winding footpaths, greensward, brick, and a bunch of trees arranged so artfully that they seemed almost accidental. There even was an occasional portico and at least one arched passageway that I drove through. I saw a number of young women, many in fine physical condition. Most of them appeared dressed to work out, or go camping. I was wearing a tee-shirt and jeans. I had my jacket off. As I drove I tried putting one arm out the window and flexing. Nobody made any attempt to flag me down and seduce me, and it was kind of cold, and it made my shoulder stiff, so I pulled my arm in and rolled up the window.

A discreet road sign said "Campus Police." I turned off

between some bushes and went in to a small parking lot behind the maintenance building. The cops were in a wing of the building, with no sign outside, hidden away like an embarrassing relative.

"My name is Spenser," I told the young cop on the desk. "I'm looking into a murder you had here about a year and a half back."

"May I see some ID?" he said. His name tag said Brendan Cooney.

I showed him some. He studied it closely and slowly before he gave it back.

"Whaddya need?" he said.

"I'd like to talk to the officers involved in the case," I said.

The young cop nodded.

"Have a seat," he said.

I sat in a straight chair near the door and read the campus parking regulations while he went into an office for a while and then came back.

"Chief will see you," he said and opened the lift top gate in the counter, and I walked through and into the chief's office.

"Sit down," the chief said. "I'm Fred Livingston."

He was a blond guy with longish hair combed back and parted on the left. His upper teeth were sort of prominent and he looked to be maybe forty-five.

"I'm working for Cone, Oakes and Baldwin," I said. "Law firm. They want to re-examine the murder thing you had out here about a year and a half ago."

Livingston nodded. "Melissa Henderson," he said.

"Who handled the thing?"

"For us? I did. But there wasn't much to handle. This isn't a big city police force. Soon as we found her we called the town cops, and they brought the State cops with them."

"You see the crime scene?" I said.

"Sure. One of our guys found her, Danny Ferris. Poor bastard. He called me, and I told him not to touch anything and I went right over."

"Can you show it to me?"

"Certainly," Livingston said. He stood, picked up a walkie-talkie from the recharge rack, put on his hat, and walked out with me.

"She was behind some bushes down from one of the dorms," he said in the car. "Probably the first corpse Danny ever saw."

"How's your experience?" I said.

Livingston shrugged.

"I've seen a few. I was Police Chief in Agawam before I got this job. Motor vehicle mostly. Some of them are pretty ugly. Couple of gun-shot homicides. Domestic one, and one involving some gang kids from Springfield. Drugs probably, we never got the perpetrators."

We went back under the archway between two buildings and bore to the left.

"Park over here," Livingston said, and I did.

We were at the foot of a hill with a long gradual grade, and a footpath that ascended the hill and curved among some bushes on the way. There's no special reason for it to curve, but landscape architects hate a straight line. Livingston led me along the path to the first clump of bushes.

"She was here," he said.

I looked back at the roadway where we'd parked.

"How'd he see her?" I said.

Livingston made a face.

"Crows," he said. "Danny saw a bunch of crows

flapping around and came up to see what was going on."

There didn't seem to be anything to say about that.

"She was on her back," Livingston said. "No clothes except for her bra pulled up above her tits. Her pantyhose were tied tight around her neck. You ever seen anybody been strangled."

"Yeah."

"Looked like she had cuts and bruises, too. 'Course, some of that might have been the crows."

"ME could probably figure that out," I said.

"Oh, yeah. He did. But I'm just telling you what we found."

"Sure," I said. "Go ahead."

"That's about it," Livingston said. "I called the town cops, and they came over, and some State cops, and we got out of the way."

I stood and looked at the crime scene. It told me what most crime scenes told me. Nothing. Students walked past us with books, and book bags, and knapsacks, and Diet Cokes in paper cups with plastic tops and straws sticking out. There was nothing interesting about two middle-aged guys standing around beside a clump of bushes. Nothing reminded them that a woman's murdered body had lain here a year and a half ago. Most of them probably knew it had happened, some of them had probably known the woman. But there was nothing they could do for her now, and there were midterms to think about, and college guys, and maybe the Dartmouth winter carnival. They had places to go, so they went there. And there was no reason they shouldn't have.

"Any clothes?" I said.

"Just the bra."

"Anybody ever find her clothes?"

"Not so far as I know," Livingston said. "The nigger

dragged her into his car. I guess he did her there and got rid of her clothes later."

"And brought her here and dumped her."

"That's what they tell me."

I looked up at the dorm on the hill.

"Odd place to dump somebody."

"Can't see it from the road," Livingston said.

"If it's on this side of these bushes," I said. "But then you can see it from the dorm."

"He probably didn't realize that," Livingston said.

"Not hard to notice," I said.

"Probably dark. I don't think they ever established just when he dumped her."

"That's probably it," I said. "Odd place for a black man from the city to dump a dead body, on a mostly white, all prestigious, suburban, women's college campus."

Livingston shrugged.

"Had to dump it somewhere," he said. "Wouldn't want to get caught driving it around."

"You'd think he'd have driven into the center of the campus?"

"Might have driven until he found a spot where he was alone. Might have been traffic near the gate, people walking by on the street, how the hell do I know. They ain't always the smartest people in the world."

"Most folks aren't," I said. "Anybody talk with the dorm residents up there?"

"Couple of State detectives were around. They probably did. College worked pretty hard to protect the students."

"From what?"

Livingston looked surprised.

"From being hassled," he said. "People pay about

thirty grand a year for their kids to go here. They don't like it much having the kids grilled by some cop, you know?"

"Where would I get the names of the students who lived in that dorm a year and a half ago?"

"Dean of Student Affairs, I suppose. But she won't want to give them to you."

"Of course she won't," I said.

chapter 7

HAWK AND I were at the bar in The Four Seasons Hotel
having a beer. It was a spacious, comfortable bar, though
one of the advantages of drinking with Hawk was that
even in crowded bars, you always had elbow room.
Nobody ever talked loud around Hawk. Nobody ever
crowded him.

"Been talking to Tony Marcus about my man Ellis."

"Marcus is out?"

Hawk nodded. He was making eye contact with an
elegant platinum-haired woman in a long dress, who was
having cocktails with a couple of suits.

"Tony got a lot of money," Hawk said.

"The Russians get a wedge into his business?" I said.

"Not after he come out," Hawk said.

"He know anything about Ellis?" I said.

"Knew him at Cedar Junction a little. Or so he say. Tony don't trust the truth."

"And?"

"And nothing much. Ellis doing the time. Tony say he a pretty bad ass."

"Anything about the Henderson murder?"

"Ellis say he didn't do it. But it don't mean much. Lotta cons say they didn't do it."

The platinum-haired woman wore a wedding ring. The suit she was sitting next to was shorter than she was and a lot heavier, and somewhat older. He rested his hand on her thigh like the proud owner of a pedigreed dog, while he talked to the other suit about something that interested him but bored hell out of her. She was still looking at Hawk.

"I can see why she's not paying attention to her husband," I said. "But why you and not me?"

"Probably 'cause she like tall, dark, and handsome," Hawk said.

Her husband was waving his hands as he talked to the guy across the table. A diamond ring glinted on his little finger. He started to tick off a series of somethings on the fingers of his left hand. Platinum Hair rose gracefully and walked toward the bar. She stopped in front of Hawk and said quietly, "My name is Claire Reston. I'm in room 508 and my husband will be out doing business all day tomorrow."

Hawk smiled at her.

"Care to sightsee?" he said.

"Depends on the sight," she said.

"We'll talk," Hawk said.

"Good," she said and moved on toward the ladies' room at the back, her elegant hips swaying under the tight dress.

"This is a positive sign," I said.

Hawk smiled thoughtfully, and drank some beer. I ordered two more. The bartender brought them and put another dish of mixed nuts on the bar where we could reach them. The platinum-haired woman glided back from the ladies' room and walked past us and smiled. Her husband was leaning forward now, drawing an imaginary something on the tabletop with his forefinger. He didn't look up when she sat down.

"You ever wanted kids?" I said to Hawk.

"I like them a little older," Hawk said.

"No, you animal, I meant have you ever wanted to be a father?"

"Not lately," Hawk said.

The piano player had been on break. He came back in and sat down and began to play "Green Dolphin Street." The husband of Platinum Hair looked at his watch and said something to the other suit. Then he jerked his head at his wife, and the three of them got up and left. As they went out, the husband had hold of the other guy's arm and was talking close to his face. Platinum Hair looked back at Hawk without any expression. Then she followed her husband and his cohort out of the bar.

"Susan wants to adopt a baby," I said.

Hawk never reacted to anything, and he didn't to this. But he turned his attention toward me and the weight of it was palpable.

"Only one?" he said.

"So far."

"What about Pearl?"

"In addition to Pearl," I said.

"Pearl won't like it much," Hawk said.

"Pearl is not alone in that."

"Susan want you to be the papa?"

"She says she doesn't want to do it without me."

"Don't blame her."

"No. I don't either."

Hawk ate a couple of peanuts and drank a little beer.

"Kind of heartwarming," Hawk said. "You changing diapers."

"Heartwarming," I said.

"Sort of what you do for a living anyway," Hawk said. "Good preparation."

"I knew talking it out with you would make me feel better," I said.

"What are friends for, Pappy?"

"Shut up," I said.

Hawk nodded. The place was filling up. It was noisier now but not loud. You could still hear the piano player. He was playing some variations on "Dream Dancing." We were drinking Saranac Black and Tan.

"Good beer," Hawk said.

"Yeah."

"She got the right to have a baby," he said.

"Yep."

"You got the right not to want one."

"Yep."

"You explain to her how we been bringing Paul Giacomon up since he was 'bout fifteen and that's enough parenting for us?"

"We?" I said.

"He a dancer?" Hawk said.

"Yeah."

"Well, he didn't get the natural rhythm from your side," Hawk said.

"I hadn't thought of that," I said.

We were quiet, the piano player had segued into "Memphis in June." My beer was gone again. I ordered more. The room was quietly full of adult cocktail sounds. Drinks being mixed, people murmuring to each other. Occasional laughter. The smell of whisky. The piano.

"You don't want to do it," Hawk said.

"No."

"You don't want to as much as she do want to?" Hawk said.

"I think so."

"You told her that?"

"No."

"Well, that's a fucking mess, isn't it?" Hawk said.

"Couldn't have put it better myself," I said.

chapter 8

THE DEAN OF Student Affairs at Pemberton College, whose name, according to her desk plate, was J. J. Glidden, said that President Evans was the only one who was authorized to discuss any aspect of the Melissa Henderson matter. So I went to see her. She would be in after lunch. I waited. Surprisingly enough, after lunch she was in.

The president was a big rangy woman with short sandy hair and humorous eyes. She was wearing high waisted black pants and a white blouse with a high collar when she met me at the door of her office and ushered me to a chair. There was a wide gold wedding band on her left hand. She looked to be about fifty-five. When she sat behind her desk the sunlight coming in the big Palladian window behind her showed up the gray in her hair. Her name was Deborah Evans.

"How may I help you, sir?"

"I'm looking into the Melissa Henderson murder," I said.

"Excuse me, but I thought that had been looked into."

"There's a feeling," I said, "that justice miscarried in this instance and I've been hired to see if that's true."

"You are a private detective?"

"Yes, ma'am."

"How does one get to be a private detective?" she said.

"I hesitate to generalize," I said. "I was a cop, found myself restless with the hierarchy, decided to go private. I was helped to that decision by getting fired."

"You speak rather well," she said.

"You too," I said.

She frowned for a moment and then her face widened into a smile.

"Good for you," she said. "I was patronizing, wasn't I."

"What I need is a list of the students who at the time of the murder were living in the dorm that overlooks where the body was found."

"Do you have some sort of, I don't know the proper terminology, some sort of legal empowerment that requires me to give it to you?"

"No."

"Then I will not."

"You academics are so evasive," I said.

She smiled. It was a nice smile, but firm.

"I'm sorry to be so blunt," she said. "But I am very clear on this, and I know the trustees will support me. The event was a severe hardship for all of us here and we do not wish it to be disinterred."

"Even if an innocent man is inside for life?" I said.

"Do you know him to be innocent?"

"No."

"My memory is that the man convicted of the crime is a career criminal who preyed on women."

"So no harm putting him away," I said. "Even if he didn't do this one."

"That may be," she said. "One could make an argument for it, I think. But that is not my issue. My issue is this college and the young women past, present, and future for whose education, in the largest sense, we are responsible."

"Especially past," I said. "Gotta raise those funds."

"If we didn't raise funds," she said, "the college could not survive. But there is no argument here. Until I know that the freedom of an innocent man is at stake, and I guess I mean 'innocent,' also, in its largest sense, I will not help you to intrude on the life of this campus."

"Well," I said. "I guess I'll have to just ask around."

President Evans didn't seem daunted.

"You are free to do that, obviously. But not on this campus. This campus is private property and I am reasonably certain that I can prohibit you from trespassing."

"How do you feel about justice?" I said.

"I am in favor of it, but I am not prepared to sacrifice this college and our young women to your definition of it."

I grinned at her.

"I hope I'm not intimidating you," I said.

The amusement that always seemed to linger around the corners of her eyes expanded into a full-face laugh.

"Not so badly that I can't breathe," she said.

"Good," I said. "I'm clear on your position. Now

here's mine. I have no desire to damage this campus or its young women past, present, and future. But I am going to find out if Ellis Alves is where he should be; and if he isn't, I'm going to get him out."

"Since we are being frank," President Evans said, "I will tell you that the victim's mother is an alumna of this college, and the wife of the governor is an alumna of this college and our board of trustees includes two U.S. Senators. None of them, including the victim's mother, wants Melissa's death exploited."

"Two U.S. Senators," I said. "Yikes."

"Are you intimidated?"

"Not so I can't breathe," I said.

President Evans laughed.

"Well, I must say, as adversaries go, you are a lot of fun," she said. "A small dose of charm."

"I've found a small dose to be safer," I said. "The full wattage, all at once, and people are sometimes injured."

"Especially women, I imagine."

"They often hurt themselves in their frenzy to disrobe."

"I've been able to conquer the impulse," she said. "You and I remain adversaries, however congenial, and are likely to remain so. You don't seem like someone who will give up easily."

"Or ever," I said.

"You also don't seem like someone who would strike a woman," she said. "Which somewhat disarms you. I imagine that your size would intimidate a lot of men."

"The power of weakness," I said.

"Yes," she said. "The world is quite ironic, isn't it."

I nodded. We sat and looked at each other. I liked her. There was a calmness in her, a quality of settled self-confidence in the way she leaned back in her chair, the simplicity of her attire, the understatement of her makeup. She knew herself and was happy with what she knew. It made her formidable.

"Is there anything you would care to tell me about the murder of Melissa Henderson?" I said.

She smiled at me.

"You take whatever you can get, don't you?" she said.

"What can you tell me?"

"It was a nightmare for this college," she said. "In personal terms, it was heartbreaking to those who knew Melissa, and frightening to all of us who are women, to whom such a thing could be done, here, in our enclosure, so to speak. It was also a nightmare in terms of publicity, in terms of student recruitment, and in many cases, alumnae support."

"Did you know the victim?" I said.

"Yes. Her mother graduated from Pemberton as did her grandmother. I was a student here with her mother."

"What can you tell me about Melissa?"

"Nothing."

"Good student? Bad student?"

President Evans shook her head.

"She have a boyfriend? Or a girlfriend?"

"How contemporary," President Evans said.

"Did she?"

"I don't know."

"Was she a girl who would be likely to have one?"

President Evans shrugged.

"I think I'll stop wasting our time," I said.

"Good," she said.

I stood. She stood. We shook hands.

"If there is something that comes up in the future," she said, "which does not threaten my college, I would be pleased to help you."

"Thanks," I said. "And if you ever need a thug . . ."

"Maybe for fund-raising," she said and smiled. And I smiled. And she came out from behind her desk and walked with me to the door and opened it. And I left.

chapter 9

THE THING I dreaded most was talking to the victim's parents, so I figured I might as well get it done. They lived in Brookline in a big red brick house with a wide porch, a couple of blocks uphill from the reservoir. Mr. Henderson was The Henderson Corporation, a firm that occupied most of the floors in the Mercantile Building that Cone, Oakes and Baldwin didn't occupy. The Henderson Corporation owned banks, and fertilizer companies, and a stock brokerage firm, and a company in Switzerland that made faucets, and a lot of other stuff that I couldn't remember, because I didn't take notes when I looked them up. He was a medium-sized guy with no hair and horn-rimmed glasses. His handshake was firm, his gaze direct. He was still in his suit, with his jacket off. He wore a white shirt and broad suspenders in a colorful pattern—the kind of no-nonsense guy that you'd trust with your money, though you might trust him more with his own. Mrs. Henderson was slim and dark with her black hair in a severe Dutch boy cut. She had on a mango-colored dress with a square neck and a short skirt. It looked good on her.

"You wish to talk about our daughter," Mr. Henderson said when we were seated in some bentwood furniture covered in floral prints in the sunroom off the formal living room.

"Yes, sir," I said.

"We had hoped to put that behind us," Henderson said.

He and his wife sat together on the sofa against the white painted brick back of the living room fireplace.

"I'm sorry," I said. "But I've been employed by Cone, Oakes and Baldwin to look into her death more closely."

"To what purpose?" Mrs. Henderson said. She held her hands folded in her lap. There was a stereo setup to my right, in front of one of the windows. On it was a picture of a young woman wearing a much too big Taft University letter sweater. The sweater had a big blue chenille T on the front. There was a pair of small tennis racquets woven into the crosspiece of the T. Beneath the racquets the word *co-captain* was embroidered.

"Is that Melissa?" I said.

"Yes," Henderson said.

"What is the purpose of your investigation?" Mrs. Henderson said.

"To make sure they've got the right guy."

They were both silent for a moment, and then Mrs. Henderson said, "You mean you're not sure?"

"I have just begun, ma'am. I'm not sure of anything. It's why I'm going around talking to people."

"This law firm, this Cone whatchamacallit, they think Alves is innocent?"

"They feel he got an inadequate defense," I said. "They wish to be sure it's the right man."

Again they were quiet.

Finally, Henderson said, "I realize you're just doing your job . . ."

His wife interrupted.

"Walton is always reasonable. He can't help it. But I don't care about your job. I care about my daughter. And I will not permit the man who murdered our only child to be set free."

Henderson looked at his wife and at me. He didn't say anything.

"You have no reason to question the verdict?" I said.

"Absolutely not," Mrs. Henderson said.

She was leaning forward on the couch, her hands still clasped in her lap. She might have been actually quivering with the intensity of her feeling, or I might have thought she was.

"Mr. Henderson?"

He shook his head.

"Your daughter ever go to Taft?" I said.

"No," Henderson said.

His voice was still reasonable, but it was sounding a little shaky.

"Do you know who her friends were?" I said. "Her roommate, maybe, at school."

Mrs. Henderson stood up quite suddenly.

"Get out," Mrs. Henderson said. "Get out of my house, you nosy fucking nigger lover."

Her daughter was too recently dead for me to debate her about race and justice. Or even nosiness. Henderson got to his feet and put a hand on her shoulder, she shrugged away from it. The skin on her face seemed too tight, and the structure of the skull showed beneath it.

"And if you do succeed in getting that son of a bitch out of jail I will find a way to kill him myself," she said.

"You'd better go," Henderson said to me. "We have nothing to say to you."

"I'm sorry I had to intrude," I said.

"Just get out of here," Mrs. Henderson said.

Which is what I did. Driving back to Boston I watched the joggers moving around the reservoir in the bright fall morning. I remembered once again why I had dreaded the parents. I'd been talking to the next of kin of various victims for a long time now and had seen all the grief I ever wanted to. It was hard to rate grief. The loss of a mate seemed to elicit as much grief as the loss of a child. But nothing came close to the rage level of grieving parents. Because she had called me a nigger lover didn't mean she would frame a black man. The police chief at Pemberton had called Alves a nigger, too. Didn't mean he would frame a black man either. On the other hand, none of this meant Alves wasn't framed. Be good to find out something that meant something.

At Cleveland Circle I turned left and went up a block to Commonwealth Ave. and headed in town that way. Near State Police Headquarters at 1010 Commonwealth, I found a convenient spot at a bus stop and parked and went in to talk with a cop I knew.

Healy was at his desk in the Criminal Investigation Division, of which he was the commander. He and I had worked on a case up in Smithfield about twenty years ago, and he'd helped me out now and then since. He was gray-haired and wiry, and not as tall as I was, though as far as I could tell it didn't bother him.

"Whaddya need today," Healy said when I walked in.

"Maybe I'm just stopping in to say hi."

"Okay," Healy said, "hi."

"And maybe to ask you if you know anything about that murder in Pemberton about eighteen months ago."

"Maybe that too, huh?" Healy said. "College kid?"

"Yeah," I said. "According to the trial transcript, a State detective named Miller was on it."

"Yeah, Tommy Miller."

"You follow the case?"

"Not really. As I remember it, it was pretty open and shut. Two eyewitnesses saw the perp kidnap her, right?"

"So they tell me."

"So why are you asking about it?" Healy said.

"Had a defense attorney right out of law school, she thinks he was innocent, and she botched the defense."

"And she hired you to get him off?"

"Sort of. She works for Cone, Oakes now, and she got them to hire me."

"Must be a nice change of pace for you," Healy said, "a client who can pay."

"Nothing wrong with it," I said. "How's Miller?"

"He's all right. Probably a little rough around the edges. Thinks being a State cop makes him important."

"Tough guy?"

Healy shrugged.

"Compared to who?" he said. "Compared to some high school kid with a loud mouth and a nose full of dope, he's tougher than scrap iron. Compared to Hawk, say, or me . . . or you." Healy shrugged.

"He ambitious?"

"He's an eager beaver," Healy said. "Probably want to be CID commander someday."

"Think he'll make it?"

"Not soon," Healy said.

"How is he as an investigator?"

"Far as I know he's pretty good. I don't like him. But he clears his cases and mostly they result in convictions that stand. He doesn't cut a lot of corners."

"How is he on race?"

Healy shrugged.

"No worse than most," he said. "Your guy black?"

"Yeah."

"You think he got railroaded because of that?"

"I don't know," I said. "Everywhere I go I keep hearing nigger nigger. And everywhere I go people stonewall me."

Healy nodded slowly. He was in shirt sleeves, sitting back in his chair, with one foot propped on the edge of his desk.

"Well, it could be," Healy said. "I'm a white Irish guy, been a cop thirty-five years. Heard a lot of nigger nigger. Sometimes it's because you're dealing with a bunch of ignorant racist assholes, and sometimes it's because the black guy has done something bad and everyone's mad at him. But they're not mad at him because he's black, you unnerstand? They're mad at him because he did the bad thing, and 'nigger's' a convenient thing to call him. I don't know about Miller. But what I do know is that race matters less to most cops than the media likes to make out. You know? You arrest some black guy with a rap sheet three and a half yards long, and the media questions you. Is it because he's black? No, it's because he's got a rap sheet three and a half yards long. For a similar crime. It's like the Stuart thing awhile back. The cops' information is that a black guy shot a white guy and his wife at the fringe of the black ghetto. They're supposed to start shaking people down at Brae Burn Country Club?"

"I would have suspected at once," I said, "that he

murdered his wife and wounded himself badly to cover it up."

"Yeah," Healy said, "happens all the time."

"Would Miller frame a guy?"

"Hey," Healy said, "the guy works for me."

"Would he?"

"Lotta cops would. Most of them wouldn't frame an innocent guy," Healy said. "But a lot of them might help the evidence a little if they figured they had Mr. Right."

"If Mr. Right were black . . . ?"

Healy shook his head.

"I don't know," he said. "It wouldn't make it less likely."

I thought about that while I got up and had a drink of spring water from the jug on top of Healy's file cabinet.

"I'm going to have to talk with Miller," I said.

"He's off today," Healy said. "I'll ask him to stop by your office tomorrow."

"Thank you."

"Don't let him scare you."

"I'll keep reminding him I know you," I said.

"I'd rather you didn't shame me in front of my men," Healy said.

"Self-defense," I said.

chapter 10

I MET SUSAN at the bar at Rialto, after her last appointment. The thank-God-it's-evening crowd was still thin and we got a couple of stools at one end of the bar. Susan had a glass of Merlot. I ordered beer. Outside the big picture window behind us, the courtyard at Charles Square was gussied up for a band concert, and fall tourists were sitting around the outdoor cafe guzzling large pink drinks, waiting for it to start.

"How is it going?" Susan said. "The Pemberton murder case?"

She drank a micro sip of wine.

"Everyone I talk to tells me that they won't help me."

"It's probably a pretty nasty wound for the people involved," Susan said.

"Even Ellis is not helpful," I said. "Hawk said it's because a lifer can't allow himself to hope."

"I wonder if Hawk has another life as a shrink," Susan said.

"I'm not sure about Hawk's tolerance for bullshit," I said.

"We don't call it that," Susan said.

"What do you call it?" I said.

"Avoidance."

"I don't think Hawk has too much tolerance for that either."

"Maybe not."

In the courtyard three musicians came and began to set up on the other side. People began to drift into the courtyard and stand around. It was still warm even though it was fall and most people were still coatless and shortsleeved.

"Have you thought about the baby?" Susan said.

"By which I assume you don't mean Pearl," I said.

"That's right," Susan said. "I don't."

I took in a lot of air and let it out slowly.

"I think it would be a mistake," I said.

"Um hmm," Susan said.

"I think we have reached maturity without children and that a baby at this point would very seriously compromise us."

"Why do you think so?" Susan said.

"A kid's a lot of work," I said.

"You're not afraid of work," Susan said. "Neither am I."

"Oh hell, Suze, I know that. I just don't want a kid, and I'm trying to think of good reasons why I don't."

"Do you mind sharing me?"

"Yes."

"Is it more than that?"

"Yes."

"Do you know what it is?"

"No."

"Maybe you will," she said.

The way I loved her never varied. But how I liked her could go up and down, and it went down most when she was being professional. I drank a little more beer.

"How come you want a kid?" I said.

She smiled.

"The old switch-the-conversation trick," she said.

I nodded.

"I guess I want to have the experience," she said. "I guess I miss participating in what so many women have done."

"Don't blame you."

"I know in some ways that sounds selfish, that it's about me, and how I'll feel, not about the still-anonymous baby and how he or she will feel."

"That would be true for anyone having a baby," I said. "Even the old-fashioned way. Until you have it, it's always about you."

"I suppose so."

We were quiet. The musicians were playing in the courtyard, but we couldn't really hear them through the insulating glass of the windows and above the chatter of the bar, now full of people glad to be out of work. Some friends of Susan's came by. Susan introduced us.

"Bill and Debbie Elovitz."

They said hello. I said hello. They talked to Susan. I drank some beer. After they had moved on, Susan said, "They have children."

"How nice," I said.

"I feel a little scared about this," Susan said, "as if maybe this could hurt us."

I shook my head.

"We'll figure it out," I said.

"But how can we?" Susan said. "You can't partially adopt a baby. We either do or we don't. One of us loses. Either way."

"We've dealt with worse," I said. "We'll deal with this."

"How?"

"I don't know. But I know that we love one another and will love one another if we do adopt a baby and will love one another if we don't."

Susan looked past me for a while at the crowd in the courtyard, listening so reasonably to the music. Then she shifted her glance back on me and put her hand on my hand where it rested on the bar.

"We will," she said. "Won't we?"

"Yes," I said. "We will."

chapter II

TROOPER TOMMY MILLER had a blond crew cut and a thick neck and looked like he might have played tackle for Iowa. He came into my office wearing plainclothes, didn't shut the door behind him, took a seat in one of my client chairs, and put one spit-shined cordovan shoe up on the edge of my desk.

"Captain Healy says I should talk with you."

I got up and walked around my desk and past him and shut the door and turned around and walked back behind my desk and sat down.

"Healy tell you why?" I said.

"Something about that nigger that did the broad in Pemberton," he said. "You're trying to get him off."

"Nicely put," I said.

"You got no prayer, pal," Miller said. "It was my case, and he did it."

"I've read the transcript," I said. "So I know what you testified. You got anything to add, stuff you knew but couldn't prove, stuff no one asked you?"

"If I did, why would I talk to you?"

"Interest of justice?" I said.

Miller laughed.

"Sure thing," he said.

"You got no eyewitness," I said.

"He's a known rapist. He's got no alibi. We got two eyewitnesses saw him grab her. We got dirt from the heel of his right shoe with traces of fertilizer. Both match samples from the crime scene. You're wasting your time and you sure as hell are wasting mine."

"Coroner says she wasn't raped," I said. "Says there was vaginal bruising but no sign of penetration, no semen."

"So he couldn't get it up. Lot of rapists can't get it up. Probably why he killed her."

"Frustration?" I said.

"Sure."

"What'd he strangle her with? Coroner says it wasn't manual."

"Some piece of her clothing, probably, what's the difference. He did her."

"You remember his name?" I said.

Miller started to open his mouth and stopped and frowned.

"Hey, pal. It was, what, year and a half ago? You think I get one case a year?"

"But you're pretty sure he was black."

"Ohhh," Miller said. "That's where we're going, huh? Poor innocent guy got railroaded."

"Did he?"

"You go down that road, pal, you're going to have a lot of people mad at you. Including me."

"I'll try to control my breathing," I said. "Who's going to be mad besides you?"

"The broad's father is Walton Henderson, for crissake. You think he'll sit around and let you fucking bleeding-heart his daughter's murderer out of jail?"

"You and Walton Henderson," I said. "Pretty scary."

"Scary enough, pal."

Miller was still sitting with his foot up on my desk, leaning back in my chair, the off-hand tough guy approach that is so popular these days.

"How did you come up with Ellis Alves?" I said.

"You read the transcript; you know."

"I know what the transcript says, I wanted to hear it from you."

"Pemberton cops got a tip, anonymous letter, mailed from Boston."

"With Alves's name and address?"

"Yeah. Pemberton bucked it over to me. They ain't used to much more than bad traffic, and I went in and busted him. Yanked his black ass right out of bed."

"By yourself," I said.

"I had troopers with me from our office and some Area B guys."

"You get many letters like that on a case like this? Naming the suspect, giving you the address?"

"High-profile case, you get a lotta stuff."

"Most of it good?"

"No, most of it's bullshit. This one was good."

"You got no idea who wrote the letter."

"No."

"Try to find out?"

"Find out?" Miller said. "Come on, asshole, gimme a

break. It's written on a computer on plain paper you can buy in any Staples. You know how many people got personal computers?"

"How many got them in Alves's neighborhood?" I said.

"Who says it came from his neighborhood?"

"They knew his address."

"I know your address. Don't mean I live here."

"Just a thought," I said.

"Well, it's a fucking stupid one."

I leaned over my desk and shoved his foot off the edge of my desk. It made his chair come forward with a bump.

"Keep your feet off the furniture," I said.

Miller stood up and leaned forward over the desk.

"You better just walk goddamned light around me, pal. I don't much like it when outsiders come in and step all over one of my cases. You unnerstan? You keep pushing at this and something bad is going to happen."

"You going to do the bad thing?" I said. "Or Walton Henderson? Or will it be you doing it because Walton Henderson told you to?"

Miller's face, which was farm-boy pink to start with, turned a darker red.

"You sonova bitch," he said. "You want to back that up?"

"By bopping you on the kisser?" I said. "It's been awhile since I thought backing things up mattered."

It wasn't quite true, but it sounded mature to me, and I went with it.

"You are making a bad mistake here, pal," Miller said. "You are walking into a swamp."

"Then I'll probably run into you again," I said and held his look, and did my best former cop dead-eyed look. We sat like that for a minute, then Miller said, "Shit," and turned and walked out. He left the door open again.

chapter 12

It was a dank fall day, drizzly, and not very cold. All the offices in the big new building across Berkeley Street from my office had their lights on, and even though it was only quarter to eleven, they made a warm pattern in the dark morning. I was having a little coffee, reading a little trial transcript. I'd been feeling overcoffee-ed lately and Susan had reminded me that I was cutting down on it. So today my coffee was an equal mixture of half-decaf and half-caffeinated coffee. Compromise is not always the refuge of scoundrels.

According to the transcript, the names of the eyewitnesses were Glenda Baker and Hunt McMartin. She was listed as a senior at Pemberton College. He was described as a graduate student at M.I.T. Nothing is easy, especially for academics. So it took me three phone calls and just under an hour to establish that Hunt had graduated from M.I.T. with a master's degree in electrical engineering. It took another half hour to get the alumni office to tell me that his current address was in Andover, where he worked at the McMartin Corp. in Shawsheen Village.

Glenda was trickier.

Since my name was anathema at Pemberton, I had to employ guile. I called the alumni office and said my name was Anathema and I was with the IRS.

"We have an income tax refund for Ms. Glenda Baker, which has been returned by the postal service. Would you have a more recent address for her?"

"What did you say your name was?"

"Anathema," I said. "Pervis Anathema, refund enactment agent."

"May I call you back, Mr. Anathema."

"Certainly. If the line's busy, please keep trying. I have calls stacked up."

Then I broke the connection, left the phone off the hook, and walked across the hall to the interior designer showroom across from my office. The receptionist was twenty years old and going to modeling school nights. When I interrupted her, she was studying the cover of *Cosmopolitan*. Her blond hair stood straight up, with a small maroon highlight streak. She wore white makeup with black lipstick and black nail polish. She was dressed for success in a plaid shirt over a scoop-necked black leotard top, and an ankle-length black dress with peacocks on it. Peeking out from under the skirt were shoes that looked sort of like black combat boots except for the high heels. When I was in Korea I'd had zippers put in on the sides because it was so tiresome to lace them all. I couldn't tell if Lila had gone that route.

"Lila," I said. "Time to pay me back for letting you leer at me through the office door."

"You see me leering," Lila said, "you'll know it."

"My phone is going to ring in a minute. You pick it up and say 'Internal Revenue Service,' with those great overtones you got. They'll ask for Mr. Anathema and you say 'one moment please' and hit the hold button. If they say something else, like 'refund department' or whatever, just say 'one moment please' and hit the hold button."

Lila looked another wistful moment at the cover of *Cosmo* and said, "Anathema? What kind of name is that?"

"Greek," I said.

Lila shrugged and said, "Sure."

She folded up the magazine and followed me over to my office. I hung up the phone and we waited.

"Ain't it illegal to impersonate the IRS?" Lila said.

"I believe so," I said.

The phone rang and Lila picked it up, said her piece, and pushed the hold button.

"Thank you," I said.

"You're welcome," Lila said. "You owe me lunch."

"Yes, I do," I said, and pushed the hold button. "Anathema."

"Mr. Anathema, Catherine Grant at Pemberton College. Glenda Baker lives in Andover at The Trevanion Condominiums."

"Is there a street address?"

"No sir, that's the only address we have. She has a married name now as well, Glenda Baker McMartin."

"Thank you," I said and hung up.

Spenser one, Pemberton zero.

chapter 13

THE MERRIMACK RIVER comes down through New Hampshire by way of Concord and Manchester and Nashua. It enters Massachusetts a little north of Lowell and weaves toward the coast through Lowell and Lawrence and Haverhill. Up until the Second World War, the textile industry was strung out along that stretch of river, the mills powered by it, the inexpensive, often female, labor force making up most of the populace in the region. It was an affluent region, and here and there, near the mill cities, residential towns like Andover sprang up to service the executives. Then after the war the labor force organized, their cost went up, the textile mills moved south where the labor was still cheap, and the big mill cities like Lawrence and Lowell were left impoverished, awaiting urban renewal, and the executive bedroom towns turned their lonely eyes toward Boston.

Andover was a little different. It had at one time its own textile mill, and the Shawsheen Village area of the town had been built largely by the mill. Its executives were encouraged to live there and walk to work; no garages were built. The mill's corporate offices were across the street from the manufacturing facility.

Unlike most of the Merrimack valley, Andover remained upscale after the mill closed. The Academy was there. The mill manufacturing facility was taken over by an electronics firm, the McMartin Corporation; and the corporate offices went through several incarnations before being rehabbed into an upscale condominium complex called very grandly, I thought, The Trevanion. Hunt and Glenda Baker McMartin lived at The Trevanion.

It took about forty-five minutes to drive up to Andover in the late afternoon, with the rain spitting against my windshield and the wipers on slow sporadic. The foliage along Route 93 had peaked and was faded mostly yellow against the early November drab. I found a parking lot in back of The Trevanion and put my car in a slot that said Guest.

Glenda and Hunt were what every couple would want to be. He was tall and athletic looking with thick dark hair expensively cut. He was dressed in the J. Crew version of after-work leisure, and sported what used to be thought of as a healthy tan. She looked like him except she was shorter and her hair was auburn. She too had an even tan, which didn't look precancerous, and had the advantage of reminding me that they could probably afford to go to the Caribbean. Or a tanning salon. She too was in freshly ironed active wear. They both looked like they belonged to a health club.

"Hello," I said. "I'm Spenser. I called earlier."

"Yes, please, do come in," Glenda said.

She looked about twenty-two and acted as if she were a bit older than I. Neither of them looked as if they'd ever had a childhood. Probably they had been too busy being rich. The condo was money. The ceilings were twenty feet high, the bedroom was a loft. There was a kitchenette with a black-and-white tile dining counter, and a ruby-colored stove and refrigerator. The windows reached the full height of the ceiling. A brightly colored Tiffany-type lamp hung on a long brass chain over a thick glass-topped dining room table. There was an antique chaise covered with leather, and a refinished carriage seat, and a carefully assembled stereo system that would play Procol Harum in every nuance. Everything about them and the place spoke of money. Including the way they talked. Both of them had the sort of tight-jawed WASP drawl that only elocution lessons, or several generations of money and private education, can sometimes instill. My sense was that they hadn't taken elocution lessons.

"A drink?" Hunt said. "Coffee?"

"Beer is nice," I said.

"I have Sam Adams," he said. "White Buffalo, Red Hook Ale, Saranac Black and Tan."

"White Buffalo would be fine," I said, as if it made a difference.

We sat in the small room dominated by the television set. Probably only used it to watch *Masterpiece Theater*. Hunt poured my beer into a fine tall pilsner glass being careful to get an inch of head on it. Glenda had a glass of white wine, and sat on the couch with her feet tucked under her. Hunt held a short thick glass of single malt scotch on the rocks, and rattled the ice cubes a little as he sat on the edge of the couch leaning forward a little with his forearms resting on his thighs. I sat on a Moroccan leather hassock across from them and slurped a little beer through the foamy head, and wiped my upper lip with my thumb and forefinger and smiled.

"You related to the McMartin Corporation?" I said.

"My great-grandfather founded the company," Hunt said.

"Nice to have job security," I said.

"Yes."

"Tell me about Melissa Henderson's abduction," I said.

Glenda looked at Hunt. Hunt was being calm, a take-charge guy, full of confidence and poise, or as full of those things as a twenty-five-year-old kid is likely to be.

"Frankly, sir, we're a little tired of telling people about that. It was unpleasant to see, and it is unpleasant to talk about."

"I'm sure Melissa would agree," I said. "But I need to hear about it again."

"You work for Cone, Oakes?" Hunt said.

"Yes."

"And you or they or both seem to think that the murderer was wrongly convicted?"

"They would like to be assured that he wasn't," I said.

"He wasn't," Hunt said.

I looked at his wife.

"You as sure as your husband?" I said.

"Oh," Glenda said, "yes."

She had on an expensive, oversized waffle weave cobalt sweat shirt over silvery tights. Her twenty-two-year-old body seemed restless under the clothing, as if her natural state was naked, and clothes were a grudging accommodation to propriety.

"What did you see?" I said.

Glenda smiled and sipped some wine and looked at her husband.

"Glenda and I were walking back from a movie," he said.

"Actually I was hoping to hear from your wife," I said.

"I'll do the talking," Hunt said firmly. "We both saw the same thing. We were coming back from a movie, walking maybe twenty-five yards behind Melissa along Main Street near the campus front entrance. And a car came along the street, driving slowly, and pulled in beside her and a black guy jumped out and dragged her in and sped away."

"Where'd he speed away to?"

"Into the campus."

"Just where I'd go," I said. "If I were kidnapping a coed."

"I started toward her to see if I could help, but I was too late and I didn't know. I thought it might have been a lover's quarrel, you know. Lot of the girls dated black guys, and it would look like because he was black : . ."

"Sure," I said. "What kind of car?"

"Big car, pink. Maybe an old Cadillac."

"Just the thing for sneaking around Pemberton," I said. "How'd he grab her?"

"Excuse me?"

"He grabbed her and dragged her into the car. What part of her did he grab?"

"I, it was dark, you know, I think he had her by the hair."

"That how you remember it, Mrs. McMartin?"

"Yes," she said.

There was a faintly dreamy quality about her, as if she were always a little disengaged, thinking of her body.

"She scream?"

"Yes."

"What'd she scream?"

"She just screamed, you know, *eeek*. A scream."

I nodded.

"You knew Melissa well?" I said.

"Oh, certainly," Hunt said. "She and Glenda were very close friends."

"She was my sorority daughter," Glenda said. "She was like a younger sister."

Hunt looked slightly annoyed, as if he wasn't used to being interrupted.

"When Glenda and I began dating," he said, "I got to know her well, too."

"So you saw a black man in an old pink car pull up, grab a female friend of yours by the hair and drag her screaming into his car and speed away."

"Yes."

"And you didn't call the cops."

"I didn't want to be one of those country-club liberals who thinks all blacks are hoodlums. I guess I made a mistake."

"I guess," I said. "Where'd you grow up?"

"Here, in Andover."

"Go to the Academy?"

"Yes, and on to Williams, and then graduate work at M.I.T."

"How about you, Mrs. McMartin?"

"Same," she said. "Hunt was three years ahead of me at Phillips."

"Did the kidnapper ever get out of the car?" I said.

Again Hunt answered.

"Yes, he had to to catch her and when he did the streetlight was right above him and I saw him clear."

"And when Melissa turned up dead you went to the cops."

"Yes."

"And they put you in front of a lineup, and you picked out Ellis Alves."

"We both knew him right away."

"That's really good," I said. "Eyewitnesses are often confused."

Hunt smiled contentedly. Glenda gazed past me into space.

"She have a boyfriend?" I said.

"A boyfriend?"

"Yeah. You were close with Melissa, you double-date at all?"

"Yeah, once in a while. Why are you asking?"

"Got nothing else to ask about," I said. "And I'm supposed to be asking something."

"Well, it's a damn waste of time," Hunt said. "The jasper did it, and he's where he ought to be."

"She date a guy from Taft? Tennis player?" I said.

"I don't know where he was from or what he played. We only doubled with them a few times. I don't know how serious they were."

"You like him, Mrs. McMartin?"

It took her a minute to come back to us.

"Sure," she said. "He was a cute guy."

"Either of you remember his name?"

Neither of them did.

"I'm afraid this is all the time we can give you, sir," Hunt said. "We haven't had dinner yet, and both of us have early days tomorrow."

"Hard day at the plant?" I said.

"I have some early meetings."

"How about you, Mrs. McMartin. What do you do?"

"I'm training," she said, "at Healthfleet Fitness Center."

"She's learning the business," Hunt said. "We'd like to open a chain of health clubs ourselves one of these days."

"Great idea," I said. "They're starting to catch on."

"The trick is to position yourself to capture a market segment that's underserved."

"That's sort of my secret," I said. "And then you say bye-bye to the family business?"

"No, I wouldn't leave my job. The company's been in our family for four generations. I'd consult, of course, especially during start-up. But Glenda would run the health clubs."

My own sense was that Glenda enjoyed being a member of the leisure class and the thought of her running a chain of health clubs made me smile, but I kept the smile to myself. Hunt was on his feet. Nobody was offering me a second beer, which was too bad, because the White Buffalo was good. Glenda smiled at me thoughtfully. Hunt was still swirling the remains of his single malt over the remains of his ice cubes.

He said, "We really do need to get to our dinner, Mr. Spenser."

I didn't like their story. It seemed glib to me, and I found both of them in their smooth, upper-class propriety entirely unbelievable. I smiled graciously, however, and shook hands with them and departed. Spenser the civilized gumshoe.

chapter 14

THE PEMBERTON INN fronts on Pemberton Green, a block from the Pemberton College Campus. The bar was small with a working fireplace, and the walls done in old barn boards. They served draft beer in small glasses. The whole place made me feel like singing boola boola when I went in. It was crowded in the late afternoon with young women from the college looking to meet men, and young men from greater Boston looking to meet women. I edged in at the left hand corner of the bar and ordered a beer. A row of college girls to my right checked me out. One of them had thick red hair that fell past her shoulders. I smiled at her.

"Come here often?" I said.

"Oh, brother!" she said.

"What's your sign?" I said.

She looked around.

"Is there a hidden camera or something?"

"Gee," I said, "I was sure that would work."

"Get a grip," she said.

"Wait a minute," I said. "I've got one more, always works . . . can I buy you a drink?"

She pointed a finger at me and smiled.

"You're right," she said. "That's the one. Sure, you can buy me a drink."

I gestured to the bartender and she brought a fresh tequila sunrise to the redhead.

"My name's Sandy," she said. "What's yours?"

"Spenser," I said. "With an S, like the English poet."

"Which English poet?"

"Edmund Spenser," I said. "You know, *The Shepheardes Calender, The Faerie Queen*?"

"Oh, yeah. Spenser your first name or your last."

"Last."

"What's your first name?"

I told her.

"I don't figure you for a sophomore at Babson," Sandy said.

"Grad student?"

She looked at me.

"Okay," I said. "I'm not in school, but I have a friend who has a Ph.D. from Harvard."

Sandy smiled.

"Close enough," she said and drank some tequila sunrise. "What do you do for a living, Spenser-like-the-poet?"

I took a card from my shirt pocket and put it on the bar in front of her. She studied it for a moment and then looked at me carefully.

"Honest to God?" she said.

I nodded.

"You got a gun?"

I nodded.

"I don't believe you."

I opened my coat a little so she could see.

"Jesus," she said, "you don't have to flash me."

Her tequila sunrise had disappeared again. I bought her another one.

"Is it like on TV?" Sandy said.

"Exactly," I said. "A lot of times I send my stunt double on the hard stuff."

"You working on a case or you got a thing for college girls?"

"Both," I said.

Sandy laughed.

"Well, I'm one," she said.

"A case, or a college girl?" I said.

"Both," she said and laughed.

It was a full-out laugh, but no one except Sandy and I could hear it, because the room was full of people talking and laughing at peak capacity. Sandy was wearing jeans and a white tee-shirt under a gray blazer. She had strong breasts, and she brushed them against me as we talked. I didn't want to make too much of that. The place was so crowded it might have been inadvertent. Either way there was nothing wrong with it.

"Did you know Melissa Henderson?" I said.

"Girl that got killed? That the case you're working on?"

"Yes."

Sandy stared at me for a minute.

"I thought that was all over. They got some black guy for it."

"I'm sort of tying up the loose ends," I said. "Make sure it was really him."

"I didn't know her well," Sandy said. "But, you know, I saw her around."

"She have a roommate?"

"I don't know."

"You know Glenda Baker?"

"Girl that saw it? No, not really, she was a senior when I was a freshman. She's graduated by now."

"Who would have known Melissa well?" I said.

"She was a Phi Gam," Sandy said. "I assume the girls in the house would know about her."

"See any of them here?"

She turned on her barstool and scanned the room. Her jeans were tight over her thighs.

"No," she said. "But they never come here anyway."

"Why not."

"They're not fun like me. Phi Gams're all Legacies. Their mother went here, you know? and their grand-mamma, and their aunt Foofy."

"They have a house on campus?" I said.

"Oh sure. Far end of the quadrangle, opposite the chapel."

We were squeezed close by the crowd. She studied my face.

"What happened to your nose?" she said.

"It's been broken a couple times."

"And you got like, what, scars, I guess, around your eyes."

"I used to fight," I said.

"Box, you mean. Like a prize fighter?"

"Yeah," I said.

She reached up and squeezed my bicep. I flexed automatically.

"You must have been a pretty good one," she said.

"I was."

"You ever like a champion or anything?"

"No."

"How come?"

"*Pretty good*," I said, "is not the same as *very good*."

She drank some more. Her breasts were now pressing steadily on my arm.

"You ever go to college?" she said.

"Yes."

"What'd you study?" she said.

"How to run back kicks," I said.

She smiled at me.

"You're a funny guy," she said.

"Everybody says that."

"You're kind of old for me," she said.

"Everybody says that, too."

"But I like you," she said as if I hadn't spoken.

"Well, I like you too, Sandy."

She stopped and looked hard at my face.

"You're kidding me, aren't you?"

"I kid everybody a little," I said.

She thought about that.

"You want to go someplace?" she said.

"And?" I said.

"And have sex," she said.

"That's a very nice offer," I said. "But Susan Silverman and I have agreed to have sex only with each other."

Sandy's face was very close to mine in the crowded room. She had a wide mouth and a lot of teeth. She had turned in her seat so that she had one thigh on each side of my leg. Her chest was against my arm. In another minute we wouldn't have to go anywhere to have sex.

"You're not kidding, are you?"

"No."

She stared at me some more.

"Well," she said. "Goddamn. You are a funny guy."

"Yeah," I said. "Everyone always says it just that way, too."

———————

chapter 15

It HAD STARTED to get dark as I walked across the leafy campus. It was a nice fall evening with just enough coolness to make my jacket feel useful. The campus was empty, and I was woefully out of place on it. I had a momentary vision of myself, a middle-aged man with a broken nose and a thick neck and a gun on his hip walking alone, remote below the darkened sky.

The Phi Gam house was a big brick house of Georgian design. The front door led into a foyer. To the right was a living room. To the left was something that appeared to be a library. Straight ahead a stairway ascended to the next floor. There were half a dozen young women in the living room. The library was empty. All of the young women turned and looked at me when I came in.

I said, "Hello."

Several of them said, "Hi."

One of them said, "Are you looking for somebody?"

They all had the quality of voice kids that age use when they're talking to somebody's parent. I walked into the living room and sat on the arm of a couch. There was a big television set on one wall. The girls were watching *Hard Copy*.

"My name is Spenser," I said. "I'm a detective and I'd like to talk with you about Melissa Henderson."

One of them said, "Melissa?"

"Yes, did you know her?"

"Sure, she lived here."

The girl doing the talking had on a black tee-shirt and gray sweatpants. She was dark haired, dark skinned, wore no shoes, and her toenails were painted red.

A pale blond woman said, "How do we know you're a detective?"

The dark girl said, "What the hell else would he be, Kim? Coming in here asking about Melissa?"

Kim was sticking to her guns.

"I think he should show us some identification," she said. "You know what Mrs. Cameron said."

Several of the girls groaned. Kim was apparently the sole law-and-order candidate in the group.

"Mrs. Cameron?" I said.

The dark girl said, "She's the housemother. She gave us all a big talk about how we had to be careful about people coming around after Melissa was killed."

"Why?"

"People would be poking around, she said, making trouble."

"What kind of people?" I said.

Another girl spoke.

"Like you," she said and we all laughed except Kim,

who was looking severe. Severe is not easy for a twenty-year-old kid.

I said, "Don't hurt my feelings, now. But what's wrong with me?"

"Not a thing," the dark-haired girl answered. "I don't think Mrs. Cameron knows why we're supposed to be careful. She's just doing what Old Lady Corcoran told her."

"Old Lady Corcoran being?"

"The dean."

"Oh, her," I said.

And we all laughed again, except Kim.

"So what was Melissa like?" I said.

"Crazy," the other girl said. She had on a man's white shirt and blue cotton gym shorts. There were two big pink rollers in her hair.

"Crazy how?"

Kim got up suddenly and walked out of the room. I suspected that my moments were numbered.

"All ways," Pink Rollers said. "Anything you wanted to try, she was ready."

Talking about the woman they had known made them all remember what had happened to her and they were suddenly silent.

"Was she rebellious?" I said.

"Hell, yes," Dark Hair said. "She'd try anything if someone told her not to."

"She have a boyfriend?"

"I think so."

"Know his name?"

"No. Melissa used to call him the Prince. She was kind of cozy about him. She never brought him around."

"He a college guy?"

Nobody knew.

"Might he have gone to Taft?"

Nobody knew.

"Anyone she was unusually close to, a roommate, somebody that might know?"

Nobody knew of such a person. Melissa had roomed alone. She had lots of friends, several among those present. But no especial one friend.

"Tell me more about Crazy," I said.

Behind me a woman said, "Just what is going on here?"

I turned halfway and looked over my shoulder at a woman in her late sixties with silver hair and rimless glasses. She had on a dark flowered dress with a white collar and modest high heels and a string of pearls. She was a housemother if I ever saw one.

I said, "Mrs. Cameron, I presume."

"I'm the housemother here. Off-campus visitors require my permission."

"You sure know how to make a guy feel welcome," I said.

"I'll have to ask you to go."

"How do you know I'm not somebody's professor come down to help them with their paper on Provençal poetry?"

"Please leave."

"Or somebody's dad. How would you feel coming in here and kicking out somebody's dad who just stopped by to see how you were spending his thirty thousand a year."

"I know who you are. You are not welcome."

I looked at the young women.

"I think Kim has ratted us out," I said.

They all laughed.

"Oh, come on, Mrs. Cameron," Pink Rollers said. "We like him. We invited him to stay."

"Take that up with Dean Corcoran, Marsha," Mrs. Cameron said.

She turned to me. Very firm.

"Will you leave or must I call the police."

"He is the police," Dark Hair said.

"He is not. He is a private detective. He's been told already that he's not welcome on campus."

Pink Rollers said, "Hey. A private eye?"

I said, "Here's looking at you, kid."

"Whoa, is that cool or what. A private eye."

Mrs. Cameron turned without a word and walked out of the room.

"Cops will be here soon," I said.

"The campus cops?" Dark Hair said mockingly. "What are you gonna do?"

"I'll probably go quietly," I said. "I don't think I'll shoot it out with them."

"Oh, damn," Pink Rollers said and we all laughed.

I took several cards from my shirt pocket and handed them around.

"If any of you, ah, undergraduate women have anything to add about Melissa, or think of something later, or want to have a nice lunch paid for by me. . . ."

"You can call us girls," Dark Hair said. "Kim's the only one that's really PC."

The familiar pulsating glow of a blue light showed through the front window and a minute later the front door opened and Chief Livingston came in with two patrolmen. Mrs. Cameron greeted him at the door.

"I ordered him to leave as soon as I discovered he was here," she said. "He basically defied me."

"He probably does that a lot," Livingston said. "Come on, Mr. Spenser, time to go."

"What charge?"

"What charge? Oh, Jesus Christ, excuse me, ladies, it is against college regulations for anyone to visit a domicile without permission of the resident supervisor."

"Oh, that charge," I said.

Livingston grinned, and jerked his head toward the door. I got up from the arm of the couch where I'd been sitting and walked to the door and turned. I'd been so successful with my Bogart impression that I tried Arnold Schwarzenegger.

"Ah'll be baack," I said.

None of them knew what the hell I was doing. But they liked me. They all waved and hollered "good-bye" as I went out the door with the cops.

chapter 16

HAWK CAME IN to my office in the morning with some coffee and a bag of donuts.

"Coffee from Starbuck's," he said. "High-grown Kenya, bright and sweet with a hint of black currant."

"They sell donuts?"

"Naw, Starbuck's too ritzy for donuts," Hawk said. "Donuts are Dunkin'."

"With a hint of deep fat," I said.

We divided up the coffee and donuts. Hawk took his coffee and one of the donuts and went and looked down from my window at the corner of Berkeley and Boylston. He was wearing starched jeans and high top Nikes, and a blue denim shirt under a black leather field jacket. He had on a pair of Oakley sun glasses with cerulean blue reflective lenses.

"You think my new shades are cool?" Hawk said.

"Cold," I said. "Can you see, wearing them indoors?"

"No. But they too cool to take off."

I drank some Kenya coffee.

"Bright and sweet," I said.

"Told you," Hawk said.

"You come up with anything that clears Ellis Alves?" I said.

"No. You adopt a kid yet?"

"No."

"You been annoying somebody though," Hawk said.

"That's sort of my job description," I said. "You wanna give me a list?"

"Ain't got the time to cover them all, but somebody's looking to have you killed."

"Moi?"

"Vinnie called me. Said one of the guys works for Gino told him there was a guy looking to have you killed."

"He want Vinnie to do it?"

"Don't know," Hawk said. "That's all Vinnie told me. He's full time with Gino now. He wouldn't be freelancing anyway."

"How much they paying," I said.

"Now that's ego," Hawk said.

"Well, how would I feel if somebody was offering five hundred bucks?"

"Be embarrassing, wouldn't it," Hawk said.

He was still looking down at the street. It was a dandy fall morning, and a lot of people were hurrying around in the Back Bay like they had important things to do.

"Lotta nice looking women walk past your office," Hawk said.

"Hoping to catch a glimpse of me."

Hawk turned and came back and sat down in one of my client chairs. His jacket was open. I could see the butt of a gun under his left arm. I could see myself in his reflective glasses.

"You working on anything but Ellis Alves?" he said.

"Nope."

"So you probably stirring something up that somebody don't want stirred up," Hawk said.

"Unless it's someone I've offended previously and they're just getting around to it."

"Ellis Alves case makes more sense," Hawk said.

"Yes."

"So if it is, it mean maybe there is something wrong with the way Alves went to jail."

"Vinnie didn't give you any idea who wants this done?" I said.

"I don't think he knows," Hawk said. "He does, I don't think he'll say. Remember Vinnie ain't one of the good guys. He's pretty far off his range already. Hell, he wouldn't even call you direct. He called me."

"Good to know Vinnie's got standards," I said.

"Why we like him," Hawk said.

"Yeah."

I finished a donut and washed it down with the coffee. It was good coffee. Too bad they didn't sell donuts. It meant I was going to have to stop twice every time I shopped for two of the basic food groups. Life kept getting more complicated. Assuming that I had stirred up somebody from long ago wasn't useful. It was possible, but it didn't take me anywhere. I'd been doing this for a long time. There were too many possibilities. Assuming I'd touched a tender spot in the Ellis Alves thing was a more productive assumption.

"Could be someone I talked to," I said. "Could be

somebody who heard I was looking into it and wanted to, ah, forestall me."

"Not everybody know how to organize a murder contract," Hawk said.

"No. But a lot of people in this deal have money. If there's enough money, there's somebody got a connection with someone that can talk to a guy."

"True," Hawk said. "We could go find the guy that told Vinnie and ask him what he knows."

"He too will not wish to tell me," I said.

"We can reason with him until he do," Hawk said.

"Make Vinnie look bad," I said.

"Yeah, it would."

"He's expecting us not to do that."

"Good to know you got standards, too," Hawk said.

"The contractor is going to find a taker," I said. "If he's offering decent money."

"Plus, I believe there a lot of people willing to do it for nothing," Hawk said.

"So maybe what we do is go about our business and let him take a run at us, and when he does we catch him and question him closely."

"What's this 'we,' white eyes?"

"You can't let me get killed," I said. "Nobody else likes you."

Hawk grinned. He swallowed his last bite of donut and finished his coffee. He dropped the paper cup in the wastebasket and went to the sink in the corner and washed his hands and face carefully. He dried himself on a white towel that hung beside the sink. The towel said "Holiday Inn" on it, in green letters. It was one of my favorites. I had picked it up in Jackson, Mississippi, once when I was driving back from Texas, with Pearl the Wonder Dog. Whenever Susan came in she replaced the

Holiday Inn towel with a small pink one that had a pale pink fringe, and a pink and green rosebud embroidered in one corner. As soon as she left, I put out the Holiday Inn towel again.

"I'll be interested to see who they get to do it," Hawk said. "And how good he is."

"Me too," I said.

chapter 17

A DARK-HAIRED WOMAN named Elayna Hurley, who was a single mother and had been in graduate school with Susan, came over to Susan's house on a Sunday afternoon while I was watching football and Susan was reading a book by Frederick Crews debunking her profession. Elayna brought her nine-year-old daughter with her. The daughter's name was Erika.

Pearl had chosen football over Frederick Crews and was sprawled on the couch beside me. I was warmed by her affection, but, in fact, had planned to sprawl on the couch myself. When they came in, Pearl sat bolt upright and eyed Erika the way a robin eyes a worm. Susan took their coats and took them into the bedroom and laid them on the bed. Erika came straight over and stood in front of me and put her hands on her hips like Shirley Temple.

She wore a maroon velvet Laura Ashley dress with a little lace collar. She had much too much blond curly hair, and she was kind of chunky. Susan returned from the bedroom.

"Who are you?" Erika said to me.

I told her.

"How come you let your dog sit on the couch?"

"She likes it on the couch," I said.

Pearl looked at Erika balefully. Erika leaned very close to Pearl and blew in her face. Pearl shook her head. The hair on her back rose, and I quickly put a hand on her collar. Erika laughed loudly.

"Erika, honey," Elayna said. "Don't bother the dog."

"I want a dog," she said.

"I know, honey, but you know Mommy's allergic."

"You always say that."

"Well," Elayna smiled lovingly, "it's always true. Come over here and sit by me and maybe Susan can find us some cookies."

Erika flounced back over to the couch and sat beside her mother and stared at Pearl.

"What kind of cookies?" she said.

"Actually," Susan said, "you know the kind of homemaker I am. There aren't any cookies."

"Oh, that's fine," Elayna said. "Erika doesn't really need one."

"I want a cookie," Erika said. "You said I could have one."

"Well, I guess I was wrong, Erika."

"You said."

"I have some V8 juice," Susan said with a smile that would have beguiled Jesse Helms.

"I hate V8 juice," Erika said.

"Some mango yogurt?" Susan said.

"I want some cookies. My mother said I could have some cookies."

Beside me Pearl was still sitting upright. The hair was still up on her back. She growled very low, almost to herself. I draped my left arm over her shoulders and patted her.

"You got that right," I said to Pearl.

Susan flashed a glance at me almost too quick to be registered. I smiled at her.

"Would you like to watch TV in Susan's bedroom?" Elayna said.

"How come I can't watch out here?"

"Well, this is where the grown-ups will be, sweetheart, and we want to talk without TV."

"He's watching TV," Erika said.

I picked up the clicker and turned off the set.

Elayna said, "Come on into Susan's bedroom, Erika, and watch TV. I'll bet we can find a real good movie for you."

"Can that dog come in and watch with me?"

"No," I said.

Again Susan gave me the glance.

"Come on, Erika," Susan said. "We'll go in and find you a movie."

"Why can't that dog come?" Erika said.

"She's not really used to children," Susan said.

"Does he bite?" Erika said.

"No, no. She's just not used to children," Susan said.

"Mom, is he going to bite me?"

"No, of course not, she's a very nice dog. Come on, we'll go into Susan's bedroom and turn on the TV."

Susan and Elayna and Erika all headed for the bedroom.

"He looks like he wants to bite me," Erika said.

"She," I said.

"Bad dog," Erika said and stomped into Susan's bedroom.

They spent awhile finding a dandy TV program for Erika to watch. My guess was that their efforts would not be worth the result. When they were gone, Pearl settled back down into her sprawl, but she kept an eye on the bedroom. Finally they came out and half closed the bedroom door.

"Don't close the door," Erika said from the bedroom.

"No, Erika. We won't," her mother said. "We'll leave it just like this."

"You know I don't like the door closed."

"I know, Erika."

"Can I get you some wine or something?" Susan said.

"A little white wine would be nice," Elayna said.

Susan went to get it.

"How's the game?" Elayna said to me.

"Patriots are getting hosed," I said.

"Oh."

"Poor Erika, she loves animals. She wants a dog so bad and I can't have one in the house."

"You're allergic?" I said.

"Can't be in the same room with one. My eyes water and itch. I begin to sneeze. My throat closes up. It's hideous."

I glanced at Pearl. Susan came back in with a bottle of white, and a bottle of red, three glasses, and a corkscrew. She set it all down on the table in front of me.

"Man's work," she said.

I opened the wine. Susan had red. Elayna had white. I declined.

"Well, isn't she a princess," Susan said.

"Erika?" Elayna said. "I suppose every parent thinks her kid is special, but she really is a darling."

"Where she get all that blond hair?" Susan said. "Her father?"

"I guess so," Elayna said. "I didn't really know him, it was all arranged by the clinic."

"Of course," Susan said. "It must be hard raising a child alone."

"Yes. It's exhausting and demanding, but very rewarding. I'm very pleased that I chose to have her."

Elayna was tall and graceful and her hair was too long for her age. There was a dramatic streak of white in the front, and hints of gray showing here and there as the sunlight through the back window caught it. She was much too advanced to color her hair.

"Do you have help?" Susan said.

"Yes, my mother and my sister live around here. So I almost always have a baby-sitter. Today it happened they were both out and I had to bring her. I hope you don't mind."

"Oh, no," Susan said. "I love seeing her."

"The first year or so she pretty well killed my sex life, she was so demanding and I was so tired, I didn't have the energy, you know?"

"I can imagine," Susan said.

"But once she got off the breast, then I could leave her with my mom or my sister . . . and I was back in circulation."

She looked at me.

"You got any single straight friends?"

I shook my head. That description fit Hawk, but he and Elayna didn't seem a match. The thought of him with Erika, however, made me smile.

"See, there, you're smiling," Elayna said, "you've just thought of someone."

"No," I said. "It's just inner peace showing through."

Erika came out of the bedroom, shuffling in a pair of Susan's high-heeled shoes, and wearing Susan's black silk robe. The girth wasn't bad because Erika was a chunky girl and Susan was a slim woman, so they measured pretty much the same around. But since Erika was about three feet tall, and Susan was five foot seven, the length was an issue. She kept stepping on the train and from the sound it made, she kept tearing it. She had also found Susan's makeup and applied it to herself lavishly, if somewhat artlessly.

"Erika," her mother said. Her voice hovered on the periphery of a shriek.

Erika kept coming, trying to flounce, stumbling on the high heels, continuing to step on the trailing fabric of Susan's black silk robe, which continued to rip. I had given her that dressing gown last Christmas and it had cost me far more than I generally earned. I looked at Susan. She looked as if she had just swallowed an armadillo.

I said, "Oh boy oh boy," very softly to Pearl, who was sitting straight up again, and flexed for attack.

Elayna jumped up and grabbed Erika and swept her into the air.

"Erika, my God, Erika," she kept saying as she scooted her back into the bedroom. In a moment we could hear Erika howling.

Between howls she kept saying, "I want to wear it, I want to wear it."

I smiled pleasantly at Susan.

"Well, isn't she a princess," I said.

"Shut up."

I turned to Pearl and put my mouth close to her ear and did a stage whisper.

"Maybe we could get one just like her if we adopt wisely."

Pearl paid me no heed. Her every desire was focused on dashing into the bedroom and biting Erika. I kept a hand on her collar, to forestall that, though I was embarrassingly eager for it to happen. Susan looked at me very hard.

"I heard that," she said. "And even if I didn't, I know what you're thinking. I knew it from the moment they walked in."

"I'm in the evidence business," I said. "When I see some, I register it."

"You can't generalize from one instance," Susan said.

"No, of course not. But you can register the instance."

I felt Pearl start to tremble slightly. Elayna walked back into the room bringing Erika with her with a firm clamp on her wrist. Erika tugged intensely to get her wrist free. But Elayna was too strong for her. The kid was wearing her own clothes again, and the makeup had been scrubbed off. She was crying determinedly.

"Tell Susan you're sorry, Erika."

Erika kept crying. And tugging.

"Erika, apologize."

Erika cried. And tugged.

"No need," Susan said. "Really. I've had that gown forever. It was just something to wear around the house."

She was careful not to look at me while she said it. I was quiet, holding Pearl's collar. I did not comment that the robe was pure silk and was meant to be worn in front of a fire while sipping champagne.

"I insist on buying you a new one."

"Oh, hell, Elayna, there's no need for it. It doesn't matter, really. I have plenty of robes."

She had one other one that I knew of, a yellow thing with cats and dogs printed all over it in various colors. I had seen it in her closet, but she only wore it when I wasn't around, along with the flannel pajama bottoms and the oversized tee-shirt.

"No, I absolutely insist," Elayna said. "What size?"

"No," Susan said. "Elayna, really. It's nothing. Don't be silly."

"Size six," I said. "If it's well made. If you buy her a cheap one, where they chintzed on the material, it might have to be an eight."

Erika continued to cry steadily. Elayna and Susan both stared at me. Erika tried to bite her mother's hand to get her wrist free. Elayna swept her up off the ground and held her kicking and struggling and crying and said loudly, "I've got to get her out of here. Susan, I'll call you."

When they were gone, Susan went and stood looking out the living room window for a while. Finally she turned and looked at me.

"Should I have let Pearl go?" I said.

"Do you think she'd really have bitten her?"

"With proper coaching," I said.

"God, wasn't she awful."

"Awful," I said.

"My beautiful silk robe," Susan said.

"Now I guess you'll have to sit around naked and drink champagne," I said.

Susan smiled at me, almost sadly.

"There's always a silver lining," she said. "Isn't there."

chapter 18

PEMBERTON DID NOT wish to acknowledge crime. The Pemberton Police Station had been moved as far from the center of town as it was possible to move it. It was barely within the town limits, on the edge of Route 128 in an old brick Department of Public Works building they had leased from the state. I parked in the spacious lot out front.

Inside they were still partitioning off some of the rooms, and the carpenters were making a lot of noise. I worked my way past the front desk officer to the detective who'd worked the Henderson case, and sat with him at a desk in a half-finished office, while the sound of power saws and pneumatic nailers competed for attention. He looked about twenty, though he was probably older. You saw a lot of cops like him on suburban forces.

High-school football player. Not good enough for a scholarship. Smart kid. No money for college. Did a stint in the Marines, maybe, came home, went on the cops. Probably got term of service credit.

"Name's Albrano," he said. "Evidence specialist. I don't know how much I can help you. We turned things over to the State as soon as we discerned that it was a homicide. We're not set up to cover a major crime like they are, sir."

"Miller?" I said.

"Yes, sir."

"You the one got the letter?"

"Letter?"

"The letter tipped you off that it was Alves."

"Well, we got it here at the department," he said. "Didn't come to me personally."

"But you read it."

"Yes, sir, and checked it for prints. Nothing we could use."

"And you bucked it on to Miller?"

"Yes, sir. He made it pretty clear he was in charge of the case."

"I'll bet he did," I said. "Who notified him?"

"I guess I did, sir."

"You remember just how you notified him?"

"How?"

"Yeah. Did you show it to him here? Did you bring it over to him? Call him up? How'd you notify him?"

"I believe I mentioned it to him on the phone and then somebody took it in to Boston and gave it to him."

"When you told him on the phone," I said, "did he call you or you call him?"

"Hell, I don't remember. This was what, year and a half ago? What's the difference?"

"Got me," I said. "You know how it goes, just keep asking questions till you find something. What did you think of Miller?"

"He has a good arrest and conviction record, sir. I know that."

"Because he told you?"

Albrano's expression of professional cooperation didn't change.

"I believe that is where I heard that, sir."

I nodded.

"The victim had a boyfriend," I said. "You happen to come across him?"

"Didn't know she had one," Albrano said. "You actually think whatsis name, Alves, is innocent?"

"It's a working hypothesis," I said.

"Be a pretty elaborate frame-up," Albrano said.

"Yeah."

"But if it was a frame-up," he said, "it was a smart move picking a loser like this Alves character."

"Jury'd figure even if he didn't do it," I said, "he did something."

Albrano shrugged.

"I don't know shit about juries," he said. "But it makes him a good-looking suspect. Arrest a guy for drunk driving that's done it three times before, you gotta like your chances."

I didn't say anything. The pneumatic nailer was banging away across the half-finished room. A uniformed Pemberton cop stuck his head through the incomplete doorway.

"Making a run, Charlie," he said. "Want anything?"

"Large black, no sugar, couple of Boston creams." He looked at me. "You want something?"

I shook my head. The uniform left. We sat thoughtfully for a little longer.

"You know," Albrano said, "now that you asked and I'm thinking about it, Trooper Miller called me and asked if we'd come up with anything on the murder of the college girl."

I nodded.

"So I told him about the anonymous letter and he said send it in to me."

I nodded again.

"I don't see that it means anything," Albrano said. "Do you?"

"Might mean he was impatient," I said.

chapter 19

MY DOOR WAS open. Hawk was sitting tipped back in one of my client chairs studying Lila in the design office across the hall. She was looking particularly Lila-esque today in a puffy-sleeved, ankle-length, black dress and a Chicago White Sox baseball hat. I was at my desk making a list of the people I had talked to about Ellis Alves. After each name I wrote a brief synopsis of what I had learned from them. It wasn't that I couldn't remember. It was that I was confused, and when I get confused I make lists. It doesn't usually solve my confusion, but it sometimes consolidates it.

"Lila know you're looking at her?" I said.

"Un huh."

"She looking right back?"

"Un huh."

"This could be the start of something big," I said.

"Be big," Hawk said. "Won't be often."

"Chatting with Lila in the morning might be wearing," I said.

"I let you know."

I was starting back through my list to see which ones I wanted to follow up when some guys came in without knocking and barred Hawk's view of Lila by closing the door behind them. I knew this would annoy Hawk, and it did. But unless you knew him like I did, you wouldn't notice. It was mostly the way his head cocked when he looked at them.

There were four of them. All chosen apparently for heft more than beauty. Two of them, who might have been related, slid to either side of the closed door and stood against the wall and looked at Hawk. The other two walked past Hawk and stood in front of my desk and looked at me. Symmetry.

"You Spenser?"

The speaker was wearing a watch cap and a pea coat. The coat, which hung open, was too long, as all his jackets would be. He was built like a beer keg.

"I am he," I said.

I saw Hawk smile as he stood without apparent effort and went without any hurry to the olive green office supply cabinet next to the coat rack. The two guys that might have been related watched him carefully.

"You're working on the Ellis Alves case," he said.

"Day and night," I said.

"I was told to make this plain to you," Beer Keg said. "You leave that case alone from here on."

Hawk opened the supply cabinet and took a sawed-off double-barreled shotgun off the top shelf and cocked both barrels. The guys by the door watched him closely as he did it, but by the time they reacted the shotgun was cocked and pointed. The sound of the hammers going back made the other two guys turn and look.

"Ten gauge," Hawk said. "Ain't even fair at close range."

Hawk leaned against the wall with the shotgun in his right hand laid idly across the crook of his left arm. He smiled at them. They looked at me. While they had been looking at Hawk I had taken the occasion to take my Smith and Wesson .357 out of the side drawer of my desk. As they looked I cocked it, and keeping it in my right hand, let it rest on the desktop. I smiled at them.

"You should have been prepared," I said. "For the off chance that we wouldn't be paralyzed by fear."

Beer Keg was a stand-up guy.

"Today was just a warning anyway," he said.

"Might be our day to shoot you in the nose, though."

Beer Keg waded right past that.

"Guy say we was just supposed to rough you up today."

"What guy?" I said.

Beer Keg shook his head. His partner was wearing a black and red Mackinaw. Mackinaw's head was shaved above the ears with long hair on top. He was taller than Beer Keg, so his coat fit better.

"Nobody you know," he said.

I raised the Smith and Wesson and sighted at Mackinaw's forehead.

"I might know him," I said.

"I don't think you'll do it," Mackinaw said and turned and walked to the door. I saw Hawk glance at me. I shook my head. Mackinaw opened the door and walked out and left it open behind him. The other three, frozen for a moment waiting for me to shoot, suddenly burst into action when I didn't and jostled each other going out the door.

"Bad luck," Hawk said. "You picked the wrong one to bluff."

"I know," I said.

Hawk walked back to the chair and sat where he could see Lila again. He put the shotgun, still cocked, in his lap. I got out of my chair with the gun still in my hand and walked to my window. In maybe a minute I saw all four of them gathered on the corner of Berkeley and Providence Street, which ran between Arlington and Berkeley behind my building. In another moment a maroon Chevy station wagon drove down Providence Street and stopped. They got in. The wagon pulled out onto Berkeley and headed toward the river. It had Massachusetts plates. I turned from the window and wrote the number on my desk calendar.

"You'd shot him dead, the others would have told you everything they knew and more."

"I know."

"Lucky you got me around," Hawk said, "to keep them from inducting you into the Girl Scouts."

"It's the physical," I said. "I always have trouble with the physical."

"You Irish, ain't you?"

"Sure and I am, bucko."

"So you don't have a lot of trouble with the physical," Hawk said.

"Just enough."

chapter 20

TAFT UNIVERSITY WAS in Walford, about twenty miles west of Boston and two towns north of Pemberton. I had been out there maybe seven years ago trying to do something about a basketball point fixing scam involving a kid named Dwayne Woodcock. In the process I had gotten to know the basketball coach, a loudmouth blowhard named Dixie Dunham, who was a hell of a basketball coach, and not as bad a guy as he seemed if you had a good tolerance for bullshit.

When I came into his office at the field house he knew me right off.

"Spenser," he said, "you son of a bitch."

"Don't get sentimental on me, Dixie," I said.

The office was pretty much the same. A VCR, a cabinet full of video tapes, a big desk, a couple of chairs.

Above Dixie's desk there was still a picture of the Portland Trailblazers point guard, Troy Murphy. Murphy had played his college ball for Dixie. Beside it there was now a picture of Dwayne Woodcock. Dixie was pretty much the same, too. He had on a gray tee-shirt, blue sweat pants with a white stripe down the leg, gray shorts over the sweats, and a pair of fancy high-cut basketball shoes, which I happened to know he got free by the case, as part of his consulting deal.

"So you come to make trouble for my program again?" Dixie said.

"I saved your damn program," I said. "You hear anything from Dwayne?"

"My players stay in touch," Dixie said. "I hear from them or I hear about them."

"How's Dwayne doing?"

"Fifteen points a game, eleven rebounds, for the Nuggets," Dixie said. "But he still plays a little soft. He toughens up, he'll double that."

"Can he read yet?"

"Hell, he's a college graduate," Dixie said.

"This place?" I said.

"Absolutely."

"Can he read yet?"

"Sure," Dixie said.

"He still with Chantel?" I said.

"Heard they got married."

"Good."

"So what brings you nosing around out here. Miss me?"

"Young woman over at Pemberton," I said. "Got killed a year and a half ago."

"Yeah, I heard about it. Some black guy, right? Raped her and strangled her?"

"No rape," I said. "I'm trying to clean up a few loose ends on that case."

"Yeah, so whaddya want from me, buddy? I didn't touch her."

"I've seen a picture of her," I said, "wearing a Taft tennis letter sweater that's obviously much too big for her."

"So you figure she was dating somebody on the Taft tennis team."

"Yes."

"And you want me to point you at the tennis coach."

"Yes."

Dixie Dunham made a low ugly sound which he probably thought was a laugh.

"Be glad to," he said. "The sonova bitch. Tried to recruit one of my players last year, right off my team."

"Tennis is a spring sport, isn't it?" I said.

"When you think the Tourney is played, buddy boy?"

"Oh, yeah."

"Coach's name is Chuck Arnold. I'll walk on down the hall with you and introduce y'all."

Chuck looked like a tennis coach. He was tall and flexible and lean and had the look of self-contentment that only expensive private education can confer. He wore a white cable stitched tennis sweater without a shirt, khaki pants, soft tan loafers, and no socks. The sleeves of the tennis sweater were pushed up over his tan forearms.

"That's him," Dixie said. "Tried to steal my back-up two guard for his fucking sissy-boy team."

Arnold smiled as if he were tired.

"Oh, give it a rest, Dixie," he said and put out a firm hand to me. "Chuck Arnold, what can I do for you?"

"Keep a hand on your wallet," Dixie said. "Fucker'll take it right out of your pocket, you're not careful."

He turned away and rumbled back down the drab corridor toward his office. Arnold stared after him with no trace of affection. Then he looked back at me.

"What did you say your name was?" he said.

"Spenser. I'm a detective. I'm looking for a guy who played tennis here sometime in the last few years. He dated a girl at Pemberton and gave her his letter sweater."

"I'm supposed to keep track of their love life?" Arnold said.

"Her name was Melissa Henderson. She was murdered about eighteen months ago."

"Yes, of course, I remember that. Some black guy raped her and killed her."

"Actually there was no evidence of rape."

"Whatever," Arnold said. "I already talked to the other detective."

"Which one?"

"I don't remember, big man, short blond hair."

"Miller?" I said.

"I don't remember."

"What did he want to know?"

"He was asking about Clint Stapleton."

"Melissa's boyfriend?"

"That's what he said."

"Who?"

"The other detective, for crissake. I try to teach them tennis. I don't delve into their sex lives."

"Is Stapleton the captain of the tennis team?"

"Yes."

"Where do I find him?"

"Why do you want to know?"

"Because I want to find him and talk with him about the murder of his girlfriend."

"Are you sure she was his girlfriend?" Arnold said. "Perhaps she was a one-night stand."

"He gave her his letter sweater."

"How do you know that?"

"I'm a trained sleuth," I said. "Where do I find him?"

"Well," he said, "I guess I really must, mustn't I?"

"Yes."

"He should be working on the bang board in the cage."

"Thank you," I said and started out.

"I'd, ah, I'd be just as happy if you didn't mention that I told you about him."

"It is quite possible," I said, "that I will never mention your name again, Chuckster."

chapter 21

I WENT OUT of his office, and along the cinderblock corridor to the cage. The cage had a lot of high windows, a dirt floor, and a pale green, rubberized, ten-laps to-the-mile indoor track around it, banked high at the curves. There was a broad-jump pit in the infield, and a pole-vault set up with thick spongy mattresses to land on. On the far curve was a chain-link hammer throw enclosure, closed on three sides so the hammer wouldn't get misdirected into somebody's kisser by an inexpert thrower.

I walked around the track to a doorway on the far side. It opened into the tennis area where two red composition courts occupied most of the space. Along the back wall behind the baselines were solid green boards against which a tall rangy kid wearing a blue-and-white kerchief on his head was banging a tennis ball with a graphite racquet. He was wearing a set of blue and white sweats, and white tennis shoes, to go with the kerchief. He alternated slicing backhands and top spin forehands, hitting effortlessly and hard, without mishitting: backhand, forehand, backhand, forehand, alone in the big empty space. The sound of the ball was almost metronomic as it whanged off the racquet, banged off the board, and popped off the floor. If he was aware of me he didn't show it. I waited for him to take a break. He didn't.

So I said, "Clint Stapleton?"

The ball clanged off the rim of his racquet and dribbled away from him. He looked up at me.

"Goddammit," he said. "I'm trying to concentrate."

"And doing a hell of a job of it," I said. "My name's Spenser. You Stapleton?"

"Yeah, but I'm busy."

"We need to talk."

"No we don't," he said. "I need to hit for another half hour and you need to get lost."

He was looking straight at me and I realized that he was . . . black certainly didn't cover it. His skin color was about the same color as mine . . . of African heritage, or partly so, seemed to say it better. I don't think I'd have noticed if the kerchief hadn't predisposed me.

"I can wait," I said.

"I don't like anyone watching me."

"Clint," I said. "Under ordinary circumstances worrying about what you like and don't like would occupy my every waking hour. But these are desperate times. And I'll have to hang around until I can talk with you."

"Maybe I could wrap this racquet around your head," Clint said.

"No, you couldn't," I said. "I'd take it away from you and play Steamboat Willie on it."

Stapleton stood and studied me for a time, slapping the racquet gently against his leg, looking as arrogant as he was able to, making sure that I knew he feared nothing.

"What do you want?" he said finally.

There was weariness in his voice, as if he was fighting off his darker impulses, trying to be civil. I was fairly sure that if I had been a short person with small bones he would have given in to his darker impulses.

"I want you to tell me about Melissa Henderson."

"Who?"

He said it too fast, and too loudly.

"Melissa Henderson, whom you used to go out with, who was murdered."

"Oh, Melissa?"

"Yeah. Melissa. Tell me about her."

"Nothing to tell. We dated a few times. Then she got killed."

"Don't you hate when that happens," I said.

He shrugged.

"How many times?" I said.

"How many times what?"

"How many times did you date her."

"How the hell would I know? I go out with a lot of girls. I don't keep track of every date."

"More than five times?" I said.

He shrugged again.

"Yeah, I imagine."

"More than ten?"

"For crissake," he said. "I told you I don't keep fucking track."

He rolled a yellow tennis ball up onto his racquet and

began to bounce it on the racquet, studying the bounce as if it was important.

"You got a girlfriend?" I said.

"What are you, Ricki Lake? Yeah, I got a girl I'm going with."

"Who?"

"None of your goddamned business."

"You give her your letter sweater?"

"No. What the hell are you asking all this crap for?"

"You gave Melissa Henderson your letter sweater."

"How the hell do you know?"

"I am wise far beyond my years," I said.

"Yeah?" he said. "Well, bullshit."

I had no idea where I was going. There was something phony about him. I didn't believe a kid would give away his letter sweater to someone he dated casually. And I wanted to keep him talking and see what came out.

"So how come you gave Melissa your letter sweater?"

He continued to watch the tennis ball bounce rapidly on the racquet face. Then he gave it a little sharper bounce and it went up in the air. As it started down he whanged the ball across the length of the tennis facility and watched it burrow into the netting that hung around the outside of the courts.

"I'm sick of you, pal," he said. "I got better things to do than hang around here and talk shit with you."

"Good for you," I said. "You know a State Police Detective named Miller?"

"Never heard of him," Stapleton said.

He zipped his racquet up in its case.

"Talk to any cops at all about this case?" I said.

"Hell, no," he said.

He put his racquet under his arm and walked away across the courts toward the exit, leaving the court area littered with yellow tennis balls. I wanted to tell him that it was bad form not to pick up the balls. I wanted to scuttle alongside him and ask more questions. But his legs were longer than mine and I decided to work on dignity. I'd already been compared to Ricki Lake. So I went looking for the Sports Information Office, instead, and found it in a wing attached to the field house.

"My name is Peter Parker, the photographer," I said to the young woman at the reception desk. "We're publishing a photo essay on Clint Stapleton, and I need some bio."

The receptionist was clearly a student, probably a cheerleader in her other life, cuter than the Easter Bunny, but nowhere near as smart.

"Could you spell the last name, sir?"

I spelled it. She wrote it down on a piece of note paper. I could see the tip of her tongue resting tentatively on her lower lip as she wrote.

She read it aloud when she'd finished writing it down.

"Stapleton, yes, sir. Now what did you want about him?"

"Biographical material," I said.

She looked a little uncertain.

I said, "A press kit maybe?"

She smiled with relief.

"Yes, sir. I'll get you a press kit on Mr. Stapleton, sir."

She stood and started to turn toward the file cabinet on the opposite wall. Then she caught herself and turned back to me.

"Would ·you like to be seated, sir? I'll only be a moment."

I said, "Thanks."

She hurried across the room to a big metal file cabinet and began rummaging through the file drawers. I didn't want to sit. But I didn't want to offend her, so I compromised by leaning on the wall while she rummaged. She was dressed in the calculated slovenliness that was *au courant*: Doc Marten shoes, baggy jeans, and an oversized white shirt under a herringbone-patterned sweater that was also too big. The white shirt tail hung well below the bottom of the sweater, and the white shirt cuffs were turned back over the sweater cuffs. The sleeves of the sweater shirt combination left only her fingers visible. The bottoms of the jeans bagged over the Doc Martens so that she stepped on them when she walked. I shifted my other shoulder onto the wall. It was slow going at the file drawers, for Ms. Grunge. I wanted to say, "After R and before T." But I feared she would find it patronizing, so I held back. And as it turned out, she didn't need my help. After five or six more minutes she came back from the file cabinet and handed me a blue folder with the Taft logo on the front and the name Clint Stapleton hand lettered in black ink on the tab.

"May I keep this?" I said.

"Oh, certainly, sir. We have them available just for that."

"Thank you," I said.

"Oh, you're very welcome, sir."

I smiled. She smiled. I left.

chapter 22

I SAT IN my office with my feet up, and the window open to let some air in, and thumbed through the press kit on Clint Stapleton. Mostly it was puffery. It did say that Clint was twenty-two, and a senior at Taft. That he had grown up in New York City, and attended Phillips Andover Academy, where he'd been captain of the tennis team.

I put the folder down for a moment. At twenty-two he was five years younger than Hunt McMartin, the guy who'd ID'd Ellis Alves. And the same age as McMartin's wife, who had also gone to Andover. This smacked of clue, but it had been so long since I'd found one that I remained cautious. The rest of the stuff was about how Clint was likely to be an all-American this year, and how he was planning to join the pro tour after graduation. His won-and-lost record was there, some xeroxed clippings, all laudatory, a head shot, and several action shots of Clint. He was wearing his kerchief in all of the action shots.

I sat for a bit and thought about the Andover connection and listened to the sounds of city traffic below my window. While I was thinking, Hawk came in with lunch.

"Nantucket Bay scallops are in," Hawk said. "Thought we ought to have some."

"What made you think I'd be hungry?" I said.

Hawk snorted and didn't bother to answer. He took out a bottle of dry Riesling, some plastic cutlery, two containers of broiled scallops, and a pint of coleslaw. I dug a corkscrew out of my desk drawer and, while Hawk opened the wine, I rinsed out two water glasses in the sink.

"Wine for lunch makes me sleepy," I said.

"Don't have to drink none," Hawk said.

He poured some in one of the water glasses and looked at me.

"I don't wish to offend you," I said.

Hawk grinned.

"'Course you don't," he said and poured some wine into the second glass.

We were quiet for a time while we sipped a little wine and sampled a couple of the bay scallops. The pint of coleslaw was communal. We took turns at it.

"Take a look at this," I said and handed the sports info folder to Hawk. "This is the guy that gave Melissa Henderson his letter sweater."

Hawk read through it. When he came to the pictures he stopped and studied the head shot.

"A brother," Hawk said.

"Sort of," I said.

"Suppose he met Melissa's parents?" Hawk said.

"Don't know."

"If he did," Hawk said, "you suppose he was wearing the do rag?"

"Looks like a trademark to me," I said.

"He tell you anything useful?" Hawk said.

"Started out pretending he didn't know Melissa," I said.

"Okay, so we know he ain't smart," Hawk said.

"He's not friendly either," I said. "He also says he never talked to the cops, but his coach says a detective who sounds like Miller, the State cop that busted Ellis, talked with him, the coach, not long after the murder and asked about Stapleton."

"So somebody knew about him right after she died," Hawk said.

"But either Stapleton's lying, or nobody talked to him."

"You talk to the cop?"

"Yeah. He wasn't friendly either. And he never mentioned Stapleton."

"Might want to talk to him again," Hawk said. "Sound like somebody lying."

"Almost certainly," I said. "Cops always talk to the husband or the boyfriend in a case like this."

"So why he lying?"

"Be good to know," I said.

"And how come the cop . . . whatsis name?"

"Miller."

"How come Miller don't mention Stapleton," Hawk said, "and Stapleton's name never come up in the transcript?"

I didn't even know Hawk had a copy of the transcript.

But I was used to that. Even I never really knew with Hawk.

"That'd be good to know, too," I said.

"And who looking to get you run off the case?"

"That'd be dandy to know."

I swiveled my chair a little and looked out my window and sipped my wine. It had rained hard last night and cleared before dawn. The morning sun was bright, and outside my window everything in the Back Bay looked clean and morally alert.

"Another thing that bothers me," I said, "is that Stapleton went to Andover three years behind Hunt McMartin and coincident with McMartin's wife."

"They the people ID'd Ellis?"

"Yeah."

"So Stapleton's girlfriend get killed, and by coincidence people he went to prep school with ID the killer and nobody mention that?"

"Not to me," I said. "And it's not in the trial transcripts."

"'Course not everybody go to Andover know each other," Hawk said.

"True," I said.

"Still a coincidence," Hawk said.

"Un huh."

"You like coincidences?"

"I hate them," I said. "How about you."

"Got no feeling on it," Hawk said. "You the detective. I just a thug."

"You're too modest," I said.

Hawk grinned.

"Didn't mean to say I wasn't a great thug," he said.

"Another thing that's bothersome," I said, "is even though, according to the ME, there's no proof of rape—

they found no semen, for instance—everybody automatically refers to the fatal event as a rape and murder."

"That 'cause the alleged perp is a brother," Hawk said.

"And all you guys think about is ravaging our women."

"Not all," Hawk said. "Sometimes we think 'bout eating fried chicken."

"While ravaging our women?" I said.

"When possible," Hawk said. "What did she die of?"

"Strangulation."

"Manual?"

"No, some kind of ligature."

"Ligature," Hawk said. "Easy to see how you got to be a detective. I assume they never found this here ligature."

"Nope."

"And they didn't find her clothes?"

"Nope."

"They ever establish a, ah, prior connection between Ellis and the deceased?"

"Nope."

Across Berkeley Street from my office the tourists were posing with the bear outside of FAO Schwarz. The coffee shop on the first floor must have changed the grease in the frialator. There was a clean smell to it as it drifted up from the alley vent.

"They ever establish how Ellis got out to Pemberton?" Hawk said.

"The eyewitnesses said he was driving an old pink Cadillac."

"Yeah, that's what we drive," Hawk said. "They ever find the car?"

"Nope."

"They get the license number?"

"Nope."

"But there was one registered to Ellis."

"Nope."

Hawk ate the last scallop. I turned back to the desk and took a healthful bite of coleslaw.

"So," Hawk said, "Alves borrows or steals a car one night, an inconspicuous old pink Caddy. He drives out to Pemberton in his inconspicuous car, where there ain't no black folks, and the cops pay attention to any that they see. He cruises around in his inconspicuous car until he spots a white girl on a busy street, drags her into his inconspicuous car in front of witnesses, drives her somewhere, takes off her clothes and strangles her, though he maybe doesn't rape her, dumps her body in the middle of the Pemberton Campus, and rides on back home with her clothes and the aforesaid ligature in his inconspicuous car, so in case the cops stop him he can incriminate himself."

"He could have dropped the clothes off in a Dumpster somewhere."

"Why take them at all?" Hawk said.

"I can't imagine," I said. "Ellis has spent half his life in the criminal justice system. He'd know better than to be caught with stuff like that."

"He'd leave them right where they fell," Hawk said.

"Sure, unless there was something about them that would incriminate him."

"Like what?" Hawk said.

"If she fought him enough to draw blood."

"But she didn't."

"According to the coroner's report there was no blood under her fingernails," I said. "No fend-off bruises on her arms. In fact, there's no sign of her putting up any resistance."

"And Ellis didn't have a mark on him," Hawk said.

"Maybe he took her to his home and undressed her there."

"And then killed her and drove all the way back out to Pemberton with her dead in the car? Or drove her out naked in the car and killed her there?"

"Don't make any sense," Hawk said.

"No, it doesn't."

"So who would take the clothes?" Hawk said.

"Someone who didn't know what they were doing and panicked."

"Don't sound like my man Ellis," Hawk said.

"No, it doesn't."

We were quiet. The scallops and coleslaw were gone. There was about one glass each left of the wine. Hawk picked up the bottle.

"Don't keep so good once it's opened," he said.

"I know," I said.

"Better finish it up," Hawk said.

"We'd be fools not to," I said.

Hawk poured out the wine, and we sat in the quiet office and looked out at the bright morning and finished it.

chapter 23

THE MAROON CHEVY wagon that had picked up Beer Keg and his crew was registered to Bruce Parisi at an address in Arlington, near the Winchester line. I called Rita Fiore.

"Can you find out if a guy named Bruce Parisi, currently living on Hutchinson Road in Arlington, has a record."

"Sure."

"And, if he does, and I'll bet he does, get me whatever you can on him."

"Sure, I'll call you back."

"No, I'm in the car," I said. "It's easier if I call you."

"Well, a car phone?"

"Modern crime fighter," I said.

It was a bright, windy day at the rim of the Mystic lakes. I turned left off Mystic Street and onto Hutchinson

Avenue and drove across the slope of a pretty good-sized hill parked a little downhill from the house and across the street. It was a white colonial with green shutters and a screened porch on the side. It sat further uphill from the road. A long hot top driveway ran up past the screen porch and widened into a turn-around in front of a two-car garage set back of the house. The Chevy wagon was in the turn-around.

I sat with the motor idling and scanned the dial for music. My favorite, Music America, had been taken off the local public radio station by the airheads who ran it. I listened occasionally to one or another of the college stations, but they tended to play fusion, and the DJs were usually painful. I hit the scan button and watched it go around the dial without finding anything I wanted to hear. While I sat with the scanner scanning, the front door opened and a man came down the front steps looking like he was going to a reception at the British Consulate in a blue Chesterfield overcoat and a gray homburg hat. He got in the Chevy wagon, backed down the long driveway, and headed out past me toward Mystic Street. I let him turn the corner and U-turned and drifted along behind him. I could afford to lay back and let him get ahead of me. If I lost him, I knew where he lived. When you have that luxury, tailing is a breeze. We went along Mystic Street, turned onto Medford Street, and went through West Medford into Medford Square. He went down an alley between two buildings. I pulled up across from the alley entrance next to a "No Standing" sign and waited. In a minute or two he came out of the alley and went into a store front. The sign in the front window said "Parisi Enterprises." I picked up my car phone and called Rita Fiore.

"I'm sitting outside Bruce Parisi's office in Medford Square," I said. "What do you have on him."

"Been arrested three times," Rita said. "Loan sharking twice, once for strong arm stuff: he contracted some goons to help break a strike."

"Where's Eugene Debs when you need him," I said.

"There's something might be interesting, though. Last time he was busted, two years ago for loan sharking, the arresting officer was a State Detective named Miller."

"Tommy Miller?"

"Yes," Rita said. "Wasn't he the man who arrested Ellis Alves?"

"Yes," I said. "He was."

"Is it interesting?"

"Yes, it is."

"You want to tell me what you're doing?"

"If I knew, I would. But I don't, so please don't embarrass me by asking."

"Fine," Rita said. "Have a nice day."

We hung up. My car wouldn't last ten minutes where I was. I swung it across the street and down the alley behind Parisi Enterprises. There were three parking spaces back there. A sign on the back of the building said "Reserved for Parisi Enterprises. All Others Will Be Towed." There was a car in each space. I parked directly behind the maroon Chevy. I didn't want Parisi leaving before I did anyway. I took my .38 out and looked to see that there were bullets in all the proper places. I knew there would be, but it did no harm to be careful. And I'd seen Clint Eastwood do it once in the movies. Then I put the gun back on my hip, got out of the car, and strolled up the alley to the front of the building.

Parisi Enterprises didn't have a lot of overhead. The office was furnished with two gray metal desks, a gray metal table, and two swivel chairs. There was an empty pizza box on the table, and several days' worth of the *Boston Herald* scattered on one of the desks. The other desk held a big television set on which a talk show host was examining the issue of cross dressing with a bunch of guys in drag. Parisi had folded his coat on the empty swivel chair and put his gray homburg on top of it. He was seated behind the newspaper-littered desk talking on the phone. His hair was black and combed back in a big Ricky Ricardo pompadour that gleamed with hair spray. That he had been able to wear a hat without messing his do was a tribute to the holding power of whatever he sprayed on it. He didn't look too tall, but he was fat enough to make up for it. Under his several chins he wore a white spread collar attached to a blue striped shirt. His tie was blue silk, and his blue double breasted suit must have cost him better than a grand because it almost fit him. He crooked the phone in his shoulder when I came in.

"Wait a minute," he said into the phone, "a guy came in."

He spoke to me.

"Whaddya want?" he said.

"You Bruce Parisi?" I said.

"You a cop?" he said.

"No."

"Then take a hike," he said. "I'm on the phone."

"Hang it up," I said.

"Fuck you, pal."

I walked over to the wall and yanked the phone wire from the phone jack. Parisi looked as if he couldn't believe what he had just seen.

"What are you, fucking crazy, you walk in here to my office and fuck with me?"

He let the phone fall from his shoulder as he stood and his hand reached toward his hip. I hit him with all the left hook I had handy and knocked him backwards over the swivel chair and into the wall behind it. The swivel chair skittered on its casters like something alive, the seat spinning and crashing into the desk as Parisi slid down the wall and landed on the floor, with one foot bent under him and the other tangled in the chair. I got a hold of his big pompadour and dragged him to his feet and slammed him face first against the wall. On his hip was a Berretta .380 in a black leather holster, the skimpy kind of holster that allows the gun barrel to stick through. I took the Berretta out of the holster and dropped it in the pocket of my coat and stepped away from him. He didn't move. He stood with his face pressed against the wall, his hands at his sides.

"Gimme a day, two at the most, I'm working on a thing. I'll have the money by tomorrow," he said.

"I'm not here about money," I said.

"What do you want?" he said into the wall.

"I want to know why four stiffs came to my office and threatened me if I didn't drop the Ellis Alves case."

"I don't know," he said. "Why should I know."

I stepped in close to him and dug a left into his kidneys. He gasped and sagged a little against the wall.

"You sent them," I said.

"I don't even know who you are," he said.

"My name's Spenser. You know a guy named Tommy Miller?"

"Yeah."

"You sending the sluggers to my office got anything to do with him?"

"I don't know what you're . . ."

I hit him again in the same kidney. He made a kind of

a yelp and his knees sagged. He turned toward me and slid his back down the wall until he was sitting on the floor, his fat legs splayed out in front of him. There was blood on the corner of his mouth. It took him a couple of tries to speak.

"Yeah. Tommy said he wanted you roughed up. I owed him a favor. I sent out some guys."

"Why'd you owe him a favor?"

"He, ah, he helped me out when I got nabbed."

"How?"

"Got rid of some stuff."

"Evidence?"

"Yeah."

"What are friends for," I said.

"No harm done," Parisi mumbled. "Nobody roughed you up. We was only going to scare you."

"If you scare me again," I said, "I will come back and kick your teeth out."

"No trouble," Parisi said. "No trouble."

"Sure," I said and walked out.

chapter 24

Susan gave a speech to a conference of professional women at the Hotel Meridien. I stood, slightly restless, in the back and listened, and afterwards we went to the august, high-ceilinged bar on the second floor for a drink. Maybe two.

"Podium magic," I said to Susan and raised my beer glass toward her in salute.

"Did you think I was good?"

"Wouldn't the term 'podium magic' imply that?" I said.

She smiled.

"Okay, I'll be more direct. Say more about how wonderful I was."

"You were profound, witty, graceful . . ."

"And stunning," Susan said.

"Isn't appraising a woman's appearance a sexist indiscretion?" I said.

"Absolutely," Susan said. "Do I look especially stunning in this dress?"

The dress was black and simple with a short skirt. She did look stunning in it, but it wasn't the dress. She still harbored the illusion that what she wore made a large difference in how she looked. I had years ago given up explaining to her that whatever she wore she was beautiful, and clothes generally benefited from being on her.

"Especially," I said.

Susan was having a martini, straight up, with olives. I was drinking Rolling Rock beer.

"If we had a child it wouldn't have to be icky like Erika," Susan said.

"Not to us," I said.

"I mean, she's had an odd and difficult childhood. No father, and Elayna is a dear friend, but she's a little flappy."

"Boy," I said, "sometimes I have trouble following you when you lapse into professional jargon."

"We might be very good parents."

"Because?"

"Because we're pretty good at everything else, why would we be bad at parenting?"

We were sitting on a little sofa with a small table in front of us. There were two chairs on the other side of the table, but four people would have been a squeeze. I ate several nuts from the bowl in front of me. Susan speared one of her olives on a toothpick.

"Well, what I think is this," I said. "You have kids when you're, say, twenty-five and you spend the next eighteen or twenty years doing little else but bringing them up. And finally you get them old enough and they are out on their own, and you let out the breath you've been holding for two decades and you look around and you're, say, forty-five. You still have a lot of time left to obsess about each other or baseball, or your job, or triple espresso—whatever it is that gets your attention."

"But because we've started late, when you and I reach that point . . ."

"Children are best had early," I said. "So that you can enjoy them in their adulthood and yours."

"Perhaps we wouldn't have to be so totally involved," Susan said.

I looked at her without saying anything. After a moment she smiled and nodded.

"Of course we would," she said.

A tall man in dark clothes slipped into one of the two vacant chairs at our cocktail table. He was wearing a charcoal suit, a dark gray shirt, and a gray silk tie. His charcoal hair was longish and brushed back on the sides. It was gray. His face was sort of gray sallow, as if he spent a lot of time indoors. His eyebrows were gray and peaked in the center over each eye, which made him seem quizzical. He had a small emerald in his right ear. His hands were strong looking, with long fingers. His nails were manicured and freshly so. They gleamed dully in the bar light. His eyes were dark and his stare seemed bottomless. If I had been a dog, the hair would have risen along my backbone. I could feel Susan's thigh tense against mine.

"I have something to tell you," he said.

His voice was soft and hoarse as if there were something wrong with his vocal cords. But it carried and I could hear him clearly. There was a kind of purr to it, like the low sound of a diesel engine.

"I thought you might," I said.

"I heard you were a tough guy," he said. "I heard they sent a local guy and you took him like he was a head of cabbage."

"Actually they sent four cabbages," I said.

He paid no attention. His deep empty eyes held on me.

"Don't let it go to your head," he said. "I ain't a local guy."

He paused and looked carefully at Susan and nodded to himself as if he approved. Then he swung his gaze back at me.

"Drop the Ellis Alves case."

There was no point talking to him. I didn't speak. It didn't bother him as far as I could see. I held his look. That didn't bother him either. He worried about me like he worried about interstellar dust.

After a moment he stood, looked at Susan, looked back at me. "You both been told," he said.

He turned and walked away. Not slow, not fast, just walking as if he had someplace to go and had decided to go there. I was aware of my heartbeat, and of the fact that I was breathing faster than I had reason to. The muscles in my back were tight, and I realized I was flexing my hands on the table top. Susan looked at me and rested her hand on my thigh.

"My God," Susan said.

"Yeah," I said.

"Is he as scary dangerous as he made me feel?"

"I would guess that he is," I said.

"Did you feel it?"

"Yeah."

"I hated him looking at me," she said.

"Yeah."

"Are you scared?"

"I suppose so," I said. "I don't spend much time thinking about it. I been scared before."

"What are you going to do?"

"First I'm going to see to it that you're safe."

"You think he might attack me?"

"You plan for what the enemy can do, not what you think he will do," I said.

Neither of us commented on the look he'd given her. It had been meant for me to see, and I'd seen it. She was too alert not to have seen it, too. And much too smart not to know what it meant. Susan nodded partly to me, partly to herself.

"He frightened me. I won't fight you on the protection."

"We're both safe until I make another move on the Alves case," I said.

"You can be so sure?"

"What makes him deadly is he says what he means, and he means what he says. It would be his trademark. He warned me off the case. If I'm off, he takes his money and goes home. If I'm not, he kills me."

"Do you know who this man is?"

"Not specifically," I said.

"But you know people like him," Susan said.

"Yeah."

Susan thought about that for a few moments.

"He's like Hawk," Susan said.

"Yeah, he is," I said.

We were quiet. Susan stared off through the doorway where the charcoal gray man had exited. She was slowly turning her barely sipped drink in a small circle on the table top. Then quite suddenly she looked back at me.

"And he's like you," she said.

"Maybe some," I said.

chapter 25

SUSAN HAD A home and office in a gray Victorian house on Linnaean Street in Cambridge that had been built in 1867. Her office and waiting room were off the entrance hall to the right on the first floor. Her home was a flight up. Across the entry hall opposite the office and waiting room, to the left as you came in the front door, was a room and bath which Susan called the study. It served as a spare room, a guest room, and a place to gather for professional purposes if the gathering were too big for her office. Though she never really used it, she had, naturally, furnished and decorated it within an inch of its life.

Hawk and I were in there. Hawk put his big gym bag on the floor and looked around. There were thick drapes and an oriental rug, and some ornate furniture and several oil paintings of American landscapes. The fireplace had a big brass fender. Hawk took a shaving kit out of the gym bag and took it into the bathroom.

He paused. The bathroom floor was tiled in some sort of thick, rust-colored tile, and the bath fixtures were Victorian, including an old-fashioned shower ring and a claw and ball Victorian tub. The walls had been painted a tone of the tile and glazed with a thin-over coat that had been dragged. There was an oval gilt-framed mirror over the pedestal sink.

"Place is so elegant," Hawk said, "I be ashamed to take out my shabby equipment in here."

"Or anywhere," I said.

Hawk put the shaving kit on the rim of the sink and came back into the study. The door was open and we could see Susan's waiting-room door across the hall. It was ajar. Beyond it, the door to her office was closed. She was with a patient. Late nights did not change that. Foul weather did not change that. Head colds did not change that. Playoff games or the arrival of Michael Jackson or implied death threats did not change that. Five days a week, Susan saw patients.

"You don't know this guy," Hawk said.

"Nope. Never saw him before."

"Funny, you'd think by now we'd know most of the gunnies around here," Hawk said.

"He said he wasn't local," I said.

"I told Vinnie about him. He don't know him. Tony Marcus don't know him."

"Neither does Quirk," I said. "And there's no one looks like him in the mug books."

Hawk took a Smith & Wesson .12-gauge pump gun from his bag and stood it behind the door. Four rounds in the magazine, one in the chamber. He put a big Ziploc bag of shotgun shells on the floor next to it. On the other side of the door, out of view of anyone in the hall, he laid a holstered Berretta Centurion, an extra magazine, and a box of 9-mm. shells on the mahogany sideboard. Beside it he put a box of .44 Magnum shells for the elephant gun he carried in a shoulder rig. Then he took a couple of changes of clothes out of the bottom of the bag and put them on the floor beside the couch.

"This thing fold out?" he said.

"Yeah. Take the cushions off, and you'll see the handle."

"Is it comfy?" Hawk said.

"I never slept on it. But I've never found a hideaway that was."

"Be sleeping in shifts anyway," he said and sat on the couch.

"What's the setup?" I said.

"Got me and Vinnie for one shift. Got Belson and the gay guy . . ."

"Lee Farrell," I said.

"Got Belson and Farrell on the second shift. Quirk say he'll come around when he can, give somebody a break."

"Nice parlay," I said.

Hawk grinned.

"Two cops, two robbers," he said.

"How'd Belson and Farrell get the time?"

"Farrell say he wants to be in on this. He didn't say why. Belson say, after you got his wife out that mess in Proctor, he owes you and he's going to pay off. They don't like it they can fire him. Quirk don't want to fire him so he assigns him and Farrell on special detail."

"Special detail," I said. "Quirk's got no authority to do that."

"Quirk don't give a shit," Hawk said.

"No, he doesn't," I said. "He never has."

"And Vinnie?"

"You know nobody understands Vinnie. He just say he'll be here until it's over."

I nodded.

"Maybe he likes me," I said.

Hawk grinned.

"Maybe he like Susan."

"More likely," I said. "I want two people always with her. This guy isn't rent-a-slug."

"There'll be me and Vinnie, or Belson and Farrell. Henry say he's going to come around with a gun and sit in, and if he does he'll make three. But I not counting him. He's a tough little bastard, but he can't shoot for shit. We know Belson's good. Quirk will be around some. How you feel about the gay guy?"

"Farrell. He's got a black belt in karate, and Quirk says he shoots better than anyone in the department."

"And he ain't going to grab me by the ass?"

"He promised me he'd try not to."

"What you gonna do?"

"I'm going to go about getting Ellis Alves out of jail."

"What you going to do 'bout the man in the gray flannel suit?"

"I'm hoping to kill him," I said.

chapter 26

CLINT STAPLETON'S HOME in New York City was on Fifth Avenue, near Sixty-eighth Street in one of those big gray buildings with a doorman, and a view of the park out the front windows. The doorman in a green uniform with gold piping held the door for me just as if I weren't a shamus, and the uniformed concierge eyed me without disapproval as I walked across the black and white marble lobby.

"Donald Stapleton," I said.

"Your name, sir?"

"Spenser."

The concierge phoned up, told whoever answered that I was down here, waited maybe a minute and said, "Yes, sir," and hung up the phone.

"Take the elevator to the penthouse," he said.

"Is there anyone else up there?" I said.

"No, sir, the Stapletons occupy the entire floor."

"How nice for them," I said.

The elevator opened into a little black and white marble foyer with a skylight. There was a thick white rug on the floor with a peacock woven into it. The Stapletons' door, directly in front of me, had a glossy black finish. In the center of the upper panel was an enormous brass knocker in the shape of a lion holding a ring in its mouth. Below and to the right was a polished brass door knob. There was a small black table next to the door, with curved legs and pawlike feet. A black lacquer vase with a golden dragon on it sat on a gold-colored doily on the table. A fan of peacock feathers plumed out of the vase, and concealed just behind them was a small functional white doorbell. The door knocker looked too heavy for me. I rang the bell.

A stunning black maid in full maid regalia opened the door. She took my leather trench coat. She would have taken my hat if I'd had one, but I didn't. She ushered me into the living room and left with my coat. I checked myself in the mirror over the immaculate fireplace. In honor of the address I had worn a blue suit and black cordovan loafers with an elegant tassel. I had on a white oxford shirt too, with a nice roll in the button-down collar. I hadn't actually buttoned the top button of the collar. My neck being what it was, I tended to choke. But I had concealed the fact by making a slightly wide knot in my maroon silk tie, and running the tie right up over the top button so you couldn't tell it wasn't buttoned. Susan says you can always tell, but what does she know about neckties?

The room was done entirely in tones of cream and ivory and white. There was a solid bank of picture windows overlooking the park. I was as impressed with the view as I was expected to be, but the rest of the room smacked of interior decorator. There was a child's fire engine, painted with an ivory gloss, on the coffee table. There was a white piano with the black keys painted vanilla. *Ordinary things used extraordinarily*, the designer had probably said. *Extraordinary things restated and personalized.* On the side board a pair of pearl-handled Gene Autry autograph toy six shooters lay at careful right angles to each other. I was pretty sure no one had ever eaten a green pepper pizza in this room, or made love on one of the off-white damask couches in this room, or sat around in their shorts in this room and read the Sunday paper. Men in dark expensive suits, with red ties and white broadcloth shirts, might, on occasion, have clinked ice in short, thick highball glasses while they tried to think of conversation to make in this room. Women in tight, long, expensive dresses with pearls that matched the decor might have held crystal flutes of Krug champagne while they gazed blankly out the window at the panorama of the park in this room. Waiters dressed in black tie, bearing small silver trays of endive with salmon roe, might have circulated in this room. And a nanny might, possibly, have walked through this room holding the hand of a small child in a zipped-up snowsuit on his way to be walked in the park on a cold Sunday afternoon, when the light was gray and the sun was very low in the southern sky. I would have bet all I had that the fireplace had never been warm.

A tall lean man with a good tan, wearing a fawn-colored double-breasted suit came into the living room with a blond-haired woman on his arm. She too had a good tan. The woman was wearing high-waisted black pants and a fawn-colored silk shirt with a stand-up collar and the top three buttons undone. There were necklaces and bracelets and rings and earrings all in gold, and some with diamonds in them.

"Mr. Spenser," the man said. "Don Stapleton. My wife Dina."

We all shook hands. Dina had big blue eyes. Her hair was thoroughly blond and worn long and curly so that it cascaded down to her shoulders. She had a small waist, and a full figure above and below it. She was maybe forty-five and she looked as if life had been easy for her.

"Let's sit over here by the window," Stapleton said. "We can enjoy the view while we chat."

He carefully hiked up his pants so as not to bag the knee and sat in a white wing chair with a heavy brocade upholstery. She sat on the edge of a white satin straight chair, folded her hands on her lap, and gazed at her husband. Her shoes were sling strap spike heels in the same fawn color as her blouse and her husband's suit.

"As I told you on the phone," I said, "I'm sort of reexamining the circumstances of Melissa Henderson's death."

They both smiled politely.

"Did you know her?" I said.

"No," Stapleton said. He had a firm voice.

"But your son did," I said.

"I have no reason to doubt you if you say so," Stapleton said, "but we have no personal knowledge that he did."

"He never mentioned her to you? Brought her home? Showed you a picture?"

Stapleton smiled patiently, I was just doing my job, it couldn't be helped that I was stupid.

"Clint is a very good looking and popular young man,"

he said. "He had a lot of girls. He didn't bother to introduce us to all of them."

"He gave this one his letter sweater."

"If so, it was merely one of many he's earned. Clint is a very good athlete."

Dina Stapleton gazed at her husband. She nodded occasionally in support of what he said. She didn't speak.

"Clint appears to be of African descent," I said. "Neither of you appears to be."

"Clint is a chosen child," Stapleton said. "We adopted him when he was an infant. Dina couldn't bear a child and we decided that if we were going to adopt, we should save a little black baby from a life of depravity."

"Of course," I said. "Does either of you know Hunt McMartin or Glenda Baker?"

Dina's expression softened a little, the way it does when you recognize a familiar name.

"Who are they?" Stapleton said.

Dina's eyes flickered a moment and then her face resumed its look of blank admiration. Stapleton put a hand on her knee. I didn't blame him. If I were in a position to do so, I'd have put my hand on her knee, too.

"Hunt and Glenda were the witnesses against Ellis Alves," I said. "The man convicted of murdering Melissa Henderson?"

"Now really, Mr. Spenser, how would we know that?"

"Close-knit family," I said.

Stapleton smiled sadly in recognition of the unbreachable gulf between them and me.

"We are not so close knit that we spend time talking about obscure sex crimes in another city."

I nodded, silently, acknowledging my coarseness. I hadn't mentioned anything about a sex crime.

"What is your business, sir?" I said.

"CEO, the Stapleton companies. I have interests in oil, in banks, commercial real estate, agribusiness, that sort of thing."

He leaned back a little and crossed one leg over the other and clasped his hands on the knee. His socks were cashmere, I noticed, and his mahogany-colored shoes were almost as stylish as mine.

"By training I am an attorney, a member of the New York State Bar, and I still maintain my law firm of course, Stapleton, Brann, and Roberts. Clint plans to attend law school after he graduates. Someday he'll run the whole thing."

"And Mrs. Stapleton?" I said.

She smiled at me and looked back at her husband.

"Dina takes care of the home front," Stapleton said.

"You don't know Hunt McMartin or Glenda Baker?" I said.

"No," Dina said. "I'm sorry, I don't."

She had a deep voice like Lauren Bacall. Her makeup was artful. Her face was calm and loving. And I knew she was lying. After another hour of conversation that was all I knew.

chapter 27

I WAS ON Cone, Oakes's dime, so I was staying at the Carlyle, which was an easy walk—eight blocks uptown and one block east. On my own dime, I usually slept in the car.

Across Fifth Avenue, the park was busy. Groups of school children were herded along the leafy walkways, a lot of third world women wheeling first-world kids in expensive prams who walked or sat on benches and chatted. Dogs chased sticks and squirrels in the park. Old men sat on benches and fed pigeons and disapproved of the third-world nannies and glared at the kids. It was still morning and the sun was shining into the park above the exclusive buildings on the east side of Fifth Avenue. It was late fall so the sun was lower in the southern sky than it would be in the warm months, and the rays slanted from behind me. Some of the sunlight fell through a stand of trees cloistering a low knoll deeper into the park and flashed on something and reflected brightly for a moment. A mirror? More like a magnifying lens. I lunged toward the doorway next to me and rolled in against the door as a bullet smacked into the limestone frame of the entryway. The whining sound of the ricochet blended with the bang of the original. I got the short Smith & Wesson .38 off my hip. It was about as useful as a tennis racquet at this distance. I waited a moment. There was no second shot. I got my feet under me and burst out of the doorway, bent as low as I could get. I ran straight across Fifth Avenue, getting honked at by the taxis, and zig-zagged through the Seventy-sixth Street pedestrian entrance, going as hard as I could go. I varied the zigzag so as not to give the shooter a pattern. A target running straight at you and moving erratically was quite hard to hit, especially with a rifle and a scope, which, I was pretty sure, was what the shooter had. My hope was that I would zig when the shooter was aiming zag, and vice versa. I must have raced past people, and some of them must have seen the gun in my hand, but I was so focused on the knoll ahead that I was not even aware of them. I was vaguely aware that a couple of people were staring up at the knoll as I got closer. It was flanked with some of the big stone outcroppings that add character to the park, and as I scrambled up them, I knew my breath was rasping and my heart was galloping in my chest. I moved from outcropping to outcropping, staying as low as I could, keeping the rocks between me and the top of the knoll. Then I was at the top, crouched behind the last sheltering rock, gasping air into my lungs. There had been no further shots after the first one. It could mean the shooter had left. It could mean that the shooter had stayed where he was and allowed me to get close enough to take me out point blank. It would have taken a lot of self-discipline, but if the shooter was who I thought he was, he probably had self-discipline. I took in more air. *Okay*, I thought, *let's see*. I cocked the .38, took a last deep breath, and dove over the rock. I landed in the grove of trees rolling. I kept rolling, and as I rolled I kept my gun sort of gyroscopically leveled, looking for someone to shoot, and there was no one there. I came to my feet. The grove of trees was completely still. I looked down the knoll. There was nothing unusual. No one was running, no one was carrying a rifle. No passersby were pointing or paying much attention. I could see several blocks down Fifth Avenue. At Seventy-fourth Street a man in a gray overcoat got into a cab. He was carrying what looked at that distance like a trombone case. The cab pulled away into the traffic. It was too far to get a number. I looked around the wooded knoll a little and scuffed the leaves and in a while I found the shell casing. It was a .458 Magnum. I was surprised it left the building standing. I dropped the shell in my jacket pocket, put my .38 back on my hip, and started back down the knoll. A couple of people looked at me briefly and went on about their business. I could feel the sweat soaking through my shirt. But my breathing was beginning to regulate, and my heart rate was probably down under a hundred and fifty by now.

I walked back to the Seventy-sixth Street entrance and crossed, waiting for the light this time, and strolled back down to the doorway I'd ducked into. There was a deep pock mark about chest high in the limestone where I would have been had I not seen the flare off the scope. I didn't see the slug and didn't look for it. It wouldn't tell me anything.

The doorman came out of the building.

"What's going on?" he said.

"I don't know," I said. "Something took a bite out of your building."

He looked at the pock mark and looked around and shrugged.

"Got me," he said and went back inside.

"Got me too," I said aloud to no one and turned back up to Seventy-sixth Street and walked the block east to the Carlyle.

The East Side was going about its upscale business just as if someone hadn't tried to shoot me. There were neat little signs in the minuscule patches of plant life along the sidewalk. The signs asked you to please curb your dog. In my memory, I had never, in any city, seen a dog being curbed. Still I liked the flicker of urban optimism that the signs embodied. Without hope, what are we?

I had no doubt who the shooter was, and he was good. The bullet would have nailed me right in the middle of the chest if I hadn't flopped at the right time. The Gray Man had known I was in New York and known where I was in New York and been able to set up and wait for me in New York. And when it hadn't worked out, he'd calmly put the rifle away and walked off and hailed a cab. The only people who knew I was in New York were Susan, and Hawk, and Don and Dina Stapleton. Only Don and Dina had known the hour of my appointment. This put them above Hawk and Susan on my list of suspects.

Plus they had lied to me. People often lied to me, but usually they had a reason and sometimes the reason mattered. Don had known the killing was sex related though he professed no knowledge of it and I hadn't mentioned it. Dina had been startled when Don said he didn't know Hunt McMartin and Glenda Baker. She didn't have much affect, but there had been enough to tell me that. Hunt and Glenda had both gone to Andover, Glenda during the time Clint Stapleton would have been there. Clint Stapleton was the black child of white parents. Saved from a life of depravity.

I turned into the small elegant lobby of the Carlyle and everyone was nice to me just as if I could afford to stay there. Maybe they thought I could. I had my blue suit on, and there were no bullet holes in it.

chapter 28

I HAD A problem. Obviously there was something wrong
with the Ellis Alves case. I needed to keep plowing at that
until it was passable. Also, obviously, somebody had
hired the Gray Man to kill me. And I probably ought to
do something about that. Except that I didn't know what
to do about that. I didn't know who had hired the Gray
Man and I didn't know who the Gray Man was. Which
made it hard to find him. The best I could do was to keep
at the Ellis Alves case and assume that the Gray Man
would find me, and that when he did, I could out-quick
him.

That decided, I acted promptly. I drove across the river
and picked up a green pepper and mushroom pizza from
Bertucci's in Harvard Square and took it to Susan's house
along with a bottle of Merlot. It was 5:30 and she was

with her last patient of the day when I went in the front door. When I opened the front door, Pearl the Wonder Dog charged out of the library and capered about in the front hall. Her eyes had the slitty look they got when she'd been sleeping on a couch. I bent over and gave her a kiss. She was returning it wetly when she got a whiff of the pizza and redirected her affections toward it. I held it up out of her reach.

Lee Farrell appeared in the open door across the hall, his body partly concealed behind the half-open door. When he saw it was me, he stepped away from the door and shoved a Glock 9-mm. back into his belt holster, butt forward.

"I guess you're okay," he said.

"There's some doubt about that," I said. "But I'm no threat to Susan."

Belson appeared behind Farrell. He was in his shirtsleeves, his gun holstered on his right hip. He was very lean with a narrow face, and a blue shadow of beard always showing no matter how recently he had shaved.

"That for us?" he said.

I went into the library and put the pizza on the sideboard, right beside two boxes of shotgun shells stacked one on top of the other. I didn't bother to answer the question. Pearl came back in with me and sat in front of the sideboard and focused on the pizza.

"She's been spending time down with us," Farrell said, "while Susan's working."

"Case the guy breaks in carrying a pizza," Belson said. "She'll be on him like a barracuda."

"How's Lisa?" I said.

"She's fine," Belson said.

"How about you," I said to Farrell. "How's your love life."

Farrell grinned.

"Most of the guys in the squad room are in love with me," he said. "But I'm playing hard to get."

"You heartbreaker," I said. "Everything quiet around here."

"Like a church," Belson said. "Pearl spends most of the time on the couch. Patients come in and out. Nobody says a word. Nobody makes eye contact."

"How do you know they're all patients?" I said.

"We got a list of her appointments each day and a little description. Susan's agreed to take no new patients until this is over, so she opens her door and sees an unfamiliar face, she hollers."

"And you can hear her if she hollers?"

Belson looked at me as if I'd asked about the Easter Bunny.

"We did a couple dry runs," he said. "You making any progress on this thing?"

"No."

"No rush," Belson said. "I'm here until it's over."

"Me too," Farrell said. "When we're on days, I get to watch *Sally Jesse*."

"You gotta get me a straight partner," Belson said. "I'm over there trying to read *Soldier of Fortune* magazine and he's sitting in front of the tube saying, 'Where did she get those shoes.'"

"Well, you saw them," Farrell said. "Were they gauche or what?"

"See what I mean?" Belson said.

The door to Susan's office opened and a young man came out buttoning up his loden coat. He didn't look at us. He went straight out the front door and pulled it shut behind him. In about two more minutes Susan came out and saw me and came across the hall and put her arms around me and we kissed.

"How about her shoes?" Belson said.

"Cat's ass," Farrell said.

I picked up the pizza and the wine.

"We're going upstairs to dine sumptuously before the fire," I said, "and perhaps later who knows."

Susan smiled.

"Actually I know," she said.

"And?" Farrell said.

"And it's none of your business," Susan said.

"Talk about attitude," Farrell said.

I went up with Susan and Pearl and the pizza. Susan put the pizza in a warm oven while I made a fire and opened the wine. In the old days, before Pearl, we would have sat on the couch to eat, but that was no longer possible, so we sat at Susan's counter where we could still see the fire and the pizza was relatively secure, unless you left it unattended. Susan had changed from her dark conservative work dress to a pale lavender sweatsuit and thick white sweat socks. She had taken off her jewelry but left her makeup in place, and when she sat beside me at the counter I felt the little electro-chemical charge of amazement that she always gave me. I had felt it the first time I'd ever seen her, in the guidance office, at Smithfield High School, more than twenty years ago. And I'd felt it, or a variation of it, every time I'd seen her since.

"How did it go in New York?" Susan said.

"Stapleton's parents lied to me," I said.

"Was it a lie that helps you?"

"Not yet. Except that I know that they're lying."

"Find out anything else?"

"They are white," I said. "The kid's adopted. His

father said if they were going to adopt anyway they may as well save a little black baby from a life of depravity."

"Oh, dear," Susan said.

"Yeah," I said, "me too."

"Anything else?"

"The Gray Man made a run at me," I said.

Susan nodded.

"Tell me about it," she said.

It seemed a shame that she had to know. It was bound to make her anxious. It certainly made me anxious. But a long time ago we'd agreed that neither of us would decide what the other one should know. I told her about it.

She was silent for a moment looking at me, breathing quietly, then she said, "He would not have expected you to charge him like that."

"I don't think he expected to miss," I said.

"But he did, and you charged him, and now he knows a little more about you than he did."

"And vice versa," I said.

"What do you know about him," she said.

"He's not caught up in macho games," I said. "He took a shot at me and it didn't work out so he walked away from it. There'll be another time, he'll look for it. He's not interested in who's tougher. He's interested in who's dead."

"What if you hadn't seen the reflection off the scope?" Susan said. "Or thought it was just a birdwatcher?"

"Well, I know somebody's out to kill me. I see a flash and dive for cover and it turns out to be some guy looking at a red-shafted flicker, the worst that happens is I'm embarrassed. If it's a guy with a gun and I don't dive for cover, I'm dead."

"Can you go through life diving for cover every time you see a light reflection?"

"Depends on how long it takes to get this guy."

Susan nodded slowly as I spoke. She picked up her glass and drank some Merlot, and put the glass back down slowly. Then she smiled slowly, although there didn't seem much pleasure in the smile.

"You are a piece of work," she said.

"Comely in every aspect," I said.

"The Gray Man thinks he's chasing you"—she shook her head once, briefly—"and you think you're chasing him."

"I am chasing him," I said. "What I don't want is for him to know it."

Susan drank again. For her this was close to guzzling.

"Perhaps you should be the one they're guarding 'round the clock," she said.

I shook my head.

"No. He's using the implied threat against you to distract me. As long as I've got you covered, that won't work for him. I take it away from you and I will worry about you all the time, and he'll have won that round."

"Are you sure it's not a macho thing with you?"

"No. But until he's disposed of, I can't do what I do and we can't live the life we want to lead."

"Yes."

"I'm sorry that what I do has spilled out all over you like this."

"I have always known what you do," she said. "I'm a consenting adult."

"I could walk away from it," I said. "I drop the Ellis Alves thing and all this goes away."

She shook her head at once.

"No," she said. "You can't walk away from it. You are

exactly suited by talent, by temperament, hell, by size, to do this odd thing that you do. You can't do something else."

"I can sing nearly all the love songs of the swing era," I said.

"Only to me," Susan said.

"You're the only one I want to sing them to."

"I'm the only one that would listen."

She got up and went to the oven and took out the pizza. She slid it out of the box and onto a big glass platter with a gold trim around the rim. She took a big pair of scissors from a drawer and began to cut the pizza into individual slices. She put the platter on the counter between us and set out two smaller plates that matched the platter, and a knife, fork, and spoon for each of us.

"Flatware to eat pizza?" I said.

"Optional," she said.

"When I'm alone I eat it from the box," I said. "Standing up by the sink."

"I have no doubt of that," she said.

I picked up a slice. By the time I had finished it and washed it down with some wine, Susan had cut a small triangle off the tip of her slice and was conveying it to her mouth with a fork. I picked up another slice.

"You matter to me," I said, "more than what I do, or who I am. If you need me to quit, I'll quit."

She shook her head again while she carefully chewed her pizza. When she had swallowed and sipped some wine and blotted her mouth with her napkin, she said, "Yes. You would. But you should not. You are an odd combination of violence and concern. You contain the violence very well, but it's there, and I would be a fool, and you would be a fool, to think it was less a part of you than the concern."

"You're right," I said. "Sometimes I wish you weren't."

"No need to wish I weren't," Susan said. "You know yourself. You understand your violence as well as you understand your capacity for kindness, maybe better."

"Maybe it needs more understanding," I said.

"Yes, it does," Susan said. "Kindness is not dangerous. You have found a way to work and live which allows you to integrate the violence and the compassion. If you had no impulse to violence, your compassion wouldn't be so admirable. If you had no compassion, your violence would be intolerable. You understand what I'm saying?"

"As long as I pay close attention," I said.

"You are able to apply the impulse to violence in the service of compassion. Your profession allows you actually to exist at the point where vocation and avocation meet. Few people achieve that," she said. "I would not have you change."

I was quiet for a moment admiring the amount of time she had spent thinking about me. Even while I was doing this I was also thinking about how beautiful she was.

"Does this mean you love me?" I said.

She plucked a single julienne of green pepper from the top of the pizza and ate it slowly while she looked at my face thoughtfully. She didn't say anything until she had swallowed the green pepper.

Then she said, "You bet your ass it does."

chapter 29

IT WAS TIME to talk with the eyewitnesses again. Glenda
seemed a better bet than Hunt, so I went up to Andover
in the middle of a cold, sunny afternoon and parked on
Main Street out front of the Healthfleet Fitness Center. I
was wearing a Navy surplus peacoat and a black Chicago
White Sox baseball cap, and when I snuck a peek at
myself in a store window I thought I looked both dashing
and ominous. Up and down Main Street, Andover, there
was no sign of the Gray Man, which didn't, of course,
mean that he wasn't there. Healthfleet was up a flight of
stairs above a coffee shop and a medical supply store.
Inside the entrance was the usual desk manned by the
usual upbeat teenybopper in designer sweats and a pony-
tail who urged everybody as they checked in to have a
great workout. I'd never figured out why cheerfulness

and exercise were so tightly linked in everybody's marketing system, but it was the official attitude in all health clubs. Made me think fondly of the old boxing gyms that I had trained in where people came to work hard, and concentrated on it. On the wall by the desk was some sort of motivational gimmick with credit given for hours on the treadmill, and a bar graph showing people's various progress. The main workout space was banked with windows over the street and mirrors around the other walls. It was a bright room with some shiny weight-training machinery lined up in front of the windows and an exercise floor behind it. I could see Glenda at that end of the room wearing painfully tight black shorts and a bright green halter top. She was leading a class of women who stepped on and off of a plastic step to the throb of rock music while Glenda yelled, "Aaand over, aaaand back, aaand nine, eight, seven . . . aaand take it on down." The Gray Man was nowhere in the room.

I told the kid at the desk that I was here to see Glenda Baker, and I'd wait until she was through. There was a small waiting area in front of the desk, a low sofa, and a bentwood coffee table. And a long coat rack, mostly filled, on the wall by the door. I took off my coat and hung it on the rack and sat on the sofa with my feet on the coffee table and my hat on. The teenybopper eyed my gun covertly. She'd probably have told me to have a great shoot if she'd seen it when I came in.

When Glenda's class ended she started across the room toward the waiting area carrying a big bottle of Evian water and taking healthful sips from it as she walked. She went straight to the coat rack without paying any attention to me.

I said, "Hello, Glenda."

She stopped and smiled and said "Hello" vaguely.

"Spenser," I said. "The sleuth."

"Oh, hello."

"May I buy you a cup of coffee?" I said.

If she saw the gun, she was too well bred to pay it any mind.

She smiled without much enthusiasm.

"Well, sure, okay."

"Good."

"Let me change and grab a quick shower," she said. "Ten minutes."

"No hurry," I said.

She went to the locker room, and I passed the time counting the number of women in spandex who should not have been wearing spandex. By the time Glenda came back out of the locker room in an ankle-length camel's hair coat and high boots, the count was up to All.

"For crissake," I said. "It really was ten minutes."

Glenda smiled faintly. She smelled of expensive soap and maybe a hint of even more expensive perfume. I stood and held the door for her. As we left, I said to the receptionist, "Have a great front desk."

She smiled even more faintly than Glenda.

It was always a pleasure to go into a coffee shop on a cold day and smell the coffee and the bacon and feel the warmth. We sat in the back in a wooden booth with blue checkered paper place mats on it. I started to slide in opposite Glenda.

"Sit beside me," she said. "It will be easier to talk."

Glenda slid in, I sat beside her, and a waitress with a white apron over jeans and a green sweater came over and asked if we wanted coffee. We did. The waitress poured it while we glanced at the menu. Since I had to stay alert for the Gray Man, I felt that caffeinated was a health necessity. In fact, it seemed to me that I'd best have more than one cup. They were out of donuts but there were corn muffins and I ordered a couple. Glenda had decaf, black, and an order of whole wheat toast, no butter. I hung my jacket on a hook on the corner of the booth. Glenda kept her coat on.

"How many classes a day do you teach?" I said.

"Varies. Today I just had the one."

"Where'd you learn to do this stuff."

"I was a sports and recreation major at college," she said. "After I got married, I took a certification course."

"Better than sitting around the house reading *Vogue*?"

"I'm a very physical person," Glenda said.

"I could tell that," I said. "Is your husband equally physical?"

"Hunt is more business oriented," Glenda said.

The waitress brought the toast and the corn muffins and freshened the coffee.

"That's decaf?" Glenda said.

"Yes, ma'am," the waitress said. "You can always tell by the green handle on the pot."

Glenda seemed not to have heard her. She was half turned in the corner of the booth, looking at me. Her gaze had that mile long quality that politicians had—the eyes were on me, but the focus was somewhere else.

"So the aerobics teaching is a nice outlet for you," I said.

"There are better outlets," Glenda said absently.

"Un huh."

"But to tell you the truth, we can use the money. Hunt's not making a very big salary."

"Doesn't his family run the business?"

"Yes, and they are cheap as hell. I tell him they're

exploiting him simply because he is family and they can get away with it."

"Well," I said, "someday it'll be his, I suppose, and then he can exploit somebody."

"Someday is a long way off," Glenda said.

"And you have to pass the time somehow," I said.

The mile-long stare disappeared, and her gaze suddenly focused very concretely on me.

"You are very understanding," she said.

I dropped my eyes a little and shrugged.

"Part of the job," I said.

"Am I part of the job, too?" she said. "Is that why you wanted to see me again?"

I finished my second corn muffin. She was looking at me in such sharp focus that I sort of missed the mile-long stare.

"I thought so when I drove up here," I said.

"And now?"

As we talked, she had been completely still, moving only to drink her black coffee. Her dry toast lay untouched on the paper plate in front of her.

"I'm glad I came."

She smiled. There was nothing faraway in the smile. It was smiled at me, and it was full of charge and specificity.

"There are a few questions I need to ask," I said as if it were an afterthought, or maybe something to be got out of the way before we got to more serious business.

"Yes," she said, "but let's go to my place. Hunt's at work and we can relax. Talk more privately."

"Sure," I said. "You have a car?"

She smiled the penetrating smile.

"I'll ride with you," she said.

I paid the check and we went to my car. No one took

a shot at me. The car was as I'd left it. Neither of us said much as we drove down the hill to Glenda's condominium. The building was silent. Apparently everyone who lived in The Trevanion worked. The heels of my rubber-soled running shoes sounded loud on the marble floors. I felt as if I ought to tiptoe. Glenda unlocked the door to her place and I followed her in and closed it behind me. One of them was a neat housekeeper. The place looked as if it were ready for company. Maybe it was always ready for company. Glenda took my coat, standing close when she did so, and I got a full scent of the milled soap and subtle perfume that had been hinted at at the health club. There was a brass hat stand beside the front door and Glenda hung my peacoat on it. Then she turned and smiled at me very idly and began to unbutton her coat.

"Can I get you some coffee?" she said. "Or something stronger?"

"Coffee would be fine," I said.

She unbuttoned the last button and shrugged out of her coat. Except for the high boots, she had nothing on under it.

"Or maybe something stronger," I said.

She walked slowly toward me, looking at me with a half smile, and pressed against me and put her arms around me and looked up at me with her head thrown back.

"How much stronger?" she said.

Her voice had a hoarse overtone to it now.

"Maybe a quart of Valium," I said. "Over ice?"

My voice had a pretty hoarse overtone, too. She pressed against me more insistently.

"Anything else?" she said.

I put my arms around her and looked down at her.

"Yeah," I said. "How come you were at Andover the same time Clint Stapleton was and you don't know him?"

She stiffened. I kept my arms around her.

"Can't you think about anything but that stupid murder?" she said.

"I can, but I'm trying not to," I said. "And what murder was it that Clint was connected to?"

She got stiffer still and tried to push away from me. I wouldn't let her. I held her tight against me.

"Let go of me," she said.

"All I said was Clint Stapleton. Why did you think I was interested in a murder?"

"Well, I mean he was Melissa's boyfriend, so I thought that's what you were talking about."

"When I talked to you last time, you said you didn't remember her boyfriend's name," I said.

She pushed hard against me now, trying to get away. I held on. She tried to knee me in the groin. I turned my hip enough to prevent it.

"Now if you went to Andover with him, and he dated your sorority daughter, and you double-dated with them a few times, isn't it odd that you didn't remember it the first time I asked you, and remembered it now in the throes of passion."

"Let me go," she said. Her teeth were clenched and the words scraped out through them. "Let me goddamned go."

She got her hands to my face and started to scratch. I let go of her and stepped away, and she stood breathing hard with her absolutely spectacular body on full display. I looked at it happily. I was all business, but I tried to be never so busy that I couldn't stop and smell the flowers.

"That is a hell of a body," I said.

"Don't you want to fuck me?" she said.

"The answer to that is actually pretty complicated," I said, "but to oversimplify—no, ma'am, I don't."

"But I thought when you wanted to see me again, alone . . ." She frowned for a minute and I realized that she was thinking, or something. "You didn't . . . you were just trying to get information."

"Still trying," I said.

"Damn," she said and flopped onto the arm of an easy chair behind her and let her butt slide over the arm and onto the seat so that she sat sideways in the chair, and her legs dangled over the arm.

"I'm not usually that wrong," she said.

She seemed entirely at ease being naked and made no effort to cover herself. Her camel's hair coat remained in a pile on the floor where she'd dropped it. The high boots only emphasized how undressed she was.

"You and your husband know Clint Stapleton," I said.

She shrugged.

"And his parents know you," I said.

She moved one foot in a small circle, watching it as she did so.

"Sure," she said finally. "They're Hunt's aunt and uncle."

"Clint is your husband's cousin?"

She shrugged, watching her boot make small circles in the air. "Yeah," she said.

"Jesus Christ," I said.

We were quiet. It was hard to think with that world-class body staring at me. I was the complete professional, and totally loyal to Susan, but I had to fight off the urge to rear up on my hind legs and whinny. She kept moving the toe of her boot in its little circle.

"Cops know this?"

"I don't know."

"You tell them?"

"I don't remember if I did or not. What difference does it make?"

"Did you really see a black man drag Melissa into his car?"

"Of course."

"Why did you pretend you didn't know Clint when I asked you before?"

"Hunt says it's better not to get Clint involved."

"Protect that pro career, right?"

"Sure."

"What makes the Stapletons related to the Mc-Martins?" I said.

"Dina Stapleton is Hunt's father's sister."

"You happily married to Hunt?" I said.

She shrugged again.

"Hunt's got a good future," she said.

"You get along?"

"He cares about me, but he's not as, ah, physical as I am."

"And you take care of that problem by, ah, branching out," I said.

"Most of the time I'm luckier than I was with you."

"I don't think luck's got much to do with it," I said.

She smiled a little but didn't say anything.

"You love your husband?" I said.

She was quiet for a moment watching her toe circles. "We get along," she said. "If I have a little adventure like this one, it doesn't mean we don't get along."

"Hell, Glenda," I said. "Maybe it means that you do."

"You can understand that?"

"I can understand that it might," I said.

"But not for you?"

"No, not for me."

"Why not."

"I'm in love," I said.

"Oh," she said.

I stood up. I knew she hadn't seen a black man pull anyone into his car. I also knew she wasn't going to make a court-useful admission of that fact, so I saw no reason to press the point. Besides that, my id was locked in grim combat with my super ego, and was going to prevail if I didn't get out of there.

"Thanks for showing me your body," I said.

"I had hoped to do more."

"Yeah," I said. I tried not to sound wistful.

She stood, and walked with me to the door.

"Would you kiss me good-bye?" she said.

"Of course," I said.

We kissed. It was a nice kiss, but I didn't quite know what to do with my hands.

When the kiss was over I opened her door behind me. She made no attempt to conceal herself. If anyone in the hall wanted to look, apparently Glenda didn't mind. I stepped into the hall and closed the door. The hall was empty. Walking out of the building toward my car, I did some deep breathing, trying to get my blood flow back into its normal pattern.

chapter 30

BY NOW THERE were several things pretty obvious about the death of Melissa Henderson. One was that it probably wasn't Ellis Alves who killed her. Another one was that there was a lot of pressure being exerted to let him take the rap for it anyway. I felt it was time to report these findings to my client, so I went and had breakfast with Rita Fiore at the Bostonian Hotel.

The dining room at the Bostonian was on the low rooftop of the hotel. It was mostly glass and from where we were you could look down at Quincy Market and Faneuil Hall, and watch the upwardly mobile hurrying through the Market carrying coffee and a bun on their way to work. Rita's mobility was so far up by now that she could watch them run while she ate sitting down. I looked around the room. It was full of suits, mostly male.

"Are we having a power breakfast?" I said.

"Yes."

"I was feeling kind of electric," I said.

"Of course," Rita said. "You confer with people at breakfast, and it makes them think you're too busy for lunch. It also gives you an excuse for coming in late."

The waiter poured us coffee, offered us juice, which I accepted and Rita declined, and presented us menus.

"If we were eating at Charlie's Kitchen," I said, "would it still be a power breakfast?"

"Certainly not," Rita said. "Don't you know anything? You read *Boston* magazine and they tell you where it's a power breakfast."

"Oh," I said. "Seems a high price to pay for knowing."

"Things don't come free," Rita said. "What have you got for me on Ellis Alves."

I told her what I knew, and what I thought, interrupting my discourse once to order some corned beef hash with a dropped egg, and a couple of more times to take bites of it when it came. I was slightly nonspecific when I reported my talk with Glenda. Rita listened quietly, sipping her coffee and eating the plain bagel, toasted, no cream cheese, which she'd ordered. It was the sort of breakfast Susan would have ordered, except that Rita ate both halves of the bagel. When I got through, Rita leaned back so that her white blouse stretched tight across her chest. It was a nice look.

"Cone, Oakes has a lot of clout in this city," Rita said, "and judges give us more leeway than some guy working out of his cellar in Weymouth Landing, but even we can't go into court with a case that consists of you standing up in front of the judge and saying that Alves's conviction doesn't make any sense."

"I understand," I said. "I just wanted to keep you, ah, abreast of the case."

"Nice phrasing," Rita said. "And you're right. It doesn't make sense."

She reached across and took a forkful of my hash and ate it.

"Oh, yum!" she said. "Don't you ever have to worry about your weight?"

"Just keeping it up."

"You bastard," she said.

We ate in silence for a moment. Rita finished her dry bagel and washed it down with her black coffee and looked distracted for a moment.

"A cigarette would taste good now," she said.

"Eventually you won't miss it," I said.

"How long for you?"

"Twenty-seven years."

"And you don't miss it?"

"Not a bit."

"How long before you didn't miss it?"

"Ten years."

Rita stared at me and said, "Oh, God!"

There was another silence while Rita gazed out the window and mourned her smoking habit. It was spitting rain mixed with snow, and the streets around the Market gleamed like polished ebony.

Finally, still staring out at the weather, Rita said, "You can quit this case, you know."

"I know."

"I don't want you to get killed for Ellis Alves. Maybe he didn't do this, but he's done a lot. You'd be a bigger loss than he is."

"I know."

"Susan want you to quit?"

"No."

Rita's eyes widened.

"No?" she said.

"No."

Rita was silent for a while.

"She's a pretty smart broad, isn't she?" Rita said finally.

"Yes."

"I didn't think you'd quit, but I wanted to be sure you knew where we stood on it."

"Thanks."

"Okay, we can establish the relationship between the eyewitnesses and Melissa's boyfriend easily enough. And I guess we can establish that Clint Stapleton was her boyfriend. That's just time and money. Send some paralegals over to Taft and ask enough questions of enough undergraduates." Rita paused and looked out the window at the Market some more, then she shifted her gaze to me. "I think that talking to Trooper Miller would pay off."

"If he'll talk. Which I don't think he will."

"You can pressure him with whatsisname's testimony."

"Bruce Parisi," I said. "He won't repeat it unless I'm punching him in the kidney."

"Okay, so you still can't take it to court. But you can threaten to take it to court and see what happens. I got some weight with the local DEA."

"Phil Fallon?" I said.

"My God, what a memory."

"What's Fallon going to do for me?"

"He could get Medford to pick up Parisi and hold him for a bit if that would do you any good," Rita said. "And make sure Miller knows it."

"Just because you ask him to?"

"Sure," Rita grinned. "In moments of despondency between marriages, I did him a couple of favors."

"That is despondent," I said.

"I know," she said. "I know, but the pompous little bastard is quite surprisingly good in bed."

"If you say so."

"Want me to speak to Phil?"

"Does it mean you'll have to schtup him again?" I said.

"No. It only means I'll have to let him think I will."

"Good," I said. "I wouldn't want to be responsible for a criminal act."

"Oh, come on," Rita said. "He's not that bad."

"So you say."

"Let me know," Rita said, "if you want Phil to have Parisi collared."

I thought about it for a little while and then I nodded. "Go ahead," I said. "Have them grab Parisi."

"Good as done," Rita said.

"And thanks for helping," I said.

Rita grinned.

"You hate help, don't you?"

"Hate it," I said.

"I do too," Rita said. "Somebody's helping you and you have to take time off to listen to them and pretend you think their ideas are great and come up with an answer that makes them feel good, which is all time wasted when you could be thinking about the problem better than they can."

"And when the idea is in fact great . . ." I said.

"Even worse," Rita said. "Sorry."

"It's okay," I said. "I got to think long thoughts about your chest."

"Just because I stuck it out a little?" Rita said.

"Yeah."

"Then I must stick it out more often."

"Please do," I said.

"You have a plan," Rita said.

"For your chest?"

"No, for Parisi and Trooper Miller."

"I think so," I said.

"You want to tell me?"

"No," I said. "Just have Parisi picked up and be sure Miller knows it. And that he knows it's got something to do with me."

"And your plans for my chest?" Rita said.

I grinned at her.

"It's a place to start," I said.

"Promises, promises," Rita said and signaled for the check.

chapter 31

THEY PICKED PARISI up in Medford the next morning, and
Miller was in to see me that afternoon. The office door
was open, in case there was an impulse buyer wandering
the corridor, and I was reading Calvin and Hobbes for the
second time because I had heard that the strip was going
to end, and I was trying to store up.

Miller came in and closed the door hard behind him.
He walked across the room and stopped in front of me
and stood looking down at me with a dead-eyed stare that
was supposed to make me hide under my desk. I gave
him a wide, friendly, open faced smile entirely suitable to
the approaching holiday season. We did that for a while.

Finally Miller said, "On your feet, asshole."

I looked around the office.

"Asshole?"

Miller jerked his thumb in a stand-up gesture.

"Surely you've mistaken me for someone else," I said.

"You want me to run you for refusing a lawful order, pal? On your fucking feet."

"Tommy, you wouldn't know a lawful order if it came by and lapped your hand," I said. "Sit down. We'll talk."

He came around the desk quicker than I thought he could move. I put up one foot and aimed for his groin, but he turned on me and caught it on his hip. He got hold of my foot and yanked me out of the chair. In someone less graceful than myself it might have been sort of ignominious. I kicked at him with my other foot and got free and rolled as he tried to stomp me and got my feet under me and came up and dug a left into his solar plexus. He grunted and made the cop move at my hair, but my hair was too short to get hold of. A perfect blend of beauty and function. I butted him on the chin. That was supposed to put him down. It didn't. Maybe Tommy was nearly as tough as he thought he was. He kept coming, and his bulk drove me back against the wall of my office. I kept my chin buried in his shoulder and my body pressed up against his so he couldn't get much of a shot at me. All he could punch was my ribs and back. He was a clumsy puncher, but his hands were heavy. I braced against the wall, got my hands against his chest, and heaved him away from me. As he staggered back, I nailed him on the cheekbone with a straight left and followed it with a hell of a right hook, and it put him down. But he didn't stay, he lunged up with his head down, and tried to tackle me. It's a dumb thing to do. I kneed him in the face and hammered him on the back of the head with the side of my right fist, and he went down on his hands and knees and stayed that way for a minute, his head hanging. My knee had probably broken his nose.

There was blood dripping onto the floor. But he didn't stay that way. Slowly he climbed to his feet. When he was upright, he tried to gather his balance around him, looking at me dully, swaying a little. Then he fumbled for his gun. I let him get it out of the holster and then stepped in and took it away from him. He was half out, and his movements were slow motion. I stuck the gun in my belt and got hold of his lapels and shoved him backwards into one of my client chairs and sat him down. As he went down he took a feeble right-handed swipe at my head. I hunched up and caught it on the left shoulder. And then he was in the chair and I stepped away from him. He sat blankly, the blood running down his face and onto his shirt. I went to the wash basin and got my Holiday Inn towel and soaked it in cold water and wrung it out and went back and put it in his hand.

"Hold that on your nose," I said.

Miller sat motionless with the towel in his hand and stared at me. His jaw was slack, his mouth was half open. I took the towel from his hand and put it against his nose gently and took his hand and placed it on the towel.

"Hold it," I said.

He had no reaction, but he held the towel. I went back around my desk and sat. And waited. In another minute or two he began to come around. His eyes began to move and he closed his mouth. He shifted the towel a little. Finally his eyes appeared to register me.

"My fucking nose is broke," he said.

"You'll need to go have somebody set it and pack it," I said.

"You ever break your nose?"

"About eight times," I said.

"Bleeds like a bastard."

"Un huh."

We sat some more.

"You are a tough sonova bitch," Miller said.

"Un huh."

Miller got up and went to the sink and rinsed the towel and wrung it out and reapplied it. Then he came back and sat down. He wasn't moving very briskly.

"I know you had Parisi send out some bone breakers to run me off the Ellis Alves case," I said.

"Yeah?" Miller said.

"And I know that Alves didn't do that coed in Pemberton."

"You do, huh?"

"I do, and I'm pretty sure your days of giving lawful orders are over."

"You think so," Miller said. But there wasn't much force in his voice.

"The question is whether Healy fires you and lets it go at that, or whether you do jail time."

Miller had restabilized enough to show some alarm.

"You talked with Healy already?" he said.

"Not yet."

"You think you can prove any of this?"

"I can prove it to Healy," I said.

"Parisi won't testify," he said.

"You think so?" I said. "You think if he's squeezed he won't talk? You think all four of the jackasses he sent to scare me won't testify if they're looking at jail time?"

Miller thought about it. He started to nod and stopped as if it hurt.

"Whaddya want," he said, his voice muffled by the towel.

"Tell me why you framed Alves."

"What makes you think it was me?"

"It's something a cop would know how to do. Especially a cop who was in charge of the investigation."

"That's just speculation."

"You came up with Ellis Alves," I said. "How? Did you investigate another case where Ellis was involved? Did you request and get a printout on known sex offenders, and pick him off that? You think when Healy starts looking he won't find a connection between you and Alves?"

I was guessing, but it was a plausible guess, and I must have been right. Miller took the towel away from his nose and looked at it. His bleeding had slowed down to a trickle. I got a box of Kleenex from my desk drawer and handed it to him. He carefully tore it into small pieces and wadded them and packed them into each nostril. It made him look funny but it stopped the trickle.

"You got a drink?" he said. His voice was thick like a man with a bad cold.

I took a bottle of Scotch from the drawer and went to the sink and got a water glass. I poured a couple of inches into the glass.

"You want water?" I said.

He shook his head very gently and pointed at the glass. I handed it to him and he took half of it in a swallow.

"You got your theories," he said in a thick voice. "And you can't prove them. And I ain't going to help you prove them. But I will tell you one thing, and you listen, you'll thank me. Leave this alone."

"Why?"

"You don't know what you're into," he said.

"What am I into?"

"Something too big for you."

"What?"

Miller started to shake his head, but that made his nose hurt, and he stopped in mid shake.

"Too big," he said.

"Tell me about the Gray Man," I said.

"Who?"

"Tall guy, gray hair, pale skin, looks kind of gray, when I saw him he was dressed all in gray."

"Don't know any guy like that," Miller said.

He sounded like he meant it. I had listened to a lot of lies and a little truth in my life, and I thought I had gotten pretty good by now at telling which was which. I didn't depend on the skill. I had been wrong often enough to make me uneasy, but Miller didn't sound like he was lying about the Gray Man.

"You got anybody else out there trying to chase me off this case?" I said.

"It's way above me," he said. "Way above me."

"How far," I said.

"Don't know."

Miller stood up suddenly. He held himself steady with one hand on the back of the chair.

"Don't feel so good," he said. "I'm going."

He turned and walked to my door with a little wobble in his walk and opened the door and went out without closing it. I didn't try to stop him. Instead I sat and thought about the interesting fact that the more I learned, the less I knew. Then I got up and went to the sink and let the cold water run over the knuckles of my left hand for a while.

chapter 32

Martin Quirk called me at ten minutes of seven while I was shaving in the shower. I got out with lather on my face and caught it on the third ring before my machine picked up.

"I'm on the sixth level of the parking garage in Quincy Market," Quirk said. "I think you should come down."

"Can I finish shaving?" I said.

"Sure," Quirk said. "We'll be here all day."

Fresh showered, clean shaven, and smelling manfully of some sort of cologne Susan had given me on my birthday, I arrived at the Quincy Market garage in the middle of a traffic jam. A motorcycle cop was trying to steer traffic away from the garage and since a lot of people who drove in from the suburbs didn't know anywhere to go but Quincy Market, there was a high

level of frustration, as people turned into Clinton Street
and were waved off by the cop.

When it was my turn, I rolled down my window and
said, "Lieutenant Quirk."

The cop nodded and gestured me into the parking
garage.

"Park along the right wall there," he said. "Don't pay
any attention to the signs."

He pointed emphatically at a Chevrolet sedan and
gestured it down Clinton Street.

"And Quirk's a captain now," he said.

"Captain Quirk?"

The motorcycle cop grinned.

"Captain Quirk," he said.

I parked where he told me and ignored the No Parking
signs like he said and walked back to the elevator and
went up to the sixth floor. Since Quirk was the homicide
commander, and there were cop cars and cops all over the
building, I pretty well knew what I'd find on the sixth
floor. What I didn't know was who.

When I got off the elevator I could see the yellow
crime scene tape stretched across the far northwest corner
of the garage, and a group of cops, mostly in plainclothes, doing what cops mostly do at crime scenes,
which is to stand around. There were only a few cars
scattered around the floor. Quirk was standing with his
back to me wearing a Harris tweed top coat with the
collar up. He had his hands in the pockets of the coat and
he was looking down at something on the floor of the
garage.

The parking garage walls were only about chest high
and the wind, funneled through the open construction,
was sharp. I put up my own collar. As I approached the
group, one of the plainclothes cops said, "Hey."

Quirk looked up and saw me and said, "Let him through," and I walked past the other cops and stood beside him. And looked down. It was a dead man, and his name was Tommy Miller.

"Know him?" Quirk said.

"Yeah. State cop named Tommy Miller."

"He had your address on a piece of paper in his pocket," Quirk said. "You know why?"

"Yeah, but it's a long story."

"Okay, we'll get to it. He'd been punched around before he was shot. You know anything about that?"

"Yeah. It was me did the punching."

"How about the shooting?"

"Nope. Where'd he get it?"

Quirk settled onto his haunches and turned Miller's head to the left. There was a small puffy hole behind his ear.

"One shot?" I said.

"Yep, no exit wound. Slug must have rattled around in there for a while."

"Twenty-two?"

"Be my guess. We're looking for a shell casing."

"Might have been a revolver," I said.

"Un huh."

"Might have cleaned up his brass," I said.

"Un huh."

"State cops know about this?" I said.

"Healy's on his way," Quirk said. "You want to wait for him, make one statement instead of two?"

"Yes."

"Anything I need to know right now?"

"Miller's involved in the case that you got Belson and Farrell assigned to in Cambridge . . . captain."

Quirk's face had no expression. He was as big as I was,

and thick. He was hatless, his dense black hair cut short and brushed back.

"I'm really something now," he said.

Across the floor the elevator doors opened and Healy got out. He had on a trenchcoat and a soft hat. He pulled the hat on harder and put his collar up as the wind swirled past him. He was alone. When he got to the crime scene he said, "Hello, Martin."

Quirk said hello. Healy nodded at me and looked down at Miller's body.

"Tommy Miller," he said. "Been in a fight."

"With me," I said.

Healy studied me for a minute.

"Looks like you won," he said. He looked at Quirk. "I got a couple of my crime scene people coming by. You got any problem with that?"

"None," Quirk said. "I'm about to gossip a little with Philo Vance, here. You want to join us?"

"Yeah," Healy said. "Let's get off this roof."

"We'll go over to the Market," Quirk said. "Get some breakfast."

chapter 33

MOST OF THE traffic in the Quincy Market Building was ambulatory. People going to work, picking up coffee on the way. We got one of the little tables at the east end of the Market and a waitress gave us coffee while we studied the menu.

When we had ordered, Quirk said, "Spenser thinks this is part of something he's working on."

"You think this has something to do with the Alves case?" Healy said.

"Yeah."

"You know the Alves case, Martin?" Healy said.

"No."

"Why don't you tell Martin about the Alves case and then go ahead and tell both of us what you know," Healy said.

So I did, sticking to what I knew and not theorizing, while eggs and ham and toast and coffee were brought and eaten and the table was cleared and more coffee was poured. No one asked us to move when we were finished. Neither Quirk nor Healy showed a badge, but there was something about them that people recognized. We were welcome all day if we wished. While I talked, neither Quirk nor Healy spoke, or even moved except to drink coffee. I could feel the weight of their concentration. When I was through, they were both quiet, thinking about what I'd told them.

"And you didn't shoot him?" Healy said.

"You know he didn't shoot him," Quirk said.

Healy nodded sadly.

"Yeah, I know," he said. "I knew it when I asked the question."

"Okay, we got the same facts you do. You want to theorize with us?"

"Sure," I said.

"You figure Miller put Parisi on you," Quirk said.

"Yeah. He'd know guys like Parisi, and he'd have leverage to make Parisi do him a favor."

"And he showed up right after Parisi got collared," Healy said.

"Why'd he do it?" Quirk said.

"Miller? I figure he talked with the kid, at the time of the murder . . ."

"Stapleton," Quirk said.

"Yeah, and the kid mentioned that his pro tennis career would be adversely affected if he got hauled in and questioned about his girlfriend's murder."

"And?" Healy said.

"And he may have mentioned to Miller that his dad had around two hundred gazillion dollars."

"So they made a deal?"

"Yeah."

"And Miller rigged it for Ellis Alves to take the fall so the pressure would be off the kid," Healy said.

"My guess," I said. "Either he came across Alves in the course of his employment or he looked him up in the case files under *Rape*."

"We can look at Miller's finances," Healy said. "See if he was involved in a case that Alves was involved in. See if we've got Alves in the *Rape* files."

"Then you show up and talk to the kid, Stapleton, and the kid gets scared," Quirk said. "And he calls Miller and Miller sends out some sluggers because he thinks you're like a regular person and a few big guys with guinea names can scare you right back to doing divorce tails."

"Guy I know heard that someone was looking to, ah, coerce me, so I had Hawk with me."

"Don't seem fair," Quirk said.

"Seemed fair to me," I said.

"Okay, I like it pretty good so far. Why'd Miller come after you himself when Parisi was picked up?" Quirk said.

"He was a cop," I said. "And a particular kind of cop. He was used to scaring people. He was a big tough guy. He was used to getting things done by slapping people around."

"Maybe so," Healy said. "But I don't see why he comes on like Conan the Barbarian," Healy said.

"He came in, wanted me to stand up, I declined, and he came for me. I think before he started trying to find out what I knew, he wanted to be sure I wasn't wearing a wire," I said. "And things got away from him."

"Meaning you kicked his ass," Quirk said.

"In a manner of speaking," I said modestly.

"Which made scaring you to death sort of problematic," Healy said.

"Yes."

"So he didn't get to find out what you knew, and he didn't get you to walk away from the case."

I shrugged.

"Tommy was a tough guy," Healy said.

"So who popped him?" Quirk said. "The Gray Guy?"

"Miller told me it was way above," I said.

"Above what?"

"Above all of us," I said.

"You figure the Gray Guy comes from above?" Quirk said.

"He's not somebody you hire out of a pool hall someplace," I said.

"Kind of guy might use a .22?" Quirk said.

"Looked like a small hole in Miller," Healy said.

"Yep."

"Guy uses a .22 is a specialist," Quirk said. "Anybody can blow a hole the size of an ashtray in some guy's skull with a .44 Magnum."

"Guy uses a .22, wants people to know he's a specialist," Healy said. "Know how good he is."

"Use the right load and know where to shoot and you can put one in his head and have it ping-pong around inside the skull," Quirk said. "Do more damage than a Mag."

"How much more damage do you need to do?" Healy said.

The people moving through the marketplace were changing character. The workers in suits and overcoats had given way to the tourists in parkas and warmup jackets. They didn't hurry. They meandered, stopping at food stalls, looking at the food.

Quirk said, "You think this kid Stapleton did his girlfriend?"

"He's a better bet than Alves," I said.

"He got the kind of reach that could orchestrate this kind of coverup?" Healy said. "The Gray Man and all?"

"I doubt it," I said. "But his father might."

"You think he hired the Gray Man?"

"He might have."

"You think the Gray Man clipped Miller?"

"Yes."

"You got any evidence for any of it?" Quirk said.

"Not a jot or a tittle," I said.

"How you going to get some?"

"I'll talk to the Stapleton kid again, see what happens."

"You want some cover?" Healy said.

I shook my head.

"No point being more macho than you need to be," Healy said.

"That ain't it," Quirk said. "He figures to keep pushing until the Gray Man makes a run at him again."

Healy looked at me. I nodded.

"You figure to take him?" Healy said.

I nodded again.

"Pretty big risk for a guy like Ellis Alves," Healy said.

"He ain't taking the risk for Alves," Quirk said.

"Then who the hell . . ." Healy stopped halfway into the sentence and closed his mouth and looked at me for a minute. Then he nodded.

"Never mind," he said.

chapter 34

It was a bright Saturday morning. I had finished the last of my breakfast as I turned off of Route 128 into Newton. Clint Stapleton lived off campus in a condominium in Newton just across the Walford line near the Charles River. It was a townhouse arrangement that shared a mutual wall with another townhouse on a carefully curved road of other townhouses. All of the townhouses were white faux colonial structures with green shutters and big brass knockers on the front door, and big carriage lamps above the front door. The street was called Fifer's Way, and wherever the developers could put up a white picket fence they had. There was no one on the street. No kids. No dogs. This was a neighborhood of the not yet married, the recently divorced, the trying-it-out-for-a-year.

Clint Stapleton came to the door in a loose-fitting ivory cable knit sweater and a pair of baggy wheat-colored canvas pants with a drawstring waist. On his feet were a pair of tasseled moccasins, no socks. He had a navy blue paisley print do rag on his head. Maybe it wasn't just a fashion statement. Maybe he was bald and his head got cold. On the other hand, if you were bald, then you really couldn't be said to have a do, so would it be possible to have a do rag?

"Now just what in the fuck do you want?" Clint said.

"You ever think of the metaphysical aspects of that question?" I said.

"I got no time for jiving," he said.

He pronounced all the letters, jive-ing, like some guy at a Princeton eating club trying to get down. I inched my foot into the doorway and hoped he wouldn't slam it. I was wearing running shoes.

"We need to talk a little more," I said.

"About what?"

"About Melissa, about your pro career, about your cousin Hunt, about Tommy Miller, stuff like that."

Clint didn't know what to do. He started to speak, and didn't. He looked over his shoulder back into the room behind him. He looked at me. I smiled.

"Can't it wait?" he said. "I got company."

I shook my head and smiled some more. Maybe if sleuthing didn't work out, I could get a job selling aluminum siding, door to door.

He backed away from the front door and opened it wider.

"Okay," he said. "Come in."

I walked into a small entry hall with a stairway along the right-hand wall. A breakfast nook and a kitchen was to my left. The living room was straight ahead. A pretty girl with no makeup and straight blond hair that hung below her shoulders appeared in the door to the breakfast nook wearing a pale pink velour robe. She too was barefooted, her toenails painted pale pink. She might have been twenty.

"I gotta talk to a guy, Trish, maybe you could make us some coffee or something."

"Sure, Clint," she said. "Cone filter okay?"

He nodded and I nodded and smiled at her, too. It was working so well I thought I'd spread it around. The blond kid smiled back at me and went to the kitchen. I followed Clint into the living room. There was a fireplace on a diagonal across the corner. It was one of those prefabbed, double-walled metal jobs that can be framed in anywhere you can run a chimney. A sawdust and paraffin log was burning in it, looking sort of cheerful but putting out very little heat.

"Whaddya want," Stapleton said.

He was trying to sound tough, but there was no iron in his voice. He was scared.

"Somebody aced Tommy Miller last night, on the sixth floor of a parking garage at Quincy Market," I said.

"Who?"

"Tommy Miller, big blond State cop who framed Ellis Alves for you."

"I don't know what you're talking about."

"How much did it cost to frame Ellis?" I said.

He stood without speaking.

"You don't know, do you?" I said. "Because your old man paid."

He glanced toward the kitchen.

"Your old man pay someone to crank Tommy, too?" I said.

The girl with the pink toenails came into the room

carrying a silver carafe of coffee, a creamer, a sugar bowl, some spoons, and three cups on a big black lacquer tray. She gave the room a big smile.

"Here's coffee," she said and set the tray down on a low table in front of the couch.

Clint looked at her as if she were a stranger, then he looked back at me the same way, then he said, "I gotta go," and walked to the front hall, grabbed a blue and gold warmup jacket from the hall closet, and went out the front door. The girl stared after him. I poured two cups of coffee, handed one to her, and added cream and sugar to mine.

"Don't feel bad," I said. "Means more for us."

"Where is he going?"

"Probably to call his father," I said. "You known him long?"

"Clint? I met him when I was a freshman, but we didn't start dating until this year."

"What year are you now, Trish?"

"Junior."

"You live here, or just visiting?"

"Oh, no. I live on campus. I just come over on weekends mostly."

"You love Clint?"

"Well, sure, I mean what's not to love, he's gorgeous, he's a big tennis star, lots of dough. He's very nice."

"You think you'll get married?"

"Oh, no, I don't think so. I didn't mean I loved him that way."

"What way do you love him?"

"Until I graduate, sort of. You know? I didn't mean, love and marriage kind of love. Who are you anyway?"

"I'm a detective," I said. "I think Clint is in quite a lot of trouble."

"What kind of trouble?"

"I'm trying to find that out," I said. "He ever talk to you about Melissa Henderson?"

She shook her head.

"Tommy Miller?"

"I don't know anything about those people. I don't know anything about any trouble Clint is in. In fact, I don't believe you. I don't think he's in trouble at all. I think you're a nasty racist. And I think you should leave."

"You ever meet his father?" I said.

"I think you should leave right now," she said.

She was frowning, and it made a little vertical furrow between her eyes that would one day be a wrinkle, depending upon how much frowning she had to do.

"Okay," I said. "Most people don't pay any attention to my advice, and are probably wise not to, but I think you should stay away from Clint Stapleton."

"You've got no right to tell me what to do," she said.

I put down my cup of coffee, half drunk.

"Of course I don't," I said and stood.

"Take care of yourself," I said and went out into the front hall and out the front door through which Clint Stapleton had only recently fled.

chapter 35

IT WAS A late Friday afternoon with a light snow falling steadily. Susan had two more patients to see and I was passing the time until she saw them by running along the Charles River. I ran east along the Cambridge side, past the boat house, and up onto the Weeks Footbridge that crossed the river and linked the rest of Harvard with the Business School. The streetlights on both sides of the river were blurry in the snow, and pedestrians coming toward me looked slightly out of focus. It was barely freezing, just cold enough for snow. The river wasn't frozen yet and the black water moved opaquely, patched with light and shadow, curtained by the snowfall, toward the harbor five miles east. The footbridge has a barrel arch to it, and as I reached the peak of it I saw a tall man in a gray overcoat coming toward me through the snow from the Boston side. The brim of his gray soft hat was pulled down to shield his face from the snow. He had a gun.

The first bullet hit me just as I dodged to my left. It got me in the right shoulder, and the gun I'd almost gotten out of my jacket pocket plopped softly into the cushioning snow. The sound of the shot was gentle in the falling snow. The second bullet got me lower and turned me sideways against the chest-high railing of the bridge. I had no feeling in my right arm. The Gray Man was maybe twenty feet away, standing square, holding the handgun in both hands, perfectly still, his outline muted in the snowfall. Nothing moving except for the slight recoil of the long-barreled hand gun. I felt the thump of his third shot in my back, near my spine, as I grabbed at the railing with what strength there was left in me. My left leg felt numb. I heaved myself mostly with my left arm and the push of my right leg up over the bridge railing and fell twenty feet into the not quite frozen water. The impact was stunning. The shock of the cold was slowed by my running clothes, but only for a moment. The cold water began to bite through the clothes almost at once. I went down under the black surface, carried by the momentum of my drop. The cold water seemed to give me a little lift at the same time it almost paralyzed me. I held my breath and let the current move me away from the bridge, treading water with one leg and one arm. I got my head above the surface, feeling already the cold and the numbness of cold and shock and, probably, blood loss. I was in the dark. I wouldn't last long in the river, but I had no chance on the bridge. I looked back and saw the blurred form of the Gray Man standing at the rail, motionless, looking into the darkness. He didn't shoot. He couldn't see me in the snow-curtained shadows. Then

I couldn't see him. My vision shrank and all there was was my nearly senseless body in the icy water and the smell of the river at my face. I paddled feebly toward the left bank with my good arm and got hold of a pole. It was a pole in the center of the earth and I clung to it trying not to spin off into space, and the pole shrank rapidly and the world spun faster and faster, and then the pole got too small to hang onto and the centrifugal pull spun me out, and I sailed, fast at first and then slower, into black space where I drifted without weight or direction forever, until I bumped against something and, still spinning, wriggled onto it in the deadly cold, and disappeared into the blackened vortex of infinity.

Infinity turned out to be busy. It revolved more slowly than the world had when I'd spun off its top-most pole. There was a lot of random noise, a lot of sudden and unexplained light coming and going. There was movement, jostling, wailing, and blaring, and long stretches of dark silence. There was an occasional blurred human sound, and the smell of chemicals, and the feel of my breath, and some pain, and the thud of my pulse that sometimes enveloped all the other sounds. The slow revolutions got slower. The thunder of my pulse quieted. My throat was sore. The light was too bright. It was hot. I shifted in the bed. There was a tube in my throat. There was an IV in the back of my right hand. There was a woman in a white uniform looking down at me. I wasn't dead.

"Welcome back," the nurse said.

She was a black woman. Her voice had a Caribbean lilt to it.

I smiled pleasantly and said, "Glad to be here."

She smiled back at me.

"You're not coherent yet," she said. "It'll take a little while."

It took a couple of hours. During which time a resident appeared and took the feeding tube out of my throat, and the nurse cranked my bed up enough that I could see Hawk sitting in a chair across the room reading a book by Tony Brown.

"Where's Susan?" I said.

"Vinnie's with her," Hawk said.

"I want to see her."

"She'll be here," Hawk said.

"Where is *here*?" I said.

"Massachusetts General Hospital."

"How long?"

"'Bout three weeks," Hawk said.

"Three weeks?"

"You been out three weeks, you been here two weeks, four days. Couple of coeds trying to cross-country ski found you on the bank of the river, 'bout opposite the foot of De Wolfe Street. They put their jackets over you and one of them stayed with you while the other one run over to Dunster House and called the Harvard cops. They got you up to Mt. Auburn. Soon as Mt. Auburn got you stabilized, Quirk had you brought over here. Officially you here as James B. Hickock."

"James Butler Hickock?"

"Un huh. Quirk's idea."

There was too much information coming at me too fast. I closed my eyes for a moment. Infinity revolved a little and I opened them. It was dark. Susan was sitting beside the bed. I put my left arm out to her and she bent over without a word and kissed me and I held her against me as hard as I was able, which wasn't very. I smelled her perfume, and the scent of soap and shampoo, and the scent of her. I felt shaky inside, but the air going into my lungs seemed fresh and plentiful, and after a while I felt the shakiness quiet. We stayed that way a long time with her face against mine, my arm weakly around her. I could feel her breath on my face. Then she sat slowly up, carefully taking my arm and putting it back down on the top of the sheet and kept her hand on top of it.

I grinned at her and said, "Here's looking at you, kid."

She patted my hand quietly.

"How am I?" I said.

"You are going to live," Susan said.

"I don't seem to have much feeling in my left leg or my right arm."

"Doctor said to expect that," Susan said.

"For how long?"

"I don't think he knows," Susan said.

I nodded, which made me feel a little funny, and I closed my eyes again for a moment. When I opened them the sun was too bright against the far wall. Susan was gone and so was Hawk. Martin Quirk was sitting where Hawk sat, and a man in a white coat was standing staring down at me over half glasses. He was a lean guy, with graying hair and a thin, sharp face. The face was tanned. There was a stethoscope hanging out of his pocket. Under the white coat he wore a white shirt with wide blue vertical stripes, and a blue tie with small white polka dots. He had a wedding ring on his left hand. His hands were tanned. His nails were square and neat as if they'd been manicured.

"My name is Phil Marinaro," he said. "How do you feel?"

"Like I got shot and fell in the river," I said.

"Makes sense," he said. "You feel like talking?"

"I feel more like listening," I said.

"Okay," Marinaro said. "If the man who shot you had used bigger bullets, you'd be dead."

"Twenty-two longs," Quirk said. "Same as Miller."

"And you were lucky. The cold water probably slowed down the bleeding a little, and some of the internal swelling. The kids who found you probably saved you from dying of exposure. They covered you with their ski parkas, and one of them, in fact, pressed herself against you until the ambulance came."

"Who can blame her," I said.

"By the time the EMTs got there, you didn't have a pulse," Marinaro said. "They got you started on the way to the hospital. With all of that, the small caliber gun, the cold water, the resourceful Harvard kids, the professional EMTs, with all of that, if you weren't as big and strong as you are, you'd be dead."

"Right now I feel about as strong as a chicken," I said.

"Right now you are about as strong as a chicken," Marinaro said. "You are going to need a lot of rehab. Can you move your right arm?"

I couldn't.

"Left leg?"

No.

"How technical do you want this," Marinaro said.

"Eventually I want it all," I said. "But right now all I want is a prognosis."

"I don't really know," Marinaro said. "I'm a good surgeon. The repair job is first-rate. But you were damned near shot to pieces and almost drowned. A bullet fractionally missed your spine. I can make some informed guesses, which is mostly what prognosis is anyway. I think if you are willing to work hard enough you can come back from this. I don't know how far. It is probably a matter of how hard you work."

"I can work pretty hard," I said.

"That's what they tell me. Once you're able to get up, we'll start you on some simple exercises with a trainer. It will be a long, slow process."

"How soon," I said.

"Don't know. We'll watch you. We'll get you started as early as possible."

"Not a big rush," I said.

"No, you're pretty battered, and the amount of anesthesia you've had is debilitating. Captain, do you wish to say anything?"

"Yeah," Quirk said.

He stood and stepped to my bedside and looked down at me.

"You know who shot you?"

"Gray Man," I said.

"We figured. Hawk brought me up to date on that."

"I saw him," I said.

"Dr. Marinaro knows who you are and why you're here. Everybody else thinks your name is Hickock and you are the victim of a jealous husband. We've told the papers that your lifeless body was recovered from the Charles River. Both papers ran an obit on you. You'll probably enjoy them."

"Call in some favors, did we?"

"Several," Quirk said.

"Aren't you a little out of line?" I said.

"Yeah."

"When you assigned Belson and Farrell to Susan, I said you weren't really in a position to do that, and Hawk said that was true, but you didn't give a shit."

Quirk shrugged.

"Why you think it took me so long to make captain?" he said.

"I always wondered."

Quirk grinned.

"Besides, from Hawk that's a compliment."

"True."

"We'll keep somebody with you while you're here," Quirk said. "Hawk will be around a lot, and Vinnie Morris, and some of our people. I'm transferring Belson and Farrell to this detail."

"The cops and the robbers," I said.

"Changes places and handy dandy," Quirk said.

"Well," I said. "You literate son of a bitch."

"I heard you say it once. I got no idea what it means."

"As long as the Gray Man thinks I'm dead, and he has no reason not to, Susan's safe. This is a guy doesn't waste time killing people for nothing."

"That's what Hawk and I thought, but we also figured he might watch her for a while just to be sure. So when you woke up, we had the Cambridge cops pick her up and take her in as if for questioning. Then we smuggled her over here."

"And no one followed her?" I said.

"Hawk brought her," Quirk said.

"I withdraw the question," I said.

I might have said something else, but I'm not sure, and then I was back in dreamland listening to the music of the spheres.

chapter 36

I LEFT IN a wheelchair. Hospital rules required it anyway, but even if they hadn't, I still had very little use of my left leg. Susan and Hawk and Dr. Marinaro and I went down in a freight elevator and into a basement garage with Dr. Marinaro pushing the wheelchair.

"Morgue's over there," Marinaro said, nodding toward a pair of double doors. He grinned. "Our mistakes go out this way," he said.

"How cheery," I said.

Quirk and Belson were leaning on the front fender of a black Ford Explorer near the overhead doors. Pearl the Wonder Dog was in the backseat, looking out the window. The rest of the garage was empty. We wheeled over to them. Belson opened the front door of the Explorer.

"I can stand," I said, "and walk a little. I'll need a little help getting in."

Hawk came around and picked me up and put me in the front seat. Pearl began to lap the back of my neck. There was luggage in the storage space in back.

"I didn't need that much help," I said.

"He ain't heavy," Hawk said. "He's my brother."

"And he's lost thirty pounds," Susan said.

"Can you shoot left handed?" he said.

"Some."

He handed me a short-barreled Colt Detective Special and I stuck it into my left-hand jacket pocket.

"Guy will have to be pretty close for me to hit him left handed with this," I said.

"He'll be close," Hawk said, "'cause he'll have gotten by me."

"Unlikely," I said.

"Very," Hawk said.

"Where'd you get the car," I said to Susan.

"Hawk arranged it," she said.

I looked at Hawk. He smiled.

"Oh, never mind," I said.

Marinaro said, "You've got my number. Call me if you need to."

I said, "Thank you."

He gave a small thumbs-up gesture, like the RAF pilots used to do when they were climbing into their Spitfires. Susan went around and got in the driver's side. Hawk got in back with Pearl. Belson closed the front door and stepped away. Susan started the car. Marinaro pressed a button and the garage door went up. It was dark outside. Quirk and Belson went outside and stood at each side of the doorway looking into the darkness. Quirk waved us forward and Susan drove the Explorer out of the garage. Quirk and Belson went back inside. The garage door closed. Susan drove down an alley and turned out onto a side street and then onto Cambridge Street heading toward Storrow Drive with the river on our right, looking as hostile as I remembered. I patted Pearl over my shoulder with my left hand. There was ice on the river now, and the Esplanade was snowy. Across the river the lights around Kendall Square looked cheerful.

"Where we going," I said.

"Santa Barbara," Susan said.

"California?"

"Yes."

"We're driving."

"Yes. It's safer."

"You mind if I sing 'California Here I Come' as we roll along?" I said.

"You're in a weakened condition," Susan said. "It's better if you rest."

"I'm just thinking of you," I said. "It's a long ride."

"Remember I got a gun," Hawk said.

"You'd shoot me if I sing? Your brother?"

"Shoot myself," Hawk said, "you sing a lot."

Pearl stopped lapping my neck finally and settled against the backseat and looked out the window.

"We're not flying because someone might see us?" I said.

"And also because we can't leave the baby behind," Susan said. "It will take you a long time to rehab . . . and she obviously isn't going in a crate in the belly of an airplane."

"Of course not," I said. "Why Santa Barbara?"

"It's far away, it's not a place anyone would look for you. It's warm. I have a friend who knows a person who knows a real estate broker out there. I was able to rent a house."

"In your name?"

"Mr. and Mrs. James Butler Hickock," Susan said.

I jerked my head toward Hawk. "Who's he," I said, "Deadwood Dick?"

"That ain't what the ladies call me," Hawk said.

"Are you guys going to talk dirty all the way across the country?" Susan said.

"I was planning to," Hawk said.

"Me too," I said.

"Oh, good," Susan said.

"What about your patients," I said.

"I have two colleagues covering for me," she said. "I've had a bit of time to arrange things."

"Good we didn't adopt that kid yet," I said.

"Yes."

We were on the Mass Pike now, heading west slowly in heavy traffic. The dashboard clock said 5:27. It had been dark for nearly an hour.

"What route we taking?"

Susan said, "Hawk?"

"Out 84 to Scranton. Down 81 to Knoxville. Turn right, take Route 40 across. Figure to reach Scranton tonight."

"Route 40 replaces stretches of the old Route 66 west of Oklahoma City," I said. "I know all the lyrics to 'Route 66.'"

"Bobby Troup be glad to know that," Hawk said.

We crept into the toll booths in Weston and Susan picked up a toll ticket. Then we were through them and the traffic thinned as the commuters peeled off into the western suburbs.

"'You go to St. Louie, Joplin, Missouri, and Oklahoma City is mighty pretty . . .'"

We slept in Holiday Inns. Me and Hawk in one room, Susan and Pearl next door. I felt that Pearl was getting the better of the deal. With Hawk holding my arm, I could shuffle in and out of the hotels and rest stops and Petro Stations.

"'See Amarillo; Gallup, New Mexico; Flagstaff, Arizona; now don't forget Winona; Kingman; Barstow; San Bernardino . . .'"

Susan and Hawk took turns driving. Susan drove faster than Hawk, and maybe faster than Mario Andretti. Pearl and I sat and gazed in semicatatonia out the window at the American continent as it scrolled past. Pearl had, quite early in the trip, edged over closer to Hawk whenever he was in the back, and leaned heavily into him and with her head on his shoulder.

"She ain't heavy, she's my sister?" I said.

Hawk sighed.

"Be a long trip," he said.

"'Get hip to this friendly tip, when you take that California trip . . .'"

chapter 37

THE HOUSE WAS in Montecito, white stucco and red tile, up in the subtropical hills, off East Valley Road, surrounded by greenery, with the hills continuing up past it and eventually easing into the Sierra Madre Mountains. From the upstairs balcony you could see the Santa Barbara Channel, with the Channel Islands in the background, and the Jurassic-looking oil platforms marching along off the coast. Around us were expensive homes and gated estates, redolent with orange trees and palm trees and vines with red flowers and vines with purple flowers. The houses weren't that far from each other, but the vegetation was so dense you couldn't see your neighbors. The streets had no streetlights, you rarely saw anyone walking along, and at night you could hear coyotes calling, and sometimes during the day you would see them, small and mongrelish, trotting through the open field behind the house. We felt like Swiss Family Robinson. Pearl ignored them.

"Would they hurt her?" Susan asked.

"She's too big for them," I said.

"What if there's a bunch of them?" Susan said.

"We shoot them," Hawk said.

"The people around here have little slogans about them," Susan said. "Like, 'You can't shoot them, they were here first.'"

"So were the Indians," I said.

About a quarter mile from the house was a hill that went up sharply at right angles to the much gentler hill we lived on. Each morning, Hawk and Pearl and I walked up to the foot of the hill and looked at it. Actually Pearl dashed. Hawk walked. I shuffled. But after the first week I shuffled without holding on. Pearl would race up the hill, barrel chested and wasp waisted. Bred to run for hours, she rubbed it in every day, looking puzzled that I couldn't do at all what she did so effortlessly. Then we'd walk back to the house and rest. Then we'd walk to the hill and back and rest and walk to the hill and back and rest. We'd do that until noon. Then we'd have lunch. I would take a nap. And in the afternoon we would work on weights. I started with three-pound dumbbells. I would do curls with them, and flies and tricep extensions, and reverse curls. That is, I would do these things with my left hand. With my right I was barely able at first to twitch the three pounds. The consolation was that Pearl couldn't do this either.

In the best of times repetitious workouts are boring. When I could barely do it, the boredom became life threatening. I would reach the foot of the steep hill each time gasping for breath, the sweat soaking through my tee-shirt. I weighed less than 170 pounds and I walked like an old man. I wasn't much of a challenge for Hawk any more than I was for Pearl, but if he was bored he didn't show it.

Susan went with us once every morning and ran up the hill with Pearl. The thought of going up that hill at any speed made me nauseous. Susan took on the responsibility for feeding us. Fortunately she found a place in the upper village that had food to take out. So we dined on an endless assortment of healthful salads and cold roast meats and pasta and fresh bread, and drank wine from the local vineyards.

One of the oddities of life in Southern California was the sense of timelessness that set in. There were no real seasons in California and each day was about like the last one. People were probably startled out here to find that they'd aged. For me the days were barely distinguishable, a repetitive sequence of effort and sweat and exhaustion and failure, briefly interrupted by sleep and food. Drinking some of the local wine each evening became more exciting than anything I'd imagined.

Susan and Pearl and I slept in a very big bed in the master bedroom. I kept the Detective Special on the bedside table. A sawed-off double-barreled .12-gauge shotgun leaned on the wall near Susan's bed. There was a nearly full moon and at this time of night it shined directly into the bedroom, through the French doors on the upstairs balcony. It was almost daylight except for the opalescence of the light.

"Could you do it?" I said.

"Hawk showed me," Susan said, "while we were waiting for you to get out of the hospital. Cock both hammers, aim for the middle of the mass, squeeze one trigger at a time. He says it is pretty hard to miss with one of those things at close range."

"It is," I said. "But could you do it?"

She turned her head on the pillow and her big eyes rested on me silently for a moment. "Yes," she said.

We were quiet together in the bright flower-scented darkness.

"Are you ever going to shave?" she said.

"Not yet," I said.

"Is this some kind of guy thing?" Susan said. "I won't shave until I've rehabbed?"

"Not exactly."

We were silent while Susan thought about this. Then in the bright darkness she smiled.

"You have a plan, don't you," she said.

"Yes."

"You are changing your appearance."

"Yes."

"So that when you're well you can find the Gray Man and he won't recognize you."

"Seemed like a good idea. Give me something to aim at."

"May I suggest that you let your hair grow and comb it differently?"

"You may."

"I do."

We lay on our backs, with our shoulders and hips touching.

"You're smart for a Harvard Ph.D.," I said.

"Yes," she said. "I know."

In the quiet night a coyote howled somewhere in earshot. For a couple of city kids it was a startling sound. Susan made a face. Pearl the Wonder Dog remained asleep. If she heard the yowl she didn't care.

"Pearl doesn't seem responsive to the call of the wild," I said.

"No," Susan said. "But I am."

"That's what all the guys at the Harvard Faculty Club say."

"The guys at the Harvard Faculty Club say nothing that visceral," Susan said. "Would you like to make love?"

I was silent for a while thinking about that. Slanted diagonally across the lower half of the bed so that she took up twice as much room as she needed to, Pearl snored softly and made occasional lip-smacking sounds as if she might be dreaming of Devil Dogs.

"What about the baby?" I said.

"We could ask her to visit Uncle Hawk for a while."

I thought about that.

"I don't think so," I said. "I think it would be better to wait."

"For what?" Susan said.

"Until I can do something better than fumble at you with my left hand," I said.

"There's nothing wrong with your left hand," Susan said.

I shrugged in the darkness.

"I think we should wait until I'm together again," I said.

"He didn't kill you," Susan said. "You shouldn't act like he did."

"Hell, Suze, I can barely turn over by myself, for crissake. I can't even walk up the goddamned hill that you run up every morning. I can barely walk to it."

"Yet," Susan said. "You'll walk up it, and eventually you'll run up it and you'll run up it faster than I can."

"Maybe," I said.

"Hawk and I didn't drag you out here for maybes," Susan said. "You're not all you were yet. But you will be. But there's no reason to be less than you are now. If you can't move around as you might wish to, I can. And would be happy to."

I thought about that while Susan got out of bed and took off her green flowered pajamas and draped them over a chair. I looked at her naked with the same feelings I always got. I'd seen her naked thousands of times by now, and it didn't matter. It was the same experience it had been the first time. She was always like the first time, always the one that wasn't like anyone else I'd ever been with.

"Maybe the machinery won't work right," I said.

"Maybe it will," Susan said and came to the bed and lay down beside me.

In a moment she said, "It appears to be working."

"That's heartening," I said.

"Just lie still," Susan said. "I'll do everything."

"Lying still is more difficult than I thought it would be," I said.

"You may yell yahoo now and then if you'd like."

Pearl shifted at the foot of the bed and made a grumpy sound as if she resented being disturbed.

"What about the baby," I said.

"It's time she knew," Susan said.

Later in the night the moon moved its location so it was probably shining into Uncle Hawk's room. In the much deeper darkness I was pressed against Susan, listening to her regular breathing. Pearl had worked her way under the covers at the foot of the bed and slept silently except for an occasional snore.

"You awake?" I said.

"Yes."

"There's no guarantee I'll come all the way back," I said.

"I think you will," she said.

"And if I don't?"

"For richer, for poorer," she murmured, "in sickness and in health."

"You'll be here," I said.

"I will always be here," she said.

And she pressed closer to me and we were silent and I smelled her, and felt her and listened to her, and knew that if I had nothing else but this, this would be enough.

chapter 38

IN THE MORNING it was raining, the low rain clouds covering the tops of some of the further hills.

When it rains in Southern California the television stations do the same thing they do in Boston when it snows. They pretend the sky is falling. They show the storm's path on radar. They give tips on how to survive the rain. They send out reporters in Eddie Bauer rain gear to ask people stuff like, "How are you coping with this rain?" Despite the emergency, Hawk and I did what we had done every morning since we'd gotten here. We walked up the road toward the hill. Hawk was wearing white Nike running shoes and black nylon sweats and a white canvas barn jacket with a corduroy collar. He had his .44 Magnum in a shoulder holster under the coat, and he was hatless, the rain beading on his shaved head.

The water drainage system all over Southern California was surface runoff, and surrounded by the subtropical growth of Montecito, babbling brooks formed along each side of the road. The water cascaded downhill through small ravines filled with trees and vines and thick-leaved green plants, went under the road in a culvert, and formed impressive waterfalls as it dropped into the cut below the roadway where flowers grew.

When we reached the bottom of the hill we stopped and looked at it, as we did every morning. It went up very steeply, turning two thirds of the way up and continuing even more steeply to the top. There were houses on the hill, and small gutters along each side of the roadway where the rain water churned downhill and spread out over the street where we were standing.

"I'm going up," I said.

"Today the day?"

"Yep."

"How 'bout we make it to that mailbox?" Hawk said.

The mailbox was maybe fifty yards up the hill.

"All the way," I said.

"Might take a while," Hawk said. "Hill's a bitch."

"Here we go," I said.

We started up. I was half dragging my left leg. Hawk walked slowly beside me. On the right there was a lemon grove, the wet fruit glistening among the green leaves. Nobody seemed to be harvesting it. The fruit was yellow and heavy on the trees and littered the ground, some of it rotting beneath the trees. I was gasping for breath. I looked up and the mailbox was still thirty yards away.

"No reason not to stop and rest," Hawk said.

I nodded. I looked back. The wet black road surface gleamed. I was twenty yards up the hill and I couldn't talk. We stood silently together in the steady rain. I was wearing an Oakland A's baseball cap, and white New Balance sneakers, jeans, and a bright green rain jacket that Susan said was the ugliest garment she'd ever seen legalized. In the left-hand pocket the Detective Special weighed about two hundred pounds.

"How . . . high . . . is . . . this . . . hill?"

"Never measured it," Hawk said. "Takes me 'bout ten minutes to walk up, five minutes to run."

"Run?" I said.

Hawk grinned.

"See that tree sticking out over the road? Let's aim for that, when you ready."

I nodded. My heart rate was slowing. I took in as much air as I could and let it out and shuffled up the hill a little further, dragging my left leg. Under the rain jacket I was slippery with sweat. I could hear my pulse so loud in my head that it seemed as if I could hear nothing else. I stared straight down at the wet roadway, concentrating on pushing my right leg forward, dragging my left leg after. I couldn't get enough air in, and by the time I reached the overhanging tree I was gasping for breath again. All that kept me from throwing up was that I lacked the strength. Hawk stood beside me. I turned and looked back at the glistening roadway and beyond at the subtropical greenery, the occasional red tile roof, and far down the hillside the Santa Barbara Channel again, gray now, and choppy, with the clouds so low over it that the Channel Islands were out of sight.

"You collapse," Hawk said, "and I gonna have to give you mouth to mouth. Neither one of us be liking that too much."

"Let . . . me . . . go," I said. "It . . . comes . . . to . . . that."

"And tell Susan what?" Hawk said.

I shook my head. I didn't have enough breath to answer.

"You want to hang onto my arm?" Hawk said.

I shook my head again. The rain was unvarying. In Boston when it rained it was often windy, and it made the rain less pleasant. Here the rain fell straight down through the warm air, undisturbed by wind. It dripped off the yellow bill of my A's cap, and dimpled the puddles that formed where the road surface was uneven.

"Mailbox," I said and we started again.

Hawk moved silently beside me, watching me, seeing everything else at the same time. I noticed grimly that he wasn't breathing hard. Again the thunder of my pulse, the struggle for oxygen, the feel of my right quadricep turning to jelly, the encumbrance of my right arm, the aimlessness of my left leg, the defiant pitch of the hill, the relentless pull of gravity as I inched along . . . I should have been a pair of ragged claws scuttling across the floors of silent seas.

I rested a long time at the mailbox, before I started again. Things began to blur: rain, gasping, pain, weakness, pounding, nausea, pressure in my head, in my chest, my left leg random, nearly lifeless, the sweat soaking through my tee-shirt, the hill rising before me as I went step by painful dragging step up it, staring at it right in front of my next step, seeing nothing else, only dimly aware that Hawk was beside me, my entire self invested in the implacable everlasting hill.

On the left was a house, set back a little from the road, with a driveway that ran level from the roadway to the garage. I stopped on the level, my head down, my breath trembling in and out in desperate involuntary gasps, as my diaphragm struggled to get enough oxygen into my bloodstream. Hawk spoke to me from somewhere outside the red vortex of my exhaustion.

"'Bout ten more yards," he said.

I looked up and the crest of the hill was before me, thirty feet away. I let my head drop again and stood entirely focused on the effort to breathe, soaking with sweat, feeling deeply shaky, as if somehow the very core of my self was beginning to fall apart. I felt like I might fall down. Hawk stood silently beside me. I waited. Hawk waited. The rain came straight down. Finally the occlusive pounding began to slow, and awareness expanded enough for me to look up at the top of the hill.

"One first down," Hawk said.

I didn't want to waste any breath talking. I took in as much air as I could, and went up the rest of the hill almost blindly, my jaw clamped, my eyes almost closed, my breath rasping, almost without feeling, barely aware of anything but my exhaustion, in a near anaerobic state, my bad leg useless, my good leg trembling. And made it. And stood at the top looking out across the valley at the vineyards on the far slope and the rain clouds just above them. Hawk stood beside me without comment. Turning a bit I was able to see Santa Barbara Harbor, and the boats in the marina, looking ornamental in the distance. I took my hat off and let the rain soak my hair and run down my face. The rasp of my breath began to slow. My leg-and-a-half felt weak but the trembling eventually stopped.

"Be easier going back," Hawk said.

I nodded. Above us, a little ways east along the ridge line, was a steep meadow, and in the meadow a couple of coyotes sat, sheltered by a rock, and stared down at us.

"Waiting to see if you make it," Hawk said.

"Next thing," I said, and took in some air, "there'll be buzzards circling."

Another coyote trotted from some trees toward the two near the rock and joined them, settling back on his haunches and staring down at us. He moved so lightly, it was as if his feet reached down to the ground. I stared back at the coyotes for a while until my heartbeat had quieted enough so they could no longer hear it on the hillside. I put my hat back on.

"Let's go down," I said.

Hawk nodded.

"Be slippery going down," Hawk said, "and all your brakes ain't working yet."

I nodded. And we started down. Going up, it had been desperately hard to go forward, now it was desperately hard not to. I fell the first time in front of the driveway, and again twenty yards beyond it, and after that I hung onto Hawk until we passed the lemon grove and reached the street, where the grade was mild, even for me, and the effort of walking was returned to human scale. I stopped and looked back up the hill.

Hawk said, "Too soon to try again."

"Tomorrow," I said.

Hawk shook his head.

"No," he said. "Skip a day."

I nodded.

"Plenty of time," I said.

"All the time you need," Hawk said.

I turned away from the hill and limped slowly down the road past the dripping bougainvillea and jacaranda and orange trees bright with fruit, toward the house.

chapter 39

I SQUEEZED A rubber ball in each hand most of the time I was in California. The first time I tried it with my right hand the ball dropped to the floor. I hadn't enough strength to hold it. Hawk hung a heavy bag from a tree in the meadow behind the house and I banged at it every day, weakly with my left hand, barely at all with my right. The next time I essayed the hill, I took Pearl on a leash and she pulled me maybe five yards further each time between stops. Progress. By the end of January, I could go halfway up, and my right leg wasn't dragging. My beard was thick and bothersome. My hair was too long. Hawk and I went up into one of the canyons back in the hills and began to shoot. I held the gun in both hands, though my left was doing all the work, and I was able to level it mainly by pulling my right arm up with my left. My only success was that I didn't shoot myself. I was up to five-pound dumbbells. With my right arm I was actually moving the weight, curling it maybe halfway so that my forearm was at right angles to my bicep. Hawk and I moved from the hill to the dumbbells to the heavy bag to the improvised pistol range to the dinner table for cold chicken and the local wine. One of the many drawbacks to Southern California was that most of the basketball games started at 4:30 local time. Another drawback was that the Clippers played in some of the games. I kept squeezing the rubber ball. Susan had gone to a drug store and bought a bunch of vitamins and I took them every morning with the local orange juice. Susan was pushing big doses of Vitamin C. She said it helped in the healing process. We spoke to no one. We called no one on the phone. We wrote no letters. As far as Boston was concerned, we were gone. As far as the Gray Man was concerned, I was dead. There was no reason to think he didn't believe that. Still, I kept the Detective Special with me even though it was like carrying a bowling ball up the hill. And Hawk was never away from me, and never without a gun. And the shotgun leaned in the corner when Susan and I went to bed. In mid-January, I made it halfway up the hill before I had to stop, and Pearl wasn't pulling me. It was a sunny day and when we came back down the road to our house, Susan was standing in the front yard watching me. She had on white sneakers and white short-shorts and a dark blue sleeveless blouse and her black hair must have been still damp from the shower because the sun glistened on it. Or maybe I just thought it did.

"You've got legs like a rainy day," I said. "I'd like to see them clear up."

"You say that to me every time I wear shorts," she said.

"Nice to be able to count on something," I said.

"Besides, my legs are hideously pale, pale, pale."

"Never my problem," Hawk murmured.

"Your legs look great," I said.

"Are you aware," Susan said, "that as you walked down the road toward me you weren't limping?"

Progress.

It was raining lightly on a Tuesday morning, but Hawk and I were out hitting the bag anyway. The way we did it was to work on one punch at a time, banging the same punch over and over again into the bag, first with my left, then with my right. And even though the right did little more than twitch, I went through the whole process in the nervous system just as if the right hand moved. By the third week in January, I was starting to thump the bag pretty good with my left, and this morning, a Tuesday, in the light rain, I got a right hook into it. It wasn't much of a right hook. It wouldn't have knocked the lime slice off a margarita, but it was a hook. I did it again, and eight more times. Neither Hawk nor I said anything. But when I finished on the heavy bag that day, I put out my left fist and Hawk tapped it gently with his. Progress.

A week and a half later, Susan brought home a bunch of Pacific lobster tails and we had them with lemon butter and rice pilaf, which Susan cooked. We ate it on a glass table out on the patio with white wine and a salad. The sun slanted in, low in the southern sky, edging down over the Pacific, highlighting the ridge line on the hills across from us. There was no wind, and the smell of flowers and trees and green grass hung in the quiet air.

"Want me to cut up that lobster?" Susan said.

I smiled at her and picked up the knife with my right hand and carefully sliced a bite off the lobster. It took me longer than it should have, and I nearly dropped the knife once.

"You've been practicing in secret," Susan said.

"Un huh."

She leaned over and kissed me on the mouth.

"Coming right along," she said.

But the sunshine was fleeting that year in Montecito. Most of the time it rained, while bits and pieces of the town washed into the ocean. There was mud clogging much of downtown Santa Barbara and the people on the tube were paroxysmal about it.

"You build on a flood plain," Hawk said, "you got to consider the possibility of a flood."

We were in the Montecito YMCA lifting weights. Or I was. Hawk was standing around with his gun hidden under a loose warmup jacket, trying to look like a trainer. I wasn't lifting a lot of weight. But I was actually moving the weights that I was lifting. Most of the equipment was Nautilus machines. There wasn't much in the way of free weights, but I couldn't do much with free weights yet. I was doing chest presses. They were very light chest presses, but I was using both hands.

"Aren't you supposed to say things like, 'You can do it!' and 'Atta boy'?" I said.

"Don't want people looking over, see what you lifting," Hawk said. "Be embarrassing."

There was a ravine between the Y and the parking lot with a wide, planked wooden bridge across it. When we left the gym, the rain was steady as it had been when we came. The ravine, bone dry when it wasn't raining, was snarling with flood waters only a couple of feet below the bridge.

"Keeps raining," I said, "Susan's going to start running in circles."

We got into the Explorer and Hawk started it up.

"She ain't had much to do here," Hawk said. "'Cept food shop and make supper, and cheer you up."

"All of which she hates."

We pulled out of the lot and out to San Ysidro Road and right up toward East Valley. The wipers were on steadily. There was something soothing, I thought, about windshield wipers.

"Maybe she don't mind cheerin' you up," Hawk said.

"Maybe not," I said. "But you know how rambunctious she is. She can't even take Pearl out running because Pearl won't go out in the rain."

"Hell of a hunting dog," Hawk said.

"And she's got no patients to work with," I said.

"'Cept you."

"And most of what I need you do better than she does."

"Like getting your sorry ass up and down that hill," Hawk said.

"Like that."

"You think you be able to handle all this weakness and pain without her?"

"I hope so."

"You handle it as well, you think?"

"No."

"I don't think so either," Hawk said.

When we got home, the door to our bedroom was closed. I could hear the television blatting inside. I opened the door quietly. One of the indistinguishable ghastly talk shows was on. The room was empty. The door to the master bath was open, and Pearl came out of it and wagged her tail and jumped up and gave me a lap. I went in. Susan was taking a bath. She had moved the shotgun in, and it leaned within reach against the laundry hamper. Pearl lay back down on the rug near the tub. I went to the tub and bent over and kissed Susan.

"Does this mean something good for me?"

"Not right away," Susan said. "I got us reservations at Acacia."

"Should I take a shower?"

"Unless you'd like to make a separate reservation for yourself," Susan said.

So I did. And Hawk did. And we dressed up with ties and jackets, and Susan put on a dress and some sort of high-laced, high-heeled black boots to subvert the rain, and Pearl got in the car with us, and we drove down to the lower village and parked and left Pearl in the locked car and went in to Acacia.

Acacia is the kind of place that people have in mind when they say they'd like to open a little restaurant somewhere. It's a small building with a patio in front and the look of bleached wood. Inside there are tables up front, a bar along the left wall in the back, and booths opposite the bar. There was a mirror over the bar, and I got a look at myself unexpectedly as we went to our booth. I was walking upright. I didn't limp. I had a hint of a tan from running up the hill in the occasional sunshine. My collar didn't look too big for my neck.

I had fried chicken with cream gravy and mashed potatoes and a gentle Chardonnay from a winery about half a mile down the road. I cut my own food. It was the first time I'd eaten in a restaurant since I'd gone off the bridge.

"For dessert," Susan said, "I think I will have something packed with empty calories and covered with chocolate."

"Good choice," I said and put my right hand out and covered hers for a moment. She smiled at me.

"Maybe I'll have two," she said.

She didn't. But she had one huge ice-cream-and-chocolate-cake-and-fudge-sauce thing, which for Susan was an Isadora Duncan-esque act of joyful abandon.

The rains abated in late February. By that time I was beginning to put some right hooks into the heavy bag with enough starch to discourage an opponent. By mid-March I was able to lift the entire stack on the chest press machine at the Y. By the end of March, I was able to shoot right handed and hit something. Hawk had a speed bag up now, bolted to the inside wall of the garage, and I was starting to hit it with some rhythm. Hawk had the big target mitts on and I was starting to put combinations together on them, as Hawk moved around me, holding the target mitts in different positions. All of us, Pearl included, after I'd slogged up the hill each morning, went down to Santa Barbara Harbor and ran along the beach, down near the water where the sand was harder. Pearl peeled off regularly to harry a sea bird, and then caught up to us easily. There were signs that said No Pets, but no one seemed to pay them any mind, except a few beach drifters who were grouchy about Pearl, but nobody paid them any mind either. Glowing with sweat, and breathing deeply, we went to the upper village and, except for Pearl who waited in the car, ate late breakfast on the terrace of a little dining room attached to the local pharmacy where movie stars ate. I had fresh orange juice and whole wheat toast and something they called a California Omelet. I drank three cups of coffee. People probably thought I was a movie star.

One morning I ran up the hill. All the way.

chapter 40

WE GOT BACK to Boston in the late summer. I weighed 195 pounds, fifteen less than I had when I went into the water, and about what I weighed when I was fighting. But I could walk, and run, and shoot. My right hook was nearly ninety percent, and gaining. I had an impressive beard and my hair was long and slicked back. Hawk was driving. We got off the Mass. Turnpike in Newton and cruised in along the last stretch of the Charles River that was navigable before you reached the falls near Watertown Square. The shells moved back and forth as they had for all the summers I'd looked at it. We cruised past the MDC Rink, and Martignetti's Liquors. In back with Susan, Pearl began to snuffle at the car window on the side near the river. Susan cracked the window slightly and Pearl snuffled harder.

"I think she knows she's home," Susan said.

"Smart," I said. "Who knows I'm alive."

"Me and Susan," Hawk said. "Quirk, Belson, Farrell, Vinnie, Paul Giacomon, Henry, Dr. Marinaro."

"And Rita Fiore," Susan said.

"Why Rita?"

"She sold the Concord house for me," Susan said. "You were presumed dead."

"Sold?"

"Where do you think we got the money to spend ten months in California with none of us working?" Susan said. "Rita arranged, or had someone from her firm arrange, to sell the Concord house in my absence. I was sure we could trust her, and she was quite upset when she thought you were gone."

"Did we make a profit?"

"Yes. We cashed in all that sweat equity," Susan said.

"I never thought about money," I said.

"You had other things to think about," Susan said. "Rita sold it and wire transferred the money to a bank in Santa Barbara where I had opened an account."

"I was a kept man for all this time?"

"Un huh."

"Me too," Hawk said.

"Yeah," I said. "But you're used to it."

"I deserve it," Hawk said.

"I feel like a jerk. I never thought about the money."

"Well, you probably are a jerk," Susan said. "But you're the jerk of my dreams, and whether you deserved it or not, you needed it."

"True," I said. "Thank you."

"The house was half yours anyway," Susan said.

We were on Greenough Boulevard on the Cambridge side of the river. Pearl was now clawing at the window and snuffling vigorously. Susan let it down a quarter and Pearl stuck her head out as far as she could, her tail wagging very fast.

"We going to your place?" I said.

"Yes," Susan said.

"Instead of my place," I said.

"We sublet your place," Susan said.

I nodded slowly. We stopped at the light near the Cambridge Boat Club. The light changed and Hawk drove on past the Buckingham, Brown and Nichols school. There were kids playing baseball on the field.

"Because otherwise the whole deal would have looked phony," I said.

Susan nodded.

"And you sublet my office?"

She nodded again.

"Gray Man had any doubts, first thing he'd do," I said, "would be check to see if the rents were being paid."

"And it would alleviate his doubts," Hawk said, "to find that they were not."

Hawk was very precise about all the syllables in "alleviate."

"Glad some of you were thinking for me."

"You were thinking about what you needed to think about," Susan said. "Not very many people would have been able to come back from where you were."

"Susan's place clean?" I said to Hawk.

He nodded.

"Vinnie's been sweeping it 'bout once a week since we been gone. Nobody paying any attention."

"And when do I see Marinaro?" I said.

"Day after tomorrow," Susan said. "Ten A.M. at his office."

"He'll probably break into applause," I said.

"Almost certainly," Susan said.

"Assuming he say you okay," Hawk said, "then what you going to do?"

"I'm going to finish up the Ellis Alves case."

Hawk nodded. Susan was quiet. We turned down Linnaean Street with Pearl straining out the window, her ears blown back, her nostrils quivering.

Hawk said, "Sometimes you looking for somebody, you set yourself up so the somebody make a run at you. You let him find you 'stead of you find him. You figure you going to be good enough to take him when he does."

"Yeah?"

"And usually you are," Hawk said. "But don't do that with the Gray Man. You might be good enough, one on one. But you ain't good enough, he got the edge."

"Sure looks that way so far," I said.

"You find him," Hawk said.

"He's a hunter," I said. "He doesn't expect to be hunted."

"And he thinks you dead."

We pulled into the driveway beside Susan's house.

"Once he's out of the way, I can finish the Alves thing," I said.

"You'll be with him," Susan said to Hawk. "When he goes after the Gray Man."

Hawk shook his head.

"He won't want me with him," Hawk said.

Susan opened her mouth to speak, and didn't speak. She looked at me with her mouth still open and back at Hawk and back at me, and clamped her mouth shut without having made a sound.

Hawk shut off the car. We got out. Susan held Pearl straining on her leash.

"You guys bring in the luggage," she said. "I'll take the baby."

Then she turned and headed for her front door, fumbling in her purse for the key. Hawk let out a deep breath that he appeared to have been holding. I did too.

chapter 41

HIS NAME WAS Ives. And he worked, as he liked to say, for a three-letter federal agency. Ten or twelve years ago, when Susan was in trouble, I had done some pretty ugly stuff for him, to get her out of trouble. I hadn't liked it then, and I didn't like remembering it now. But Ives didn't seem to care, and, as far as I could tell, neither did the universe.

Ives had an office in the McCormick Federal Building, in Post Office Square. There was no name on the door when I went in. And no one at the reception desk. The blank door to the inner office was ajar. I went in. Ives was sitting behind a desk wearing a cord suit and a blue and white polka dot bow tie.

"Spenser, isn't it?" Ives said.

"Yes, it is," I said.

"The beard threw me," he said. "Your Lieutenant Quirk said you might be coming by."

"He's not mine," I said. "And he's a captain now."

Ives had one of those red rubber erasers in his hands and he kept turning it slowly in his thin fingers as he talked.

"Well, good on him," Ives said. "You look well."

"I'm looking for a guy," I said.

Ives smiled. He slowly turned the eraser on its axis.

"Gray-haired man," I said. "Gray eyes, sallow complexion, forty to sixty, six feet two or three, rangy build, athletic, when I saw him he was dressed all in gray."

"And what does this gray man do?" Ives said.

"He's a shooter," I said.

"And where does he do his shooting?"

"Boston and New York, to my knowledge, but I assume he goes where his vocation takes him."

"Is he an American national?" Ives said.

"I don't know. He speaks English without an accent."

"You know of course that this agency has no domestic mandate."

"Of course not," I said.

The eraser revolved slowly. Ives gazed off into the middle distance.

"You wouldn't, naturally, know the varlet's name, would you?"

"No."

"You have solid municipal police connections," Ives said. "Why come to me?"

"Cops can't find him. They have no record of him or anyone like him. Not here. Not New York. Not on the national wire."

"How distressing," Ives said.

"Yes."

"And why do you think I'll help you?"

"I helped you twelve years ago," I said.

Ives smiled gently and shook his head. The eraser did a complete revolution.

"We helped each other, as I recall. The agency got what it wanted. You got the maiden and a clean record. How is the maiden?"

"Susan is fine."

"You're still together?"

"Yes."

"Glad to hear love has triumphed. But I still don't see why either of us owes the other one anything."

"How about old times' sake."

"How about that, indeed," Ives said. "It's quite a charming idea, isn't it."

We were quiet. Except for a desk with a phone on it, and a green metal file cabinet, Ives's office was entirely empty. The morning sun was shining in through the big window to our right and made a clear stream for dust motes to sail through. Ives got up and looked out his window for a while, down at Post Office Square, and probably, from this height, the ocean, a few blocks east. High shouldered and narrow, he stood with his hands loosely clasped behind his back, still turning the eraser. Where his trouser cuffs didn't quite touch his pebble-grained oxford shoes, a narrow band of Argyle sock showed. The dust motes drifted. Ives stared down at the square. He probably wasn't thinking. He was probably being dramatic. He had, after all, gone to Yale. Finally he spoke without turning away from the window.

"There's a fellow fits that description, an Israeli national, who was a covert operative. He left Israeli service under prejudicial circumstances, worked with us for a little while, and then dropped out of sight. I had heard he was in private practice."

"Name?"

"Barely matters," Ives said. "He called himself Rugar when he was with us."

"How was his English?"

"American accent," Ives said. "I believe he was born in this country."

"You know where he is now?"

"No."

"Any suggestion where I might look for him?"

"None."

"Anything else?"

"He had gray hair and a sallow complexion. Attempting, presumably, to turn a liability into an asset, he affected a completely gray wardrobe."

"Funny," I said. "A guy in his line of work trying to give himself an identity."

Ives turned from the window.

"How so?"

"It's in his best interest to have no identity," I said.

"By God," he said. "You know, I never thought of it that way."

"Bureaucracy clogs the imagination," I said. "Is there anything else you can tell me about this guy?"

Ives pursed his lips faintly. He was turning the eraser at belt level now using both hands. There were liver spots on his hands.

"He is," Ives said gently, "the most deadly man I have met in forty years."

"Wait'll you get a load of me," I said.

"I've gotten a load of you and the black fellow, too."

"Hawk," I said.

"Yes, Mister Hawk. He's still alive?"

"Yes."

"He's still your friend?"

"Yes."

"You are a stable man," Ives said. "In an unstable profession. But I stand by what I said of our friend Rugar."

He smiled softly and squeezed his eraser and didn't say anything else.

chapter 42

I SLID THE pin into the bottom notch of the weight stack on one of the chest-press machines at the Harbor Health Club, and sidled in under it, and took a wide spread grip and inhaled and pushed the weight up as I exhaled. Things creaked in my right shoulder, but the bar went up. I eased it down, pushed it up again. I did this eight more times and let the bar come back to rest. Henry Cimoli was watching me.

"Ten reps," he said. "You got another set in you."

I nodded, breathing deeply, waiting. Then I did ten more reps, struggling to keep form. And rested and did ten more.

"That's as good as you did before," Henry said.

I slid off of the machine and stood waiting for my oxygen levels to normalize, watching the rest of the club members exercise. Most of them were women in spandex. Across the room was a bank of treadmills and Stair Climbers each with a small television screen so that you could exercise while watching an assortment of daytime talk shows, with maybe a videotape of a public dismemberment thrown in to cleanse the palate.

"Weigh in," Henry said, and we walked to the balance scale. I got on, Henry adjusted the weights. I weighed to 210. The same weight I'd carried into the river almost a year ago.

"I'd say you're as good as new," Henry said.

"Too bad," I said. "I was hoping for better."

"We all were," Henry said. "But you can't shine shit."

"You're awfully short for a philosopher," I said.

"Hell," Henry said. "I'm awful short for a person. But I'm fun."

I got off the scale and went and drank some water and wiped my face with a hand towel. There were mirrors on all the walls so that you could admire yourself from every angle. I was doing that when Vinnie Morris came in and glanced around the room and walked over to me.

"I tried your office and you weren't there," Vinnie said. "Figured you'd be here."

"Ever consider a career as a private investigator?"

"Naw," Vinnie said. "Gino wants to see you."

"You told him I was back," I said.

"He's out in the car," Vinnie said.

I went to Henry's office, got my jacket and my gun, put both of them on, and went out with Vinnie. There was a big silver Mercedes sedan double-parked on Atlantic Ave. The street was already narrowed by construction, and the traffic was having trouble getting around the car. There was a lot of honking, to which, as far as I could see, no one paid any attention. Gino Fish was in the backseat. A guy with a thick neck and a black suit was behind the wheel. Vinnie opened the back door and I got in beside Gino. Vinnie got in the front. Gino was wearing a blue suit, a blue striped shirt, and a gold silk necktie. His hair was cut so short that he seemed bald, though he actually wasn't. He was wearing bright blue reflective Oakley sun glasses, which seemed totally out of keeping with the rest of his look.

"Drive about, please, Sammy," Gino said.

And the Mercedes pulled into traffic, cutting off a maroon van and causing more honking of horns. Neither Sammy nor Gino seemed to hear them. We cruised slowly north along Atlantic Avenue.

"I understand you were injured," Gino said.

"Yes."

"Specifically you were shot."

"Yes."

"Vinnie tells me this man dresses in gray and may be named Rugar."

"Or he may not be," I said.

"Yes," Gino said. "It is good to be precise."

We passed the garage in the North End where the Brinks job went down almost fifty years ago, and the Charlestown Bridge to what had once been City Square. Sammy kept on straight on Atlantic, under the elevated trains in front of the old Boston Garden, with the new Boston Garden behind it.

"I know of such a man," Gino said.

"Gray man?"

"Yes."

"Called Rugar?"

"Yes."

I waited. We bore right past the Garden and North Station, past the ruins of what used to be the West End.

There was a single defiant three-decker remaining, surrounded by pavement, like the isolated tombstone of a neighborhood that disappeared.

"This Rugar, who affects gray all the time—so tacky—is a gunman. He works out of New York and he is very expensive and, hence, very exclusive."

"Ever use him?" I said.

"I have Vinnie," Gino said.

"Before you had Vinnie," I said.

Gino smiled gently.

"His arrangement is simple. You pay nothing until it's done. Then you pay him promptly in full and in cash and he disappears. Once he commits to a project he stays on it until it is done, no matter how long it takes, no matter how far he has to travel. He guarantees results and he requests no payment until he gets them. Anyone who has dealt with him is not likely to try and, ah, renege on payment.

"And it prevents him from getting stung if the client turns out to be an undercover cop. He doesn't take money, he can just say he was humoring them and had no intention of killing anyone."

We went past the old Registry building and the new Suffolk County jail, past the Charles River dam, and onto Storrow Drive, going west at a leisurely pace.

"Where do I find Rugar?" I said.

"One might be better not to find him," Gino said.

"One might."

Gino sort of smiled. If it was a smile. Whatever it was, it was devoid of warmth or humor.

"People who wish to hire him," Gino said, "see an attorney in New York who arranges a meeting."

"And if the cops ever backtrack to him," I said, "he can

claim that all his dealings with Rugar are privileged communication between a lawyer and his client."

"You are an astute man," Gino said.

"Yeah, and a swell dancer. How come you're telling me this?"

"Vinnie holds you in high regard."

"Good employee relations?" I said.

Gino spread his hands. They looked like the hands of a violinist.

"You know the attorney?" I said.

"Not anymore," Gino said.

"But the one you knew was a New York guy?" I said.

"Yes."

"And you don't know who replaced him?"

"No."

"No reason to think it wouldn't be a New York guy," I said.

"No reason," Gino said.

"Thanks," I said.

"You're entirely welcome," Gino said. "Where would you like us to drop you off?"

The sublet had run out, I had my office back. "My office is fine, corner of Berkeley and Boylston."

"I know where your office is," Gino said.

He leaned forward slightly.

"Did you hear that, Sammy?"

"Yes, sir," Sammy said. "Berkeley and Boylston."

"While we drive you there, may I offer another thought? I'm a thoughtful man, and what I think is often valuable."

"And your diction is *très* elegant," I said.

"Thank you. My dealings with Rugar remain my business. I have spent a long and successful life among very deadly people. If I were a fearful sort, I would fear

Rugar more than anyone I've ever known. I advise you to stay away from him."

"How's he compare with Vinnie?" I said.

"I would not ask Vinnie to go against him alone."

Vinnie sat in the front seat looking at the coeds from Emerson College as we turned off Storrow Drive and onto Beacon Street. He didn't seem interested in our conversation. In fact, Vinnie wasn't interested in many things. What he could do was shoot. I had never met anyone I wouldn't send Vinnie up against—except maybe Hawk. Or me.

We went up Beacon to Clarendon, turned up to Boylston, and drove back down to Berkeley. Sammy pulled up and double parked outside my building.

I said, "Thanks for the information, Mr. Fish."

"And the advice," Gino said. "You would be wise to heed the advice."

"And spend the rest of my life waiting for him to come back?"

"Perhaps he'll never learn that you survived," Gino said.

Several drivers behind us blared their horns. Sammy ignored them.

"He will if I do what I signed on to do."

"Get that schwartza out of jail?"

"Yes."

"The world is a better place," Gino said, "with him in jail."

"He didn't do what he's there for. I said I'd get him out."

"And you keep your word," Gino said.

"Yes."

Gino nodded slowly, looking past me at the corner of the Public Garden that showed on the left at the end of the block. Then he looked at me. His eyes were pale blue and as flat as a couple of one-inch washers. Again he made the motion with his face that might have been a smile.

"I don't think the beard becomes you," he said.

I got out of the car and watched as it pulled away and headed down Boylston. I watched it until it turned left on Charles Street and disappeared. Then I turned and went up to my office.

chapter 43

"CAN'T YOU SIMPLY turn over what you have to Rita and her big law firm," Susan said. "And let them get Ellis Alves out of jail?"

"I have knowledge. I have no evidence."

"You know that the witnesses against Alves are cousins of Clint Stapleton," she said. "You know that Clint Stapleton was the victim's boyfriend. You know that that State Police Detective . . ."

"Tommy Miller."

"Tommy Miller was involved in some kind of cover-up and then was shot when you were threatening to find out what it was. You know that a man shot you, to prevent you from looking further."

"And I know who it was," I said. "But none of that proves that Alves was framed, and so far there is no demonstrable connection between the Gray Man and the Stapleton family."

"But you know they hired him, don't you? You know that you were shot right after you confronted Clint Stapleton."

"I don't think I can get a court to just take my word for it," I said. "I think I have to be able to prove it. Especially with a guy like Alves. Even Gino Fish thinks the world is a better place with Ellis in jail."

"So how can you prove it?"

"Keep pushing. Stapleton, his father, his mother, cousin Hunt and his wife Ms. Congeniality. They're not pros. One of them will break."

"But pushing them makes you vulnerable to the Gray Man."

"So I'll have to deal with him first."

"You think you can find him through this lawyer?"

"Yes."

"You have to do it alone?"

"The goal is to decommission the Gray Man. How is not as important."

"Hawk would help you, and Vinnie. Chollo would come if you asked him."

I nodded. We were lying in bed together in Susan's bedroom. Pearl was draped diagonally across the foot, having been but recently allowed back in. The room was dark, lit only by the odd tangential light of the mercury street lamps on Linnaean Street.

"You're going to do it alone, aren't you?"

Susan's head was on my shoulder, my right arm was around her. A Browning 9-mm. semiautomatic pistol lay unholstered right beside the alarm clock on the table next to the bed.

"We'll see," I said.

"Is it like being thrown from a horse? You have to get right up and ride it again so you won't be scared?"

"Something like that, maybe."

"Are you afraid?"

"It's not a question I ask myself," I said. "It's sort of like flying. Most people I know, in fact, are a little afraid of flying. But you fly anyway because life's too complicated if you don't, and you don't pay much attention, unless you're phobic, to whether in fact you are afraid."

"Do you intend to kill him?"

"I guess that's up to him," I said.

"You plan to give him a chance to surrender?"

"I'm not sure what I'm going to do, Suze. Some things become self-evident as they develop. Readiness is all."

Susan raised up on her elbow and put her face very close to mine. Her voice was very soft, and very fierce.

"Fuck readiness is all," she said. "And fuck Shakespeare. Don't give the Gray Man a chance. Kill him as soon as you can."

"Fuck Shakespeare?"

"And the whole English Renaissance for that matter," Susan said.

"And you a Harvard grad?" I said. "A resident of Cambridge?"

"This isn't some sort of knightly errand," Susan said. "This is your life, our life. Bring Hawk with you, and Vinnie. Kill him on sight."

"I'll try to do it the best way I can," I said.

Susan settled back down with her head on my shoulder again. We were quiet.

"Yes," Susan said finally, "you will. Which is the way you should do it."

Pearl got off the bed and went purposefully to the

kitchen, where I could hear her lapping water from her dish.

"Have you noticed that I have no clothes on," Susan said.

"This was brought to my attention quite forcefully," I said. "About an hour ago."

Susan ran her forefinger along the line of my bicep.

"I suppose, since you've been wounded, and since you are not as young as you were when we first met, that bringing it forcefully to your attention again would be too much."

"Probably," I said. "On the other hand, it seems a shame to waste all that nudity. Maybe we should fumble around a little and see what develops."

Susan reached over and closed the bedroom door.

"Pearl won't like being shut out," I said.

"It'll only be for a little while."

"Maybe it'll be a long while," I said.

"One can only hope."

I heard Pearl return to the closed door and snuffle a little, and sigh and lie down against it. She seemed to have figured out that there were times when we had to be alone. And accepted it philosophically.

"Well, for heaven's sake," Susan whispered. "Something seems to be developing already."

"Strong," I said. "Like a bull."

Susan giggled a little bit.

"The resemblance ends there," she said.

chapter 44

I TALKED WITH Ellis Alves again, alone, in a small conference room on the thirty-second floor at Cone, Oakes and Baldwin. He was as hostile and interior as he had been the last time. I remembered what Hawk had said: *You in for life, hope will kill you.* There was nothing on the conference table except a water carafe and some paper cups stacked upside down. Ellis paid no attention to it. He stood motionless, silhouetted against the bright picture window with the early fall light filling the room.

"Where's Hawk?" Alves said.

"Elsewhere," I said. "I have some things to tell you."

He didn't say anything. He simply waited, standing on the other side of the small conference table, for what I might have to say. I imagined in prison you learn to wait.

"I know you didn't kill Melissa Henderson," I said.

Alves waited.

"I can't prove it yet, but I will."

Alves waited.

"You interested in what I know?" I said.

"No."

"You're going to get out," I said.

Alves stood without speaking or moving.

"You got any questions?"

"No."

"Okay, then that's all I got to say."

"Make you feel better?" Alves said.

"No. I just figured you ought to know you're going to get out pretty soon, so you wouldn't do something dumb in the interim."

"Yeah," Alves said.

"Don't try to escape. Don't get into a fight. Don't break any rules. Nobody much wants you to get out, so don't give them an excuse to keep you."

Alves didn't say anything. He was looking at me, but I felt no contact. It was like exchanging stares with a statue.

"You got anything else you want to say before I get the guards?"

"No."

"Okay."

I got up and started for the door.

Behind me, Alves said, "How long it going to take?"

"I don't know, weeks probably, maybe days. I need to make somebody confess."

"What happens they don't?"

"I'll force it," I said.

"Been almost a year," Alves said. "How come you still doing this?"

"I was hired to do this."

"What happens to me, somethin' happen to you?"

"Hawk will finish it," I said.

We stood looking at each other for a minute.

"Couple niggers fighting the system," Alves said.

"Couple niggers and the biggest law firm in Boston," I said.

Alves walked stiffly over to the window and looked out at Boston Harbor.

"I ain't counting on nothing," Alves said.

"Best way to be," I said.

Alves nodded once, his eyes flat and meaningless, his face empty.

"Yeah," he said. "It is."

I knocked on the door and the guards opened it.

"All done," I said.

They went past me into the conference room and I walked out to the corridor and punched the button on the elevator. It arrived in time, and I got in it with mail room clerks and young female secretaries and a couple of suits, and down we went.

I stopped in the lobby for a minute and watched the people hurrying freely about. They would have taken Ellis down in the service elevator and out the back. In an hour he'd be back in the joint, looking at life; his only chance to get out in the hands of a white guy he neither knew nor trusted . . . *breeding/lilacs out of the dead land, mixing/memory and desire . . . If you're a lifer, hope will kill you . . .* Was I mixing up my poets? At least no one was calling me the hyacinth girl.

I walked over to the parking garage where they'd found Tommy Miller's body and got in my car and headed for New York.

chapter 45

PATRICIA UTLEY HAD moved uptown. She had a townhouse
on Sixty-fifth Street between Park and Madison with an
etched glass front door, which I noticed had been covered
with a thick sheet of clear Lexan. On either side of the
entrance there were little pillars, like the entrance to
some sort of Greco-Roman shrine. Steven opened the
door. He was still black and well set up, still moved with
a light springiness. His short hair had started to gray. In
keeping with the times, he had turned in his white coat
and was wearing a blue blazer. He recognized me, though
the recognition didn't overpower him.

"Mister Spenser," he said.

"Hello, Steven," I said. "Is Mrs. Utley in?"

Steven stepped back from the door so I could come in.

"Come into the library," he said, "while I find out if she can see you."

The room was in the front of the house. There was a clean fireplace with a green marble hearth on the left wall. The big arched windows looked out onto Sixty-fifth Street. There were filigreed metal inserts on the inside of each, which effectively barred someone from breaking in. I sat on a big hassock covered in green leather. All of the furniture was leather covered in green or a kind of off blue. The walls were paneled in oak, and the whole room looked exactly like the library of someone who never read but watched *Masterpiece Theater* a lot. There was a bookcase on either side of the cold fireplace. She seemed to have moved all her books up from Thirty-seventh Street. I remembered some of them: *The Complete Works of Charles Dickens, A History of the English-Speaking Peoples, Longfellow: Complete Poetical and Prose Works, The Outline of History, The Canterbury Tales.* They didn't look as if they'd been taken down and thumbed through fondly in the twenty years since I first saw them.

Patricia Utley herself, when she came into the room, didn't look like she'd been thumbed through much either. She was as pulled together as she always was. Her hair was maybe a little brighter, and thus a little less credible, blonder than it had been when I'd first met her. It was short and full but it didn't look lacquered. There were crow's-feet at her eyes, and only the subtlest hint of lines at the corners of her mouth. She was small, trim, stylish in a black pantsuit with a white blouse. The blouse had a low neck line, and a short rope of pearls lay against her skin above it. Her glasses were big and round and black-rimmed. I had no idea what age she was, but whatever it was she looked good. She put her hand out as she walked across the room. I stood and took her hand. She leaned gracefully forward and kissed me on the cheek.

"Still a detective?" she said.

"Yes," I said. "Still a madam?"

"Yes, and a fabulously successful one, if I may say so."

"As the move uptown would suggest," I said.

"My previous home was not impoverished," she said.

"No, it wasn't."

"Would you like a glass of sherry?" she said. "A real drink?"

"No, thank you," I said. "Just some talk."

"I hope you won't mind if I have a glass."

"Not at all."

She walked to a small sideboard between the big windows and poured herself a pony of sherry from a cut-glass decanter, and turned, standing in front of the window so the light silhouetted her.

"So what stray are you looking for this time?" she said.

"Maybe I just dropped in to say hi," I said. "Maybe I miss you."

"I'm sure you do," Patricia Utley said. "But I do know that in the past, whenever you have come to see me you were looking for someone's little lost lamb."

"More like a wolf this time," I said.

"Really?"

"Guy named Rugar, he's been hired to kill me, and he almost did."

"I would have thought that would be hard to do."

"He didn't succeed," I said.

The library door opened and Steven came in with what appeared to be a black and white aardvark on a leash. The aardvark had a bright red choke collar around his neck. His lost-and-found tag dangled from one of the loops on the collar. The tag was bright red also, and heart shaped.

"She's had her walk," Steven said. "And the maid says she was very good."

He leaned over and unsnapped the leash and the aardvark dashed over to Patricia Utley and wagged its tail. Astonishingly, Patricia Utley went to her knees and put her face down where the aardvark could lap it. It wasn't a very big aardvark. Maybe it was too small to be an aardvark.

"Did you have a lovely tinky tinky?" Patricia Utley said.

As I studied it, it was definitely too small to be an aardvark. But whatever it was, it was a lapping fool. It lapped Patricia Utley's face very intently.

"This is Rosie," Patricia Utley said.

She was turning her face to avoid losing all her makeup.

"That's great," I said. "Rosie is not an aardvark, is she?"

"No, of course not. She's a miniature bullterrier."

"That was going to be my next guess," I said. "Like Spuds McKenzie in the beer ads."

"I don't watch beer ads," Patricia Utley said.

She stood and Rosie turned and wiggled over to me and rolled on her back.

"She wants you to rub her stomach," Patricia Utley said.

I sat back down on the hassock and bent over and rubbed Rosie's stomach, which was quite pink.

"She likes it if you say *rub rub rub*, while you're doing it."

"I can't do that," I said. "You'd tell."

"Rub, rub, rub," Patricia Utley said for me.

She brought her sherry to the blue leather couch and

sat on the edge of it, her knees together, her hands, holding the sherry, folded quietly in her lap. Rosie turned immediately over onto her feet, trotted to the couch, and elevated onto it without any apparent effort, as if somehow she had jumped with all four feet equally. She lay down beside Patricia Utley, put her head on Patricia Utley's lap, and stared at me with her almond-shaped black eyes that had no more depth than two slivers of obsidian.

"And now you are looking for this Rugar person?"

"Yes."

"I don't know anyone of that name."

"He works through a lawyer," I said. "Or he used to."

"Is he based in New York?"

"I think so."

"Do you know anything else about him?"

"Rugar or the lawyer?"

"Either," Patricia Utley said.

She was smoothing the fur on Rosie's tail, which looked like it belonged on a short Dalmatian. Rosie would occasionally open her mouth and close it again.

"He's American born, worked for the Israelis for a while. He's in his forties or fifties. Tall, athletic, gray hair, gray skin, seems to dress all in gray. Rugar probably isn't his real name. Very expensive, very covert."

"And if I wished to hire him I would go to a lawyer?"

"A particular lawyer. Who would set up an appointment with Rugar."

"And you don't know who the lawyer is?"

"No, hell, I don't even know if his name is Rugar."

Patricia Utley ran the tip of her tongue along her lower lip. I waited. She sipped her sherry and swallowed and repeated the tongue-on-lower-lip movement. Rosie kept looking at me. Occasionally she wagged her tail.

"I don't know of any such lawyer," she said finally.

"Where would you go if you needed someone killed?" I said.

"I have never had to consider that," she said. "Bribery has always been entirely serviceable."

"And so much more genteel," I said.

She smiled and sipped her sherry again.

"Will you be in the City long?"

"Depends how long this takes," I said.

"You would be amazed at the diversity of my client list," she said.

"No, I wouldn't," I said.

She smiled and made an assenting gesture with her head.

"No, probably you wouldn't be. But I have contact with a vast range of rich and important people. If this man, who might be named Rugar, is truly expensive, my clientele would be his market."

"Can you ask around without being too direct?"

She gave me a look as flat and impenetrable as Rosie's.

"Of course you can," I said.

She smiled.

"Where are you staying?" she said.

"Days Inn on the West Side."

She wrinkled her nose. "Really?"

"I'm on my own time," I said, "and Susan's not with me."

"Don't you yourself deserve to go first class?" she said.

"I probably deserve whatever I can get," I said. "But all I need is a room and a bath. Days Inn will do fine."

She nodded as if she weren't really listening to me.

"I'll get in touch with you there," she said.

I stood. Rosie sprang from the couch and dashed over
to me and did a quick spin.

"She wants you to pick her up," Patricia Utley said.

I did. She weighed more than I would have thought.

"Dog's built like a Humvee," I said.

"But much cuter," Patricia Utley said.

"And her nose is longer," I said.

Rosie lapped me slurpily under the chin as I walked
toward the door carrying her. Patricia Utley walked with
me. Steven appeared in the hall. I had noticed over the
years, both on Thirty-seventh Street and now here, that
the front door never opened unless Steven was present.
He opened it. I handed Rosie to him and leaned over and
kissed Patricia Utley on the cheek and went down the
steps and turned west on Sixty-fifth Street. West Fifty-
seventh Street was only about ten blocks away, but it was
a lot farther than that from where Patricia Utley lived.

chapter 46

I HAD DINNER with Paul Giacomon that night in one of those SoHo restaurants where the wait staff all look like members of a yuppie motorcycle gang.

"What do you think?" Paul said as we studied the menu which the head biker had slapped down in front of us before returning to her real job, intimidating tourists.

"Interesting," I said.

"Does that mean it really is interesting, or is it the kind of interesting like when you see a Jackson Pollock painting and you haven't got a clue and somebody says how do you like it?"

"The latter," I said.

Paul grinned.

"But it's very downtown," he said.

"I think maybe I'm more a midtown guy," I said.

"Food's good," Paul said.

And it was. We had a bottle of wine with it. And we talked. It was fascinating to me to see how at home in this environment Paul was.

"You look good," he said. "Susan told me after you got shot you were down to like 170 pounds."

"I was slim," I said, "but I was slow and clumsy."

"You okay now?"

"Good as new," I said.

"Susan says you and Hawk worked like slaves for almost a year."

"If I'm to pursue my chosen profession," I said, "I can't be slim, slow, and clumsy."

"I suppose you wouldn't pursue it for very long," Paul said, "if you were."

"How's your love life?" I said.

"More like a sex life at the moment," Paul said.

"Nothing wrong with a sex life," I said.

Paul grinned at me again.

"Nothing at all," I said. "Though finally it seems to me that a love life is better."

"If you find a Susan," Paul said.

"True," I said.

"And the Susan finds you."

"Meaning?"

"Her first marriage, for instance, didn't work," Paul said.

"Meaning?"

"Meaning Susan is not a simple woman."

"Not hardly," I said.

"Not everyone could be happy with her," Paul said.

"Maybe not," I said.

"But you can."

I nodded.

"You dating anyone regularly?" I said.

"Three people," he said.

"They know about each other?"

"Of course they do," he said. "Who brought me up?"

"Mostly me, I guess."

"All you," Paul said. "And the psychiatrist you got me. My first fifteen years were without upbringing."

"Well," I said. "We did a hell of a job."

"Me too," he said. "You in town on business?"

"Yeah."

He nodded. Paul never asked about business.

"You okay?" I said.

"Me? Yeah."

"Enough money?"

"Yeah. I still get a check every month from my father. I'm getting a lot of bookings for my choreography, and I've started acting a little. Got a part in a thing called *Sky Lark* about ten off-offs."

I nodded. Paul looked at me carefully.

"Why do you ask? You never ask questions like that."

"Just wondering."

Paul didn't say anything. He drank some wine, poured some into my glass and some more into his.

"You're all right?"

"Absolutely," I said. "Healthy as a horse, and damned near as smart."

Paul chimed in on the damn near as smart so that we spoke it simultaneously. We both laughed.

"Okay," I said, "so maybe you've heard my act."

"And maybe I know it pretty well," Paul said. "You're worried about something."

"Not worried exactly, just alert to all possibilities. If something happened to me, you could count on Hawk to help you in any way you needed."

"I know."

"And Susan."

"I know that, too."

"And if she were alone you could be very helpful to her."

"And would be. You and she are the closest thing I ever had to real parents."

"Good," I said. "Can we come down and see you in this play?"

"You don't want to talk about all the possibilities you're alert to," Paul said.

"No."

"Okay."

Paul drank some wine and cut a piece off his sushi-quality tuna steak and ate it. Then he looked at me for a minute and nodded silently.

"Whatever it is," he said, "my money is on you."

"Smart bet," I said.

chapter 47

PATRICIA UTLEY'S MAN Steven showed up at my hotel the next morning. He called from the lobby. I gave him the room number and let him in when he knocked. He handed me a lavender note-sized envelope with my name written on it, purple ink in a beautiful cursive hand.

"Mrs. Utley asked me to give you this," he said.

I opened the envelope and found a piece of matching note paper with the name Attorney Morris Gold written on it, and an address in the East Nineties. Under that was written in the same beautiful script, *"You will need a place to receive calls. You may use my home. You know the number."*

"Tell Mrs. Utley thank you," I said.

"She also instructed me to offer you any help you might need."

"Thank you, Steven, but I think this will be a solo dash."

He nodded.

"If you decide otherwise," he said, and let it hang. I nodded.

"I'll go see this guy, then I'll come to the house."

"Very good," he said, and left.

I had no plan. All I had was the name and address of a guy who might get me to the Gray Man, and a Smith & Wesson .357 Mag, with a four-inch barrel, which I slipped onto my belt and positioned on my right hip. No machine guns, no siege cannon. This would be a simple deal. Either I'd get him or I wouldn't. No more than a couple of shots would be fired. And they'd be at close range. I put some extra bullets in my shirt pocket and went out of the hotel.

I walked through the park to the art museum and then up Fifth to Ninety-seventh Street and across to the East Side. The address was next to a Spanish grocery store. On the second floor. The door had a pebbled glass window and on it was lettered "Morris Gold, Attorney at Law." The lettering was in gold with a black outline. I went in. The room was barely big enough for a big old gray metal desk and a large swivel chair. Behind the desk was a short very fat man. He wore glasses and a powder blue sport coat, and a dark blue shirt that was too tight around his neck to button. His white tie was narrow and loose and hung crookedly as if he hadn't tied it right. The wider part was shorter than the narrow part. His hair was artificially dark and he wore it long in the back and swooped it up over a large bald spot. On the desk was a computer and a telephone. On the left wall was a file cabinet that matched the desk. Behind him was a window with a crack in it. The overhead light was on. He was reading the *Daily News*, the paper open flat on the desk in front of him. As I came in he licked his thumb, turned a page, looked at it briefly, then looked up at me.

"Whaddya need," he said.

"Morris Gold?"

"Yeah."

"I have some work for Rugar," I said.

"Don't tell me what it is," Gold said.

I nodded.

"Who are you?" he said.

I shook my head.

"Who sent you to me?"

I shook my head again.

Gold nodded, and turned and picked up the phone and dialed.

"Guy wants to see you," Gold said.

He was silent.

Then he said, "Big guy, beard, wears his hair long, over the ears. Black Oakley shades. Wearing a blue blazer, a white tee-shirt, chinos, and white running shoes."

He listened again.

Then he said, "Okay," and hung up.

"You from around here?" he said.

I didn't answer. Gold nodded with approval, as if he admired reticence.

"You got a phone you can be reached at?" he said.

I gave him Patricia Utley's number.

"Ask for Mr. Vance," I said.

"Okay, somebody will call you at this number at"—he looked at his watch—"two P.M. You got that?"

"Yes."

"You got any questions?"

"No."

"*Hasta la vista*," Gold said and began to read his newspaper again.

I left without saying anything else. I walked the forty-five blocks back to the hotel. I took off the blue blazer, and the tee-shirt, got a black mock turtleneck shirt and a gray silk tweed sport coat out of the closet and put them on. I took off the chinos and put on a pair of jeans. I left the black Oakleys on the bureau and put on a pair of horn-rimmed Ray Bans. I went into the bathroom and got some hair spray that I'd brought for the purpose, and drenched my hair with it. I combed my hair straight back, being careful to tuck it behind my ears. Then I headed back to Patricia Utley's house and got there at a quarter to two. Steven put me in the library next to a phone, and left me alone. At three minutes past two, it rang.

The voice said, "Mr. Vance."

It was the same voice, deep, flat, disinterested with an internal vibration as if a vast and infernal machine were generating something deep below the surface.

"Yeah."

"Wear what you were wearing this morning. Carry a paperback copy of *Hamlet*, and stand by the entrance to NBC studios at three-fifteen."

"Okay."

He hung up the phone. I took out the .357 and checked it and put it back. Normally I left the chamber under the hammer empty. This time I had all six rounds in the cylinder. I knew it was loaded. I had reloaded it carefully an hour ago in my hotel room. It was just sort of a practice swing before going to bat. Ritual. I put the gun back and left the strap unsnapped. I made sure my coat was unbuttoned and made a couple of practice draws. Everything was just like it always was. The holster was old and broken in. I'd pulled a gun—often in practice and sometimes for real—enough so that it was as automatic as checking my watch. I did it again. A couple of practice swings. Then I left Patricia Utley's library and went to the front door. Steven was there to let me out. On the front step I turned and put out my hand. Steven took it and we shook. I went down the steps, turned right, walked the block and a half to Fifth Avenue, crossed to the park, and walked down Fifth Avenue on the park side toward Rockefeller Center. I got there at twenty of three, walked past the skating rink and the statue of Atlas and went into Thirty Rock from the Fifth Avenue side. It was eight minutes to three . . . I waited behind my Ray Bans just inside the door while my pupils dilated in the diminished light. I didn't see the Gray Man, but I would, and I'd see him before he saw me. He'd be looking for a guy wearing a blue blazer with his hair hanging over his ears. When he'd last seen me I was clean shaven with a crew cut. Now I had a beard and a Pat Riley slick back. He'd only seen me two or three times in his life. And the last time was nearly a year ago. He didn't expect to see me. He thought I was dead . . . I walked slowly along the lobby toward the NBC studios. There was a steady movement of people in both directions through the lobby. I didn't see them. Everything I had was focused on the Gray Man. He was not at the studio entrance in the pass-through in the middle of the lobby. I kept on going along the lobby, circled it slowly, came back past the studio entrance on the other side of the pass-through. It was 3:15. The foot traffic through the lobby was steady, enough to swell a progress, but no more than that. I had time to look at everybody. And I did, without seeing them. He was the only one I'd see. The rest were so peripheral as to be without meaning, blurred by their inconsequentiality. Amorphous. Their footfalls must

have made sound in the black marble space, but I heard
nothing, the procession of passersby was spectral and the
space through which I walked was soundless and
narrow . . . I circled slowly through the inessential
lobby, through the ethereal silent crowd, and he was
standing by the shop window across from the pass-
through appearing to look at nothing. His gray raincoat
was unbuttoned over a gray turtleneck shirt and dark gray
slacks. His shoes were black suede with thick gray rubber
soles. His thick gray hair swept back smoothly from his
face as if it had never been otherwise. He was clean
shaven. His skin was still sallow. And deep lines ran from
the flare of his nostrils to the corners of his mouth. He
still had his earring. His hands were strong and thick and
long fingered. His nails were manicured and buffed. He
hadn't changed since he'd almost killed me. His face was
without expression. His bearing without affect. He was
completely still as he waited, looking for a guy carrying
a book by William Shakespeare . . . I looked at him for
a while, feeling nothing. Things never stirred the feelings
that you have invested in them. Rugar was merely a man
in a gray coat looking blankly at the people walking
past. . . . I walked past him too, and when I was close
I turned and hit him in the face with my left hand and
then my right. If you've been a fighter, you have learned
how to hit. You know about shortening your arm exten-
sion and getting mostly body into the punch. The two
punches were good ones. They rocked him back against
the black marble wall. His head banged against it. His
hand went inside his coat. I pressed my body hard against
him, trapping his hand between his stomach and mine. I
put my gun up under his chin and pressed the muzzle
hard into the soft tissue under the point where his jaw
hinged on the right side. With my left hand I got a

handful of his hair and banged his head back against the marble wall again. My face was an inch from his. I could see his eyes refocus and the intelligence begin to work in them. He knew me. It hadn't taken him ten seconds to understand what was up. I wanted to keep banging his head. I wanted to bang it until it split open and his life seeped out. But I didn't. It wouldn't get Ellis Alves out of jail. I got the genie far enough back into the bottle to do what I had set out to do more than a year ago. I held him against the wall while I got my breathing under enough control to speak. Around me I was vaguely aware of a lot of scuttling and movement.

"It's me," I said to Rugar. "Lazarus . . . come back to tell you all."

chapter 48

I KNEW SOMEONE would call the cops, and the first one showed up about forty-five seconds after I hit Rugar. It was a young black guy walking toward me very fast from the Sixth Avenue end of the building. There was a Rock Center security guy with him, pointing toward me. The young cop had his gun drawn and pointing at the floor, held in against his right thigh as he walked. His finger was outside the trigger guard.

When he got close enough he said, "Put the gun down."

I said, "I'm a private detective. This guy's wanted for attempted murder in Boston."

"Maybe he is," the cop said. "But I want that gun down on the ground, now."

"Guy's too dangerous," I said. "He's got a gun, left side."

"I'll take care of the gun," the young cop said. "You lay yours down and step away."

"Call Manhattan Homicide," I said. "Detective Eugene Corsetti. My name's Spenser."

"First put down the piece," the cop said. He was in a shooter's stance now, gun held in both hands, steady on my back.

"Don't drag this out," I said. "You aren't going to shoot until you know the deal. Call Corsetti."

Rugar started to speak and I jammed the gun barrel harder up under his jaw hinge. His head was bleeding. Blood smeared the marble wall behind him.

"Not a sound," I said.

Two more cops came hot-footing it in from the Fifth Avenue end and I could hear sirens in the distance. The black cop was silent for a moment. Then as the other two cops arrived he spoke to them.

"Got a hostage deal here. Guy with the gun wants to talk to Corsetti at Manhattan Homicide. Call it in."

The three cops stayed in a circle around me, pointing their guns at me while one of them talked into the radio mike clipped to his lapel. As he talked some of the sirens stopped outside while others called in the distance. Cops, mostly uniformed, came pouring into the building wearing bullet-proof vests. The circle of pointing weapons enlarged. I kept a firm hold on Rugar's hair and a continuing pressure on his underjaw with the barrel of my gun. It was probably uncomfortable for him. I didn't care. And he didn't flinch. And that's how we stayed while more cops arrived and the crowd milled apprehensively trying to see, trying to stay safe in case there was shooting. Some of the cops started working at the crowd.

The crowd got bigger and harder to control. Here and there people yelled, "Shoot him." I didn't know if they were talking to me or the cops. There were more sirens. More cops. More flack jackets. Fewer uniforms. More plainclothes. More crowd. The media arrived. Cameras. Tape recorders. Note pads. Somebody popped a flash bulb and a uniformed cop slapped the camera down and jawed at the camera man. A woman with a television camera was on the shoulders of a big sound guy trying to get a clear shot of the scene. The young black cop had relaxed into his shooter's stance, his gun still steady, his eyes still steady on Rugar and on me. There were five other cops ringing us, in the same stance. A rangy white-haired police captain with a bright red Irish face arrived. He told me to stay calm, and we'd all wait for Corsetti. Then he turned his attention to making sure there was no way for us to run. He ordered some guy in civvies to check the lines of fire so that if the cops had to shoot they wouldn't hit a civilian. He instructed other subordinates to get the crowd the hell out of the way. The subordinates weren't having much luck. The crowd got bigger. There was a lot of horn beeping outside and more sirens and then through the mob walking the way cops walk, a little arrogant, a little careful, a lot of I'm-on top-of-this, came Detective Second Grade Eugene Corsetti. I had met him ten or eleven years ago when I was looking for a kid named April Kyle, and since then when I had time on my hands in New York, I'd go have a beer with him. Corsetti was a short guy, maybe five feet seven or eight, with a body like a bowling ball and an eighteen-inch neck. He had on a dark blue Yankees warm-up jacket and a white dress shirt open at the neck. As far as I knew, all his shirts were worn, of necessity, open at the neck. His natural cop swagger was enhanced by his build so that he almost rolled from side to side as he pushed through the crowd and slid with surprising delicacy through the perimeter of shooting-stance cops. He put his own hand gun into Rugar's ribs and grinned at me.

"Film at eleven, buddy."

"Gun on his belt," I said. "Left side."

Corsetti nodded. I stepped away and handed my gun to the young black cop. Corsetti flipped Rugar's coat open and took out a 9-mm. Berretta and dropped it in his coat pocket. With his eyes on Rugar he spoke over his shoulder.

"This guy's legit, captain."

He reached with his left hand to the small of his back and got a pair of handcuffs off his belt and handcuffed Rugar.

"We can take them over my place," Corsetti said, "and get statements."

The captain nodded.

"Sergeant, clear us a path," he said.

Then he pointed a finger at the young black cop.

"You come too," he said.

Corsetti and I took Rugar through a corridor of onlookers and press toward the Fifth Avenue end of the building. We were behind a phalanx of cops the captain had designated to clear an egress. Behind me came the young black cop and four guys in plainclothes that had arrived with Corsetti. Behind us a uniformed employee of Rockefeller Center was already cleaning Rugar's blood off the wall with some Windex and a roll of paper towel.

Outside Thirty Rock on the little side street behind the statue of Atlas, where the limos normally let people off for television interviews, there was a mosh of police vehicles and behind them the mobile units of television stations, spilling out onto Forty-ninth and Fiftieth streets, blocking crosstown traffic back beyond the Delaware Water Gap. There was a bank of cameras set up along the far side of the street and Corsetti turned toward them and smiled as we moved toward his car.

"Eugene Corsetti," he yelled, "Detective second grade, NYPD."

chapter 49

I was with Rugar in a holding cell. There was no furniture so we both stood. There was still force in Rugar. But before it had been a force field that radiated from him. Now it was contained, as if the genie had gone back into the bottle for the moment. He stood motionless near the far wall of the cell, his arms hanging loosely at his sides, his face expressionless, looking straight at me without blinking. There was a big bruise on his chin and another on his cheekbone. His gray hair was matted and dark with dried blood. I was leaning on the wall near the door with my arms folded looking back at him.

"You know who I am?" I said.

"Of course."

His voice was still a reverberative purr.

"Then you know we got you."

"For the moment."

"Forever," I said. "No better witness to attempted homicide than the survivor."

"I was told you would be difficult," Rugar said.

"By whom?"

"By people I asked, people who know of you."

"If it's any consolation," I said, "you almost succeeded."

"It is no consolation," Rugar said.

The cell was a cage of heavy wire mesh backed against a yellow-tiled wall in the basement of the precinct house. The cells on either side were empty. The area was lit by a ceiling fixture in the hallway, where a low wattage bulb was overmatched by the space it had to light. Outside in the corridor, under the ineffective ceiling light, a uniformed cop with a thick moustache rested his back against the far wall out of earshot and watched us. The moustache was partly gray though his hair was dark.

"They don't know who you are," I said.

Rugar was quiet.

"They can't match your prints anywhere. You seem to have no arrest record."

Rugar was still quiet.

"You want to bargain?" I said.

"What have I to bargain?"

"The name of the guy who hired you."

"And what have you?"

"My testimony."

"Without your testimony, there is no case against me."

It was my turn to be quiet.

"On the other hand," Rugar said, "even with your testimony there is simply word against mine."

I waited.

"You can prove that you were shot last year."

Rugar seemed to be thinking out loud. I nodded and let him keep thinking.

"I have been so successful, for so long, I had begun to think I was impregnable," he said.

I waited some more. I didn't say anything. Rugar looked at me as steadily as he had.

"The longer they hold me," he said, "the more chance they have to look into my identity."

"Good point," I said.

"And giving up the man who hired me would cost me nothing."

"Another good point," I said.

He paid no attention. As far as I could tell he was talking to himself.

"I promised him nothing. I never expected to fail, so there was nothing to promise. Had I succeeded, I could not implicate him without implicating myself, and he could not implicate me without implicating himself. Each had to keep the other's secret."

"But that's not how it is now," I said.

"No," Rugar said. "It isn't, and that is my fault. I have failed in my assignment. I am forced to compromise myself."

"There's another way to look at it," I said.

"Yes?"

"You didn't fail," I said. "I succeeded."

"My present situation remains the same," Rugar said.

"It can be changed," I said. "You give me the guy who hired you, and you testify against him, and you walk away from this."

"You are willing to let me go free after I came so close to fulfilling my assignment?"

"Yep."

"Do you fear I will try again?"

"No."

"Really," Rugar said. "Why not?"

He seemed genuinely interested.

"You are a professional. You do this for money. You don't allow ego or fear or compassion to motivate you. If you give me your client, you have no further reason to chase me."

Rugar looked past me for a moment at the cop leaning on the wall outside the cage. Then he shifted his eyes back to me.

"And how do you know this about me?" he said.

I shrugged. He kept looking at me for a moment and then, oddly, he smiled.

"It is because that is also how you are," he said.

"Gimme a name," I said.

"Donald Stapleton," Rugar said.

"That's the right name," I said.

"You knew it."

"Yes."

"But you couldn't prove it."

"Correct."

"Now you can," Rugar said.

chapter 50

WHEN I CAME back from New York I went straight to the Inn Style Barbershop and had Patty cut my hair the way it's always been cut. Then I went home and shaved off my beard. Which, if you've never shaved off a beard, is not as easy as you might think. I rinsed out the sink, took a shower, and patted on some Club Man aftershave, which Susan laughed at but I liked. I put on beige slacks, sand-colored suede loafers, a white oxford shirt with a button-down collar, and a blue blazer to hide my gun. I put a white silk handkerchief in the display pocket of the blazer, checked myself in the mirror, and noticed that I looked entirely dashing, and went to Susan's house. I got there just as her last patient was coming out the front door. I went in, making no eye contact, and was standing in her front hall when she came out of her office in her tailored blue suit with the white blouse and her dark hair perfectly in place. She froze in mid-step when she saw me. I opened my arms and she stared at me for a moment as if she didn't understand, then the angularity went away and she stepped in against me and pressed her face against my chest.

"He didn't kill you," she said after a long time.

"Not hardly."

"Did you kill him?"

"He's in jail," I said.

"Will he get out?"

"Maybe, but he's no threat to us anymore."

She stayed with her face against my chest and her arms around my waist under the handsome brass hanging lamp that ornamented her front entry hall. I could feel her body trembling slightly. I didn't say anything. Neither did she. Finally she pulled away and looked at me. Her eyes were red. There were tears on her face.

"You appear to be crying," I said.

"Yes, and it's beating hell out of my eye makeup."

"Doesn't make you look less beautiful," I said.

"Yes, it does," she said. "I had talked myself into it, that maybe this time you wouldn't come back. That this time you met somebody too good for you and you'd been hurt, and I knew you had to do this. I knew I wouldn't even want to be with the man you'd be if you didn't do this and you allowed me to talk you out of it, and I told myself that loving you meant letting you be you, and I was ready when Quirk, or Belson, or Hawk came and told me."

She was holding herself from me at arm's length looking straight at me with the tears washing down her face.

"And when they did I would have been brave and when they left me I would have wanted to die."

I didn't have anything to say.

"And here you come, looking just like you always have, with your hair cut and your face shaved and smelling, good God, is it Club Man?"

"Yes."

She shook her head.

"And we're supposed to be all right again and just like we were."

"Yes."

"Well, maybe I can't rebound that quickly."

"I think you can," I said.

"Who gives a fuck," Susan said, "what you think."

"Good point," I said carefully.

"Yeah, well, maybe I do care what you think."

"I bet you do," I said.

"And maybe I can rebound. God knows I'm glad you're okay."

"Both of us have had to rebound," I said. "We'll be okay."

"Okay?" Susan said. "Just okay?"

"How do you think we'll be?" I said.

"I think we'll be goddamned sensational," she said.

"Would you like me to hug you again?" I said.

"Yes, but there have to be changes."

"Like what?" I said.

"Like you have to get rid of that goddamned Club Man."

I pulled her slowly in against me and held her.

"Would you be able to love the man I'd be if I let you talk me out of it?" I said.

"Oh, fuck you," Susan said and put her face up and I kissed her and she kissed me back so hard that I was grateful I was bigger.

chapter 51

THE NEXT MORNING, clear eyed, clean shaven, close cropped, and contumescent, I went to see Clint Stapleton again.

He wasn't at his condo. I found him on the indoor practice court at Taft playing against a short red-haired scrambler who kept getting the ball back over the net without looking very good doing it. The tennis coach was watching them closely, and maybe ten undergraduates were in the stands. Stapleton had graduated from Taft last June while I was fighting the hill in Santa Barbara, but he'd redshirted his first two years and had another year of eligibility left. And, according to my research, his coaches didn't feel he was ready yet for the pro tour. Stapleton's game was serve and volley, and he looked overpowering. Except the red-haired kid kept returning his serve and lobbing Stapleton's volleys to push him back to the base line. It was annoying Stapleton. He kept hitting the ball harder, and the kid kept getting to it and getting his racquet on it and getting it back over the net. Sometimes he'd hit it on the rim of the racquet. Sometimes it would come back over the net like a damaged pigeon. But he kept getting it back and Stapleton kept hitting it harder. And the harder he hit it, the more erratic he became. They played three games while I watched. The red-haired kid held serve in the second one, and broke Stapleton's serve in the third. Stapleton double-faulted on the game point and threw his racquet straight up into the air. It arced nearly to the top of the arena and fell clattering on the composition court five feet from the red-haired kid, who was grinning. I stood in the shadow of the stands for a while and watched.

"Control, Stapes, focus and control," the coach said to him. "He's not beating you. You're beating yourself."

"Control this," Stapleton said and walked off the court and out the runway through the stands past me.

I fell silently in beside him as he walked, and we were out of the indoor facility and into the bright fall sunshine before he took notice of me. His focus on being mad seemed good. On the walkway that led toward the student union, Stapleton stopped abruptly and turned and looked at me.

"Are you following me?" he said.

"I prefer to think of it as you and me forging ahead together," I said.

Stapleton recognized me. I could see the stages of recognition play on his face. First he realized he knew me. Then he realized who I was. Then he realized I was supposed to be dead. And finally he realized that I wasn't dead. The effect of the sequence was cumulative. He stepped back two big steps.

"What the fuck are you doing here?"

"We need to talk."

"I heard you were dead," he said.

"Where'd you hear that?"

"It was in the paper."

"Media distortion's a drag, isn't it?"

Stapleton started walking again. I stayed with him.

"I can talk with you this way, but we've got hard things to talk about," I said. "And it might go better if we sat on that bench there by the pond."

He looked at me for a time without stopping, then he sort of sighed and gave a big forbearing shrug and walked over to the bench and sat. I sat beside him. Several ducks waddled promptly over expecting to be fed. They were brown ducks for the most part except one which had a green head and was probably a male duck, though I wasn't sure. I didn't know a hell of a lot about ducks.

"Your old man," I said, "hired a guy named Rugar to kill me."

Stapleton didn't say a word. He didn't look at me. He sat straight upright on the bench with his feet flat on the ground and stared at the ducks.

"He'll testify to that in court," I said.

Stapleton didn't speak. The abyss was starting to open in front of him.

"But the question still to be answered is why did he?"

The abyss opened wider. Stapleton stared harder at the ducks.

"You know why he did that?" I said.

Stapleton shrugged, just enough to let me know he'd heard the question. The ducks waddled briskly back and forth in front of us, looking anxious about the possibility of scoring some stale bread.

"I think he did it to keep me from finding out that you killed Melissa Henderson."

The abyss was beneath him. Looking at the ducks didn't help.

"You want to talk about that?" I said.

He shook his head.

"You're going to have to," I said. "Sooner or later. I know you did it. And I know you and Miller and your old man set up a guy you didn't even know named Ellis Alves to take the fall for it. And you or your father got your cousin Hunt to testify that he did it. What I don't know is why did you kill her?"

Stapleton seemed frozen in his position, looking at the ducks but seeing the abyss. No more big man on campus, no more cold beer, no more women, no more picture in the paper, no more condominium in a nice section. No more leisurely Sunday mornings with oranges and a green cockatoo. The abyss was too wide and too deep and he was in it. He stood suddenly and began to walk away from me. I didn't bother to follow him. He walked faster and then broke into a run. I watched him running away until he passed the corner of the gym and was out of sight.

I looked at the ducks. The one with the green head looked back at me with black eyes that held no expression of any kind.

"Yeah," I said to the duck, "I know."

chapter 52

SUSAN AND I were making dinner together at my place. The sublet tenant had finally departed. Pearl was demonstrating why she is known as the Wonder Dog by managing to sleep soundly while lying flat on her back on my sofa with all four paws in the air. I had bought a Jenn Air stove a couple of years back and it had a rotisserie unit on which I was roasting a boneless leg of lamb, which I had seasoned with olive oil and fresh rosemary. After it's seasoned and put on the spit there isn't a great deal demanded of the guy that's cooking it, so I stood at the counter while the roast turned slowly and watched Susan as she made beet risotto.

"I saw a woman on the *Today* show make this," she said.

"And you loved it because it was such a pretty red color," I said.

"Yes. Does this rice look opaque to you?"

I looked and said that it did. Susan ladled some broth into the rice and began to stir it carefully. While she stirred, she looked in the pot and then at the rice.

"Do you think I have to put this broth in a little at a time, the way the recipe says?"

I said that I did. She stirred some more.

"It has to all absorb before I put in more?" she said.

"When you see the bottom of the pan as you stir, add some more broth," I said.

She nodded. The counter around the stove and the space on the stove not occupied by the risotto fixings and the roast was covered with pans and plates and dishes and cups and measuring spoons and forks and knives and a grater and two wooden spoons and a platter of grated beets and a dish of grated cheese and some onion skins and three pot holders and a crumpled paper towel and a damp sponge and her glass of barely sipped red wine and a lip-liner tube and a copy of the recipe written in Susan's pretty illegible hand on the back of a paperback copy of *Civilization and Its Discontents.* Susan was not a clean up as you go kind of cook.

"They always lie to you on television," Susan said.

"I know," I said.

"This woman never said you had to stand here for an hour and stir the damn stuff."

"When you tear away the mask of glamour . . ." I said.

Susan stirred some more, studying the rice, looking for the bottom of the pan.

"Hurry up," she said into the pan.

I thought about explaining to her how a watched pot

never boils, but it might have seemed contentious to her, so I skipped it and went and looked out the front window at Marlborough Street. There was an east wind coming off the water, slowing down as it funneled through the financial district and downtown, picking up speed as it came down across the Common and the Public Garden, driving some leaves and some street litter past my building at a pretty good clip. I watched it for a while, keeping my mind on the wind, trying not to think of anything, sipping red wine.

"Look how pretty," Susan said behind me.

I turned and left the window. The big white pot of bright red rice was in fact pretty, though had we been eating at Susan's house the pot it was in would have been pretty, too.

"Keep it warm in the oven," I said, "while I make the salad and then we'll eat."

"You didn't say it was pretty."

"The beet risotto is very pretty," I said.

"Thank you."

Susan set the table while I made the salad. Then we ate the lamb and risotto with a green salad and some bread from Iggy's Bakery.

"You feel sort of mad about having to sell Concord?" I said.

Susan shrugged.

"It had to be done," she said. "But yes, I probably resent it a little. If you were a stockbroker maybe I wouldn't have had to."

I nodded.

"How about the baby, any new thoughts on that."

"Yes."

"Care to tell me?"

Susan drank some of her wine and touched her lips with a napkin.

"I can't bring a child into this kind of a life," Susan said.

"A life where I may be off getting shot on her first day in kindergarten?"

"Or his," Susan said. "Yes, that kind of life."

"I think you're right," I said.

"You have thought that since I first mentioned the idea," Susan said.

I shrugged. We ate together for a moment in silence. The risotto was very good. Susan put her fork down.

"And I suppose that makes me a little angry as well," she said.

"Yeah," I said. "I can see where it would."

"And I suppose I'm angry sometimes because the man I love keeps getting in harm's way and I have to be frightened that he might not come back."

"It's the only thing I'm any good at," I said.

"Not entirely true, but I understand. I don't want you to change. I just wish I didn't have to be scared as much as I am."

"Me too," I said.

Pearl, with her hunter's instinct, had come instantly awake when we started to eat and was now sitting alertly on the floor between us, watching closely.

"Life is imperfect," Susan said.

I nodded.

"But it is not so imperfect that we cannot enjoy it," Susan said. "We don't have our country house, and I will probably never be a mother. But I love you, and you love me, and we are here, together."

"Works for me," I said. "And what about the anger, what are you going to do with that?"

"I'm not going to do anything with it. Anger doesn't have to be expressed. It is enough to know that you're angry, and know why, and not lie to yourself about it."

"You mean it's not repression if I keep my feelings to myself?"

"No," she said. "It's repression if you pretend to yourself you don't have them."

"Does Dr. Joyce Brothers know about this?" I said.

"I doubt it," Susan said. "Our life together has not always been placid. You must certainly have some anger at me. What do you do with it?"

"I know that I'm angry," I said. "And I know why, and I don't lie to myself about it."

"Very good," Susan said and smiled at me. "We'll both keep doing that."

"Till death do us part?" I said.

"Or hell freezes over," Susan said. "Whichever comes first."

"You sure adorable little Erika didn't have any influence on your decision to adopt a child?"

Susan smiled slowly.

"You are a cynical bastard," she said.

"Of course," I said.

Pearl put her head on my lap and looked up at me by rolling her eyes up. I gave her a spoonful of the risotto. She liked it. On the other hand she liked just about everything. Things were quite simple with Pearl.

chapter 53

THE CHANCES OF a black man being elected DA in Suffolk County were comparable to discovering that the pope is a Buddhist. But there he was, Owen Brooks, the son of a New York City cop, a graduate of Harvard Law School, neat, well dressed, pleasant, and as easy to fool as a Lebanese rug merchant.

We were in Pemberton Square in Brooks's office: Brooks, Quirk, Donald, Dina, and Clint Stapleton, a guy named Frank Farantino from New York who represented Donald Stapleton, and me.

Brooks did the introductions. When he finished, Farantino said, "Why is Spenser here?"

"Mr. Spenser is here at my request," Brooks said. "Since he has been both the primary investigator in this case, and one of its victims, I thought it might serve us all to listen to him, before we get into court and this thing turns into a hairball."

"Is this a formal procedure?" Farantino said.

"Oh, of course not," Brooks said. His smile was wide and gracious. "Nothing's on the record here, I just thought we might get some sense of where the truth lies if we talked a little before we started grinding the gears of justice."

Quirk sat in the back row of chairs, against the wall of the office, next to the door. Clint sat rigidly between his parents. He was stiffly upright. His face was blank. Don was regal in his bearing. Dina rested her hand on her son's forearm. Farantino was to the left of Don. I was to the right of Dina.

"Spenser, you want to hold forth?"

"Here's what I think happened," I said.

"Think?" Farantino said. "We're here to see what he thinks?"

Brooks made a placating gesture with his right hand.

"He can prove enough of it to require us to pay attention," Brooks said.

"Clint Stapleton killed Melissa Henderson," I said. "I don't know why. But he concocted a story about a black man kidnapping her and he got his cousin Hunt McMartin and his cousin's wife Glenda to say they saw the kidnapping. When a State cop named Tommy Miller came in on the case, he took one sniff and it smelled bad. It would have smelled bad to any cop. But Miller also knew that Stapleton had dough and that his father had more money than Courtney Love, and Miller saw a chance to get some of it. So he supported Clint's story and even supplied a fall guy, guy named Ellis Alves. Maybe he busted him once for something else. Maybe he just pulled him up off the known offenders file. We look hard, we'll find a connection. And it all works, and Alves goes to Cedar Junction and everybody else gets back to being a yuppie."

Nobody said anything. From his place by the door, Quirk's eyes moved from person to person in the room. Otherwise he was as motionless as everyone else.

"But because Alves's lawyer won't quite quit on the thing, I get brought in and I start to poke around and pretty soon people are having to lie to me, and the lies are the kind that won't hold if I keep on looking, and I keep on looking and Miller tries to scare me off and that doesn't work out, and it implicates Miller so somebody killed him before he can say anything, and Clint's father hires a guy to kill me. We have that guy, he probably killed Miller, he tried to kill me, and he'll testify that Don Stapleton hired him."

"In exchange for what?" Farantino said.

"We've made no deals with him," Brooks said.

"So he's looking at major time," Farantino said.

"I would think so," Brooks said without expression. "If Spenser testifies against him."

Farantino looked at me very quickly. "Why wouldn't you testify," he said.

I shrugged and shook my head.

Farantino looked back at Brooks just as quickly.

"What's your case against Rugar."

"Eyewitness," Brooks said. "Rugar shot Spenser and Spenser saw him do it."

Farantino's head swiveled back at me. "You sonova bitch," he said. "You have a deal with him, don't you?"

I shrugged again.

Don Stapleton said, "What's going on, Frank?"

"You see how cute they are?" Farantino said. "The DA's got no deal with him, but unless Spenser testifies against Rugar they've got no case. So Spenser makes the deal. Rugar gives them you, and Spenser won't testify. So they may as well give him immunity and use him to try and get you."

"And he goes free?"

"He goes free."

All three of the Stapletons stared at me.

I said to Clint, "Why'd you kill her? Did you mean to or did something happen?"

Farantino said, "Don't answer that."

He turned toward Brooks.

"That's an entirely inappropriate question and you damned well know it, Owen."

Brooks nodded vigorously. "Entirely," he said.

"It was an accident," Clint Stapleton said softly.

Don Stapleton said, "Shut up, Clint."

"We were having fun, it was rough but she liked rough, and there's a thing you do, you know where you choke someone while having sex and it makes them come . . ."

Dina Stapleton put her hand over her son's mouth.

Don Stapleton said, "Clint, that's enough, not another word out of you. I mean it."

Clint gently turned his head away from his mother's hand. "Great White Bwana," he said without looking at his father. "You think you can fix this?"

Don Stapleton was on his feet. "You goddamned fool, I can if you'll keep your mouth shut."

Clint shook his head staring at the floor between his feet. "Get fucking real," he said.

"Don't you speak to me like that," Don said.

Dina began to cry softly, her hands clasped in her lap, her head down. Farantino was on his feet now, beside Don. "Everybody just shut up," he said.

"Well, Melissa loved that, we'd done it before, but this time we both got too excited and . . . she died."

It had been said. There was no way to reel the words back in. They hung there in the room, surprisingly inornate after all that had been done to keep them from being said.

Clint was trying not to cry, and failing. His mother cried beside him, her shoulders slumped hopelessly. His father, still on his feet, was white faced, and the lines at the corners of his mouth seemed very deep.

"And I got scared and left her body and called my dad." Clint's voice was soft and flat and the emptiness in it was uncomfortable to hear. "My dad," he said, "the Great White Fixer. He fixed it good, didn't he."

"Clint, you're my son," Don said. "I was doing what I had to do."

"You been fixing it all my life," Clint said in his affectless voice. "Fix the pickininny. Well, you fixed it good this time, Bwana."

There was a rehearsed quality to Clint's speech as if it were a part he'd learned, the fragment of a long argument with his father that had unspooled silently in his head since he was small.

Farantino said, "You simply have to stop talking, both of you. You simply have to be quiet." He looked at Brooks, who was listening and watching. "This is informal," Farantino said. "This is off the record. You can't use this."

Brooks smiled at him politely.

"Goddamn you," Don said to his son. The tension trembled in his voice.

"He already has," Clint said and the words seemed clogged as he started to cry hard and turned toward his mother and pressed his face against her chest and sobbed.

Dina put her arms around him and closed her eyes. She cried with him, the tears squeezing out under the closed eyelids. I glanced back at Quirk. He was expressionless. I looked at Brooks. His face was as empty as Quirk's. I wondered what mine looked like. I felt like a child molester.

"You hired Rugar to kill Spenser, didn't you?" Brooks said quietly to Don Stapleton.

Farantino said, "Don!"

Don said, "Yes," in a voice so soft it was almost inaudible.

"And Miller," Brooks said, "to cover your tracks."

"Yes."

I was looking at Clint when his father confessed. The dead look left his eyes. For a moment he looked triumphant.

"I think we need a stenographer," Brooks said and picked up the phone.

chapter 54

WHEN THEY LET Ellis out, Hawk picked him up and brought him to my office. I had just finished endorsing the check from Cone, Oakes, and was slipping it into the deposit envelope when they came in.

"What are you going to do now?" I said to Ellis.

He was as tight and watchful and arrogant as he had been before, but now that he was out he was more talkative.

"You been in the place four years, what you do?"

"Whatever it was would involve a woman," I said.

"You got that right," he said.

"Try to make it voluntary," I said.

"You got no call talking to me that way," Alves said. "Ah'm an innocent man."

"You didn't do Melissa Henderson," I said. "That's not the same as being innocent."

"You get me in here to talk shit?" Alves said.

"You need some money?" I said.

"'Course I need money," he said. "You think being inside a high-paying fucking job?"

I took two hundred dollars out of my wallet and gave it to him. It left me with seven, until I deposited the check, but the bank was close by. Ellis took the money and counted it and folded it over and slipped it into the pocket of his pale blue sweat pants.

"Ah'm supposed to say thank you?"

"We know you an asshole, Ellis," Hawk said. "You don't have to keep proving it every time you open your mouth."

"I just figure Whitey owe me something, and he making a down payment," Alves said.

Hawk looked at me and grinned. "Way to go, Whitey."

I nodded modestly.

"You got a job anywhere?" I said.

"No reason for you to be asking me about no job," Alves said. "It got nothing to do with you."

"Know a guy runs a trucking service out of Mattapan," I said.

"Don't need no help from you," Alves said.

"You did yesterday," Hawk said.

"I'm supposed to be grateful?" Alves said. "I'm in for four years on something I didn't do, that some honky rich kid done, and they let me out and ah'm supposed to say thank you?"

"Actually it was a nigger rich kid," Hawk said. "And they didn't let you out, Spenser got you out."

"And he got paid for it too, didn't he? Who gonna pay me for my four years?"

"Actually," I said, "two hundred is probably about what four years of your time is worth. You want that trucker job give me a call."

"Don't you be sitting 'round waiting," Alves said.

He turned toward the door and hesitated fractionally while he looked at Hawk, saw no objection, and walked out of my office.

"Glad he didn't get all sicky sweet with gratitude," Hawk said.

"Yeah," I said. "It's always so embarrassing."

"He be back inside in six months," Hawk said.

"I hope so," I said.

We were quiet for a moment.

"I probably wouldn't have made it back without you," I said to Hawk.

"Probably not," Hawk said.

I picked up the deposit envelope and looked at it.

"What do you think he'll do with the two hundred?" I said.

"Depends," Hawk said. "If he don't have a gun, he'll buy one. If he does, he'll spend it on a bottle of booze and a woman."

"Nice to know he's got priorities," I said.

"Good to know what they are, too," Hawk said.

I nodded and looked at the deposit envelope again. It was a lot of money.

"I might have made it back alone," I said.

Hawk smiled his charming heartless smile.

"Maybe," he said.

chapter 55

RUGAR'S TESTIMONY CONVICTED Don Stapleton. Clint's confession was supported by Hunt McMartin and the lissome Glenda. He too was convicted. Both convictions were being appealed when they let Rugar out. Brooks told me when he was getting out, and I met him on the steps of the new Suffolk County jail. The first snow of the season had begun to fall, it was only a degree or two away from rain, and it fell like rain, straight down, and small.

"You kept your word," Rugar said.

He was wearing a gray tweed overcoat with a black velvet collar. He turned the collar up as he stood in the falling snow. He was still gray. I wondered if his color was connected to some internal coldness, like a gray reptile.

"You kept yours," I said.

We walked down the steps together, carefully, because they had already become slippery, and turned right toward North Station and the new Fleet Center.

"The nigger get out?" Rugar said.

"Yes."

"They tell me Stapleton's got that appellate specialist from Harvard," he said, "working on the convictions."

"They've got a lot of money."

"Probably have enough," Rugar said. "You have enough and the law makes a lot less difference."

Time in jail had made no difference to him. He still spoke with the voice-under harmonic of some internal force.

"So young," I said, "yet so cynical."

"If there's a retrial, I won't be around to testify," Rugar said.

I shrugged.

"I do what I can," I said. "Alves is out of jail."

"You like him?" Rugar said.

"No," I said.

Rugar nodded slowly. "Work is work," he said.

"You ought to know."

Rugar made a motion with his mouth which he probably thought was a smile. "Yes, liking or not liking has never had much to do with my work either," he said.

We were on Causeway Street now. There were cabs lined up in front of North Station. Rugar signaled to one and waited while it pulled forward to him.

As he waited he turned and looked at me.

"You won this time."

"Yep."

"There may never be a next time."

"Yep."

"But if there is," he said, "I plan to win."

He stared at me. His eyes had no animation in them. It was like looking at the underside of two bottle caps.

"I like a cheery optimism," I said. "It's good to get up each morning as if your hair were on fire."

Rugar continued to look, the way you might survey a project you might someday undertake. He stood stock still while he looked. But the low throb of deadliness seemed somehow alive between us, as if his gray corporeal self was an insignificant replication of the near Satanic energy that was his real self. Then the cab pulled up and he turned toward it.

"Rugar," I said.

He turned half bent to step in the cab and looked back at me.

"I took you once," I said. "I'll take you again."

Rugar's expression didn't change. For all I know he didn't hear me. He turned back to the cab and stepped in and shut the door. He said something to the driver and the cab pulled away in the steady straight-down snowfall. I watched it until it was out of sight.

Not killing him may have been an error.

chapter 56

SUSAN AND I were standing with Pearl on the sidewalk of the Larz Anderson Bridge, leaning on the parapet, looking down at the river on a late afternoon in early winter, while the homebound traffic edged toward Harvard Square. The light that lingered after sunset colored the atmosphere blue, and the snow along the river looked whiter than I knew it to be. A couple of hundred yards downstream, the Weeks Footbridge was a graceful arch over the current.

"A year," Susan said, staring down at the slick black surface of the water. Between us, Pearl reared up on her hind legs and put her forepaws on the parapet and stared downriver, too. I didn't wonder what she was thinking. It was aimless, and I was glad I didn't know. It was one of the things about the link between people and dogs that

I liked. Neither would ever fully know the other. Maybe it was true of the link between people and people, too.

"Why was the relationship between Clint and Melissa such a secret? Was it Clint being black?"

"Yes."

"How awful."

"Yes."

"How awful for her parents," Susan said. "How awful for the Stapleton family."

"Yeah."

"They had everything, money, position, each other. The girl was lovely and successful, wasn't she?"

"So they tell me."

"The boy was handsome and accomplished."

"And he didn't mean to kill her," I said. "Just a little exotic sex."

"And it destroys his whole family, the father, the son—the mother must be devastated . . ."

"To save a career criminal who'll be back in jail in no time," I said.

"And a professional killer goes free to accomplish it."

"Yeah."

"You don't even need his testimony, now," Susan said. "The Stapletons confessed."

"Yep."

"But he goes free anyway."

"A deal's a deal," I said. "We needed the threat of his testimony to get the confessions."

"And the Stapletons go to jail while two career criminals go free."

"Couldn't have said it better myself."

"They are both guilty of things," Susan said. "But the people going free are probably guilty of more things."

"Almost certainly."

"And the father was trying to save his son."

"Yep."

"Doesn't seem right, does it."

"No."

"On the other hand, you can't make it seem righter by letting the Stapletons go."

"Probably not," I said.

"Do you think the boy confessed to get his father?" Susan said.

"Yes," I said. "There was something ugly there. I don't know what it was, but it had to do with race."

"Sometimes interracial adoptions are very painful. The parents get caught up in a racism they didn't know they had. Fearful that the child will be black, which is to say bad, they work too hard to make him be good, which is to say white."

"Pygmalion," I said.

"Something like that. It fosters dreadful resentments within a family."

"Something did that here," I said. "On the other hand, they are very rich. They are appealing the convictions . . ."

I shrugged.

"I'm not criticizing you, in all of this," Susan said.

"I know you're not," I said. "The confusion of guilt and innocence just looks a little starker in this case and it interests you."

She smiled. Pearl got sick of looking at the river, or sick of standing on her hind legs, or both, or neither, and dropped down to all fours and looked up at us questioningly. I scratched her ear.

"How do you feel about all this?"

"As little as possible," I said. "The Stapletons are not without resources. They'll get the best justice money can buy. The kid especially. A good lawyer may convince a jury that Melissa Henderson was complicit in her own death, that Clint was doing what she wanted. But I know a couple of things. I know that Melissa Henderson shouldn't be dead. I know that no one should have framed Ellis Alves."

"Or hired someone to kill you," Susan said.

"I might do that to save my son," I said.

Susan looked up at me in the now thickening darkness.

"No," she said, "you wouldn't. You might kill someone to save your son, but you wouldn't hire someone to do it."

I put my arm around her and she leaned her head against my shoulder. "But since we don't have a son, and won't, I guess the question is moot."

"We have Paul," she said softly.

"True."

"You'd kill someone to save him."

"Yes," I said.

"And we have Pearl."

"A son and a daughter," I said. "No need to adopt at all."

Susan laughed softly. Pearl looked up at the sound and wagged her tail. And we stood together like that as night fell and the river ran.

If you enjoyed *Small Vices*, you won't want
to miss Robert B. Parker's newest novel . . .

NIGHT PASSAGE

Here is an excerpt from
this provocative new novel—
available in hardcover from
G. P. Putnam's Sons

AT THE END of the continent, near the foot of Wilshire Boulevard, Jesse Stone stood and leaned on the railing in the darkness above the Santa Monica beach and stared at nothing, while below him the black ocean rolled away toward Japan.

There was no traffic on Ocean Avenue. There was the comfortless light of the street lamps, but they were behind him. Before him was the uninterrupted darkness above the repetitive murmur of the disdainful sea.

A black and white cruiser pulled up and parked behind his car at the curb. A spotlight shone on it and one of the cops from the cruiser got out and looked into it. Then the spotlight swept along the verge of the cliffs and touched Jesse and went past him and came back and held. The strapping young L.A. patrolman walked over to him holding his flashlight near the bulb end, the barrel of it resting on his shoulder, so he could use it as a club if he needed to. The young cop asked Jesse if he were all right. Jesse said he was, and the young cop asked him why he was standing there at four in the morning. The cop looked about twenty-four. Jesse felt like he could be his father, though in fact he was maybe ten years older.

"I'm a cop," Jesse said.

"Got a badge?"

"Was a cop. I'm leaving town, just thought I'd stand here a while before I went."

"That your car?" he said.

Jesse nodded.

"What division you work out of?" the young cop said.

"Downtown, Homicide."

"Who runs it?"

"Captain Cronjager."

"I can smell booze on you," the young cop said.

"I'm waiting to sober up."

"I can drive you home in your car," the young cop said. "My partner will follow in the black and white."

"I'll stay here till I'm sober," Jesse said.

"Okay," the young cop said and went back to the cruiser and the cruiser pulled away. No one else came by. There was no sound except the tireless movement of the thick black water. Behind him the streetlights became less stark, and he realized he could see the first hint of the pier to his left. He turned slowly and looked back at the city behind him and saw that it was almost dawn. The streetlights looked yellow now, and the sky to the east was white. He looked back at the ocean once, then walked to his car and got in and started up. He drove along Ocean Avenue to the Santa Monica Freeway and turned onto it and headed east. By the time he passed Boyle Heights the sun was up and shining into his eyes as he drove straight toward it. Say good-bye to Hollywood, say good-bye my baby.

TOM CARSON SAT in the client chair across the desk from Hastings Hathaway in the president's office of the Paradise Trust. He felt uneasy, as if he were in the principal's office. He didn't like the feeling. He was the chief of police; people were supposed to feel uneasy confronting him.

"You can quietly resign, Tom," Hathaway said, "and relocate, we'll be happy to help you with that financially, or you can, ah, face the consequences."

"Consequences?" Carson tried to sound stern, but he could feel the bottom falling out of him.

"For you, and if necessary, I suppose, for your wife and your children." Carson cleared his throat, and felt ashamed that he'd had to.

"Such as?" he said as strongly as he could, trying hard to keep his gaze steady on Hathaway.

Why was Hathaway so scary? He was a geeky guy. In the eighth grade, before Hasty had gone away to school, Tom Carson had teased him. So had everyone else. Hathaway smiled. It was a thin geeky smile and it frightened Tom Carson further.

"We have resources, Tom. We could turn the problem over to Jo Jo and his associates, or, depending upon circumstance, we could deal with it ourselves. I don't want that to happen. I'm your friend, Tom. I have so far been able to control the, ah, firebrands, but you'll have to trust me. You'll have to do what I ask."

"Hasty," Carson said. "I'm the chief of police, for crissake."

Hathaway shook his head.

"You can't just say I'm not," Carson said.

"You don't make the rules in this town, Tom."

"And you do?" Carson said.

His face felt stiff as he spoke and his arms and hands felt weak.

"We do, Tom. Emphasis on the 'We.'"

Carson was silent, staring at Hathaway. The mention of Jo Jo had made him feel loose and fragmented inside. Hathaway took a thick stationery-sized manila envelope from his middle drawer.

"You aren't much of a policeman, Tom, and it was just a sad accident that you learned things. But you did, and you were right to come first to me. I've been able to save you so far from the consequences of your knowledge."

"What if I went to the FBI with this?"

"This is what I'm trying to forestall," Hathaway said. "Other people, people like Jo Jo, would prevail. And your family . . ." Hathaway shrugged and held the shrug for a moment, and sighed as if to himself, before he continued.

"But we both know, Tom, you are not made of that kind of stuff. The better choice for you, and I'm sure you recognize this, is to take our rather generous severance package. We've found you a house and we've contributed some cash to help you in relocation costs. The details are in here."

"What if I promise not to say a word about anything, Hasty. Why can't I just stay here. You'd have a chief of police that won't give you any trouble."

Hathaway shook his head slowly as Carson spoke. He smiled sadly.

"I mean, you know, the next chief," Carson said, "might be harder to deal with."

Hathaway continued his sad smile and slow head shake.

"I am trying to help you, Tom," Hathaway said. "I can't help you if you won't help yourself."

"I'm no troublemaker," Carson said. "How can you be sure you won't just get a troublemaker."

"We have already chosen your successor," Hathaway said. "He should be just right."

He held the envelope out toward Tom Carson and, after a moment of empty hesitation, Carson reached out and took it.

JESSE DROVE OUT Route 10 past Upland where he picked up Route 15 and followed it north to Barstow where he went east on Route 40. He didn't turn on the radio. He liked quiet. He set the cruise control to seventy and kept a hand lightly on the steering wheel and slowly settled into himself and allowed his feelings to seep out of the compacted center of himself. He no longer had a badge. He'd turned it in with his service pistol. There was no wedding ring on his left hand. He smiled without pleasure. Turned that in too. It made him feel sort of scared to be without a badge or a wedding ring. Not quite thirty-five and no official status anymore. With his right hand he fished in the gym bag on the front seat beside him until he found his off-duty gun, a short-barreled Smith & Wesson .38. He arranged it near the top of the bag, where it would be easy to reach, and he let his hand rest on it for a time. It made him feel less insubstantial. He stopped at a truck stop outside of Needles, sat at the counter and had orange juice, ham, eggs, potatoes, wheat toast, and three cups of coffee with cream and sugar. It made him feel good. The place was full of truckers and tourists, and he was alone among them. No one paid any attention to him. They were going where they would and he was on his way east. He went to the men's room and washed his hands and face. Back in the car, cruise control set, he felt a small freshet of excitement. It was afternoon now, the sun was behind him. Shining on what he had left. The road spooled out ahead of him, straight to the horizon, nearly empty. Freedom, he thought, and smiled again, no badge, no ring, no problem. You look at it the right way and that's freedom. He nursed the excitement as long as he could, trying to build on it.

He stayed the night in Flagstaff 250 miles north of where he had been born, and went to the motel bar for supper. He ordered scotch on the rocks and a chicken breast sandwich on a croissant. There were a couple of guys in plaid shirts and those little string ties they wore in places like Arizona, the kind with the silver hasp where a knot should be. Both bartenders were women wearing white shirts and black ties and short red jackets. One was a fat blond woman, the other a more slender dark-haired Hispanic girl who would be fat in five more years. Beyond the bar was a room with tables and a dance floor, and the setup for a disc jockey. No one was in the room yet. An unlit piece of neon script over the disc jockey stand spelled out "Coyote Lounge." He sipped a little scotch, felt the cold heat spread from his esophagus. A tall well-built man in his thirties came into the bar wearing a big Stetson hat and earphones. He seemed to

be bouncing slightly to music that only he heard. He had
on a plaid shirt with the sleeves rolled up and tight jeans
and two-toned lizard skin cowboy boots. The tiny tape
player was tucked into his shirt pocket and the slender
cord ran up under his chin. He looked as if he'd just come
from a shower and a shave and his cologne came into the
bar ahead of him. Clubman, maybe. Jesse watched him.
There was nothing particularly interesting about him
except that Jesse watched everything. The cowboy ordered a nonalcoholic beer and when it was served he left
the glass and picked up the bottle and carried it with him
as he walked along the bar looking everything over.

"When's that dancing start?" he said to one of the
bartenders.

He spoke loudly, perhaps because he needed to speak
over the music in his ears. He drank his nonalcoholic
beer from the bottle, holding it by the neck.

"Nine o'clock," the Hispanic girl said. She had no
accent.

The cowboy looked around the bar at Jesse, at the two
guys in plaid shirts drinking beer, at the two bartenders.

"Anybody know a happening place around here?"

One of the beer drinkers shook his head without
looking up. Nobody else even acknowledged the question. Everybody knows it, Jesse thought. Maybe it's how
loud he talks. Or how he looks like a model in one of
those western-wear catalogs. Or the way he walks around
in the little backwater bar, like he was strolling into the
Ritz. Whatever it was, everyone knew he was a guy who,
encouraged by an answer, would talk to you for much too
long. The cowboy nodded to himself, as if his suspicions
were confirmed, and walked into the empty dance hall
and walked around it, looking at the caricatures of dapper
semi-human coyotes hanging on the walls. Then he put

his half-finished bottle of nonalcoholic beer on the bar, surveyed the bar again, and walked out.

"Takes all kinds," the blond bartender said.

A jerk, Jesse thought. A good-looking jerk, but just as lonely and separate as the homely ones. His sandwich came. He ate it because he needed nourishment, and drank two more scotches and paid and went to his room. Nothing was going to happen when they opened up the dance floor that Jesse wanted to watch.

In his room he got the travel bottle of Black Label out of his suitcase and poured some into one of the little sanitary plastic cups he found in the bathroom. The walk down the hall for ice seemed too long so he sipped the scotch warm. He didn't turn on the television. Instead he stood at the window and looked out at the high pines that rimmed the hill behind the motel. He'd grown up in Tucson when *The Brady Bunch* was hot, and while it was only four or five hours away it could have been another planet. Tucson was sunlight and desert and heat, even in January. Up here they had winter. It was 7:45, getting dark. He was still in the same time zone. Jennifer would be home from work. Actually she'd probably be fucking Elliott Krueger about now. He let the images of his wife having sex roll behind his eyes as he stared at the now-dark window pane and sipped his Scotch. His reflection in the window pane looked somber. He grinned at it, and raised his glass in a toasting gesture. Go to it, Jenn, fuck your brains out. It's got nothing to do with me. The bravado of it, buoyed with the scotch, made him feel intact for a moment, but he knew it was scotch, and he knew it was bravado, and he knew there was nothing behind the smile in the empty window.